The Missing Heirloom Mystery

ALSO BY RACHEL WARD

THE SUPERMARKET MYSTERIES

THE
MISSING
HEIRLOOM
MYSTERY

Rachel Ward

The Supermarket Mysteries Book 5

Joffe Books, London
www.joffebooks.com

First published in Great Britain in 2024

Cover art by Nick Castle

ISBN: 978-1-83526-816-2

For Ozzy, Ali and Pete — my treasures — and for my Mum, Shirley, who continues to inspire me.

CHAPTER ONE

'Cheeky pint after work, Ant?'

Ant, sprawled next to Bea on the stained and lumpy sofa in the staff room, didn't seem to have heard. He was studying an article on one of the inside pages of the *Kingsleigh Bugle*, his index finger resting on the text and his lips moving as he worked out the words.

Bea was a staunch supporter of his burgeoning literacy and would normally have left him alone, but their lunch break was nearly over and she wanted something to look forward to this afternoon. She gave him a little nudge in the ribs.

'Whassat?' Ant muttered, finally looking up.

'We keep saying that we should have more fun. I just wondered if you wanted to go to the Ship after work today. Bit of a session on a school night. What do you think?'

He closed the paper and put it on the low coffee table in front of them.

'Ah, not today. I've got to go to the allotment. Bob's off with Dot looking at wedding venues, poor sod, and I need to keep an eye on things.'

Bob, the master of the meat counter, had been helping Charles, an elderly customer and friend, with his allotment for years. This summer they had recruited Ant, too. Initially reluctant, Ant had really taken to it — something which rather baffled Bea, who had never seen him as the green-fingered type. Now, as the date for the annual flower and produce show drew near, Ant seemed to be spending all his free time there.

'You should come, Bea. We could get some goodies from the cold cabinet, have a picnic.'

Bea shuddered. She hadn't been to the allotments since the fateful night in February when she'd had an unpleasantly close brush with death in Charles's potting shed. Even now, in the familiar surroundings of the staff room, she felt a stab of anxiety, remembering the claustrophobic dark space, the musty smell and the terror of being trapped there with a murderer.

'No thanks. I still can't face it.'

Ant pressed his lips together and nodded. He knew how close he had come to losing his best friend that night.

'I understand, I really do,' he said, 'but it's okay there. It's not the place that was the problem, it was the people. And they're taken care of. They can't hurt you, Bea.'

Bea screwed up her face. 'I know. I just can't. Besides, I don't get the attraction. What would we even do there?'

Ant smiled. 'You can put your feet up, if you like. I'll do a bit of watering and check in on Marvin.'

'Who's Marvin? Your neighbour up there?'

'No, our prize marrow. He's an absolute unit and he's going to win us a prize at the show. Charles has been doing this for thirty years or so and he says he's the best marrow he's ever grown.'

Bea shook her head. 'Men and marrows. It's a really big one, is it?' She held her hands parallel and drew them apart. 'I bet you've even measured it.'

'I haven't, but that's a top idea. Do we sell tape measures? We should take one up there. You can hold one end.'

Bea burst out laughing. 'It's not that big, is it? I have to hold one end while you walk down to the other? Oh, Ant!'

He grinned. 'Come on. It'd be a blast, and then we'd set up some chairs, eat a couple of Cornish pasties, crack open a can or two and sit in the evening sun. It's quiet there, Bea, really peaceful. Might see a robin or a blackbird. They're usually around. I'm trying to train one of the robins to eat worms out of my hand. I'm nearly there, too. He comes really close.'

Bea shifted round to face him.

'Who even are you?'

He laughed. 'I know! I don't recognise myself these days. I thought growing things was all old blokes with their trousers held up with string, smoking pipes and stuff, but it's not like that. Well, it is, but that's not all there is. Bob, Charles and I have right laugh and you'll never guess who's got the plot next to us — Mr Bradley from school.'

Bea remembered her History teacher well. She'd got a grade 7 in the subject at GCSE and Bradley had tried, unsuccessfully, to persuade her to take it for A level. Given Ant's intermittent school attendance and difficulties with anything academic, she knew that he might have a very different view of him.

'Bit awkward?' she said.

'Yeah, I was pretty sick about it when I first spotted him up there, but he's really chill outside school. He's teased me a bit about what I was like then, and he can take a bit of banter back. And he likes a drink and a smoke on the quiet, so we've actually got stuff in common.'

Bea shook her head. 'Ha! Who'd have thought?'

'Sometimes when everyone else has gone home, we just drink a beer and talk. He's an interesting guy, actually. He retired this year, so he's been up the allotment loads and he's on the council now, shaking things up a bit.'

'Now you mention it, I think he was in the paper this week.'

She leaned forward and picked up the *Bugle*. There was Dylan Bradley on the front page — young-looking for a recent retiree, with a kind, open face and rather wayward greying hair. He'd been photographed in front of the town council offices, looking friendly, yet serious, underneath a headline declaring, '*Our Missing Treasures — Councillor Calls for a Town Museum.*'

'He was telling me about that a few days ago,' Ant said. 'Do you remember him banging on about Kingsleigh's past in History lessons and assemblies and stuff? Roman villas and something about an abbey?'

'I do. He was very passionate about it. He took us to see the remains of Kingsleigh Abbey in Year 7. They're in the corner of the park. Did he do that with you?'

Ant shook his head.

'The abbey is just a pile of stones now, but he was telling us about some of the artefacts which were found. They're not on display anywhere at the moment. Here we are,' she said, putting her finger next to a paragraph in the article and then reading aloud. '*Councillor Bradley said, "Kingsleigh has an amazingly rich history and there are some wonderful treasures kept under wraps in the basement of the town hall, including stone carvings, pots and coins, and, of course, Kingsleigh's crown jewels — the magnificent chalice which was used by the monks in the abbey, six medieval chess pieces made of jet and bone, and the bishop's seal. It's criminal that these local heirlooms have been missing from public view for so long and I'm making it my mission to establish a museum and have these on permanent display for the people of Kingsleigh."*'

Ant chuckled. 'He means business, all right. Not sure I'd be queuing up when a museum opens its doors.'

'Don't be such a philistine, Ant. It'd be really interesting.' She caught his expression. 'Well, it would be interesting to see them once, anyway. Is that what you were reading about in the paper just now?'

'No, I was looking through to see if there was anything about some argy-bargy up at the allotments, but it hasn't made it into the paper.'

'What sort of argy-bargy?'

'Someone's nicking veg. Tomatoes going missing. Spuds and onions dug up.' He shook his head sadly.

'Well, I'm not surprised that isn't in the *Bugle*.' She feigned a yawn.

He jostled his shoulder into hers. 'This is serious stuff. It's less than a fortnight to the big show and it's starting to get tense now. Bob said that one of the guys whose produce was taken, Cyril, was actually in tears. He reckoned his heirloom tomatoes were prize-winners. He might have been right, too. He's two plots along from us and his tomatoes are — *were* — pretty impressive.'

'Sounds like sabotage. Bit of unfriendly rivalry.'

'Could be. That's another reason for going up there this evening. I need to make sure Marvin's all right. Don't want somebody nobbling him.'

'Well, obviously the Ship and I can't compete with a giant vegetable and your new mates,' she said.

Ant looked at her quizzically. 'Wait. Are you jealous?'

'No, course not.' She paused. 'Maybe just a bit left out. Dot's busy planning her wedding and you've turned into Alan Titchmarsh.'

'Ha! You daft doughnut. Come up and meet everyone. Have a chat with Dylan. He'd be chuffed to see you again.' He could tell she was wavering. 'It's good vibes up there, Bea. We'll only be there in the light — it's a beautiful day. Maybe it's time for you to get over what happened before. I'll be with you the whole time. I can show you why I love it there.'

He was looking at her so earnestly, and she really did miss hanging out with him, so she caved. 'All right, then. Shall we get some bits from here to take with us? Sausage rolls and crisps and stuff?'

'Yeah. Not those fancy sausage rolls, just the ordinary ones.'

'Okay, and a box of little tomatoes to be healthy.'

'No need, Bea. You can have some of ours. Nothing better than stuff you've grown and picked yourself.' He rubbed his hands together. 'You're going to love it.'

The afternoon passed pleasantly enough, although Bea missed the effervescent presence of Dot in the neighbouring checkout. Her stand-in, Kirsty, although nice enough, wasn't such good company.

Bea was used to the rhythms of the retail year and rather enjoyed times like this. By the second week of September, the 'back to school' stock had been moved to the 'last chance to buy' section and the Halloween merchandise wasn't due in for another ten days or so. So, for the time being, Costsave could just be itself — a small-town supermarket, offering decent prices and friendly service. Nothing fancy, but none the worse for that.

She had already seen some of her regulars today — the older ones were usually out and about in the morning, many popping in daily, to buy the few bits and bobs they needed for lunch and dinner for one. They were there as much for the change of scene and a chat as for the ready meals, crumpets or individual apple pies. She imagined that during the afternoon most of them were either having a well-earned nap or watching the quizzes on TV, or perhaps a bit of both, which is why she was a bit surprised to see Charles approaching her checkout at what was, for him, a lively pace. He had his shopping bag on wheels with him, with a basket perched on the top and the end of his walking stick clicked loudly on the hard floor.

'Afternoon, Charles,' she said, beeping through three tins of dog food, a large pork pie, a bag of new potatoes and some toilet rolls. 'Ant's persuaded me to go and have a look at your allotment this evening. Will you be up there?'

'Hello, Bea. Not tonight. It's a bit too far for me to walk these days, so I only go there if Bob can give me a lift. He's away today.'

'He and Dot were looking at somewhere posh, down near Frome. Hope he put his best bib and tucker on.'

'I can't see Bob somewhere like that, but weddings are special, aren't they?'

'Yeah. Dot's so excited about it. It's lovely to see her so happy.'

'He's a good man.' Charles nodded.

'And she's a good woman,' said Bea, and they both laughed.

He put his shopping into his trolley and paid. 'Has Ant told you about our marrow?'

'Oh yes, I've heard all about Marvin.'

'He's a bobby dazzler. Best marrow I've ever grown.'

She grinned. 'Can't wait to meet him.'

Charles left the store, pulling his trolley behind him. The final hour passed smoothly enough, with the usual harassed parents and gaggles of teenagers, but Bea was glad when it was time to clock off. Ant called by her checkout, they collected their coats and bags from upstairs, then went round the store together, selecting their favourites for a tip-top picnic, Costsave style — sausage rolls, vegetable samosas, sweet chilli flavour crisps and a couple of bottles of cider.

They headed out and walked along the high street and then followed various paths, alleyways and residential roads. It was a glorious afternoon. The September sun, strong enough to make their jackets redundant, seemed to infuse the town with goodwill. Dog walkers said hello. Neighbours were chatting outside their houses. Even the surliest teenagers were lounging about on the rec, listening to music and minding their own business.

As they approached the allotments, Bea felt her resolve start to crumble. She hadn't been here for seven months, but her last visit suddenly seemed like yesterday. She hadn't really talked about it with anyone. After she'd been checked over and released from hospital, she'd gone home, spent a couple of days on the sofa binge-watching her favourite dramas, and then resumed her usual routine, figuring that the sooner she got back to normal the better.

Ant sensed her hesitation. 'It's all right, you know. Everything's fine.'

'Yeah, I do know, it's just . . .' She was reluctant to put her feelings into words, as if naming them would somehow breach a dam that she'd built in her mind, and her emotions would come flooding out and overwhelm her.

'Hey—' Ant dug into his pocket and produced a chunky black-and-yellow tape measure — 'I found this in the stores.

Reckon it might be up to the job of measuring Marv. Come on!'

He danced away from her and, fears banished at least for now, Bea broke into a jog to follow him through the gates.

The allotment site on this warm afternoon was almost unrecognisable as the place she'd last seen on a dark February night. The changing seasons had worked their magic to create a patchwork of green, leafy plots, full of life and vigour. Vegetables and fruit bushes mixed with flowers here and there, with one plot in the far corner providing a blast of colour, almost like Dutch tulip fields that Bea had seen online, with stripes of red, yellow, orange and purple, and rows of sunflowers as a backdrop.

Various people greeted Ant as he walked along the path, mostly older men. An upright old chap wearing mustard-coloured corduroy trousers and a green waistcoat festooned with pockets nodded to them as they passed the central hut and noticeboard.

'I trust you're keeping the shirt on today,' the man said.

'Of course. Rules is rules,' Ant replied, then, as soon as they were past, he rolled his eyes and muttered some choice phrases under his breath.

'Friend of yours?' said Bea.

'Lionel.' He said the word as if it tasted bad in his mouth. 'He's in charge. There's always someone in charge, isn't there? Even in a place like this.'

As they got nearer to the far end, a young woman with hair in two braids looked up from the middle of the flowery plot and waved at them.

'That's Lily,' Ant said. 'See, it's not all old fogeys up here.'

Bea wondered if Lily was part of the attraction for Ant but didn't say anything.

'Here we are. This is us,' Ant announced.

Bea had thought she might have to fake enthusiasm, just to encourage him, but in fact she was impressed. The long rectangle of land was beautifully kept with rows of different plants of various heights, including beans sprawled over structures made of bamboo poles and pristine, weedless soil in between.

'Blimey, Ant, it's lush!' she said.

He beamed in response. 'It is, isn't it? Come and meet Marvin.'

He led her part-way down the plot to a patch of low-lying plants with a jungle of large, dark green leaves.

'That's odd.' He picked his way carefully towards the middle of the patch. 'Someone's been here. Look.'

Bea followed carefully in his steps as he pointed to where two leaves lay on the ground, sheared from their stems.

'I reckon someone's stood on these. They'd better not have hurt Marv . . .'

He carefully moved some other leaves to reveal an enormous plump marrow, lying on a bed of straw.

Bea couldn't help smiling at the sight. 'Wow,' she said, 'he's a big boy all right. Is he okay?'

Ant ran his hands over the surface. 'Yeah, I think so. Bloody hell, I don't know what I'd do if someone damaged him. Let's measure him. Do you want to do the honours, while I hold the leaves out of the way?'

Bea took the tape measure from him and held the end against the far end of the marrow, then stretched the tape along its stripey body to where the stalk started. 'I make it sixty-seven centimetres.'

'Do it again to check.'

She sighed, then measured again and confirmed the result. 'Hey, Ant, let me take your picture with him.'

Ant's eyes lit up and they took a series of shots.

'If I crouch down, he looks even bigger,' said Bea.

She showed Ant her phone screen and he flipped his fingers in delight at the photo of Marvin filling up two thirds of the frame with him in the background looking proud.

'That's the one!' he said. 'Straight to Insta. Let's do some selfies.'

They larked about for a bit until they'd exhausted the photo opportunities.

'How do they judge marrows, anyway?' said Bea. 'Is it length?'

'Maybe weight.'

'Girth?'

They both started laughing so hard that they doubled over. Bea ended up sitting on the grassy path next to the marrow patch, clutching her stomach.

'Stop, stop, I can't breathe!' she gasped.

'You started it.' He offered her a hand and helped her up. 'I need to check with Charles about the judging next time I see him. Dylan will know. He was reading through all the rules last week. I wonder where he is. He's usually up here by now.'

Ant looked across at the neighbouring plot and Bea followed his gaze. It was less manicured than Charles's. Bea would never have thought that plots could have different characters, but she could see that they did now, reflecting those of the people who tended them. Dylan's plot showed a kind of exuberance. His bean supports were tied together with odd bits of colourful string, rather than the regulation green twine which everyone else seemed to use.

On the plot beyond this, a diminutive man with a bald head and glasses was watching them.

'Hey, Cyril, have you seen Dylan today?'

Cyril seemed embarrassed at being caught looking.

'Not today,' he said with a clipped tone. 'Why are you asking me?'

'Just cos you were here before me. I just thought you might have—'

'Well, I haven't.' He picked up a nearby watering can and started walking towards the top of his plot.

'Someone's been over here,' Ant called. 'They've trampled round my marrow. Has anything else gone missing from yours?'

'No, not since last week.' Cyril had paused by a fine array of healthy plants, some of which Bea could see were bearing round green tomatoes.

'You've got some more coming,' said Ant. 'Looks like they might be ready in time for the show.'

10

Cyril made a noise like a bull snorting at the sight of a toreador and stalked off towards the tap.

'He's a bit shirty,' Bea whispered.

'He's been uptight since his tomatoes got nicked. Can't really blame him. Do you want to sit down while I do my checks and water some of the plants?'

'Okay.'

'The chairs are in the shed.' He clocked the look of panic on Bea's face. 'Don't worry, I'll get them. You stay here.'

Ant fished in his pocket and found a key. He unlocked the padlock on the shed door and fetched two chairs and a little folding table.

Bea sat down and set the food out on the table, watching a little robin flitting about. It seemed to be keeping one eye on Ant and the other on her, or perhaps on the pies and crisps. When Ant joined her, collapsing with a sigh into the other chair and opening one of the bottles of cider, the robin perched on the top of a potato plant, only a few metres away.

'Is this your mate?' Bea asked.

'Yeah, that's him. Hang on. Watch this.'

Ant broke off a little bit of pastry, put it in the palm of his hand and stretched his arm out towards the bird, holding it very still. Bea watched, fascinated, as the robin tipped its head to one side and then the other, as if weighing up the risks. She held her breath as it launched itself from its perch and flew towards them. At the last minute it flipped around in the air and retreated to a more distant perch on top of a spade sticking into the ground on Dylan's plot.

'Nearly,' said Ant. 'He'll do it one day. Maybe next time.' He dropped the crumb onto the ground and crammed the rest of the sausage roll into his mouth.

The sun was dropping towards the horizon and starting to give off a more mellow glow. Bea savoured the warmth on her face and closed her eyes for a moment or two. 'You're right, Ant. It's pretty nice here,' she said. 'Thanks for asking me.'

'Thanks for coming. I'll put you to work next time.'

She smiled. 'No, I'm all right just sitting watching you, ta.'
She opened her eyes to find that Ant was, in fact, watching her.

'What?' she said, putting her hand up to her face. 'Have
I got a spot or something?'

'No, silly. You just look happy there.'

She shifted in her seat and reached for a samosa.

'It's a shame you didn't get to see Dylan,' he said. 'Although,
despite what Cyril said, he must be around somewhere because
he never leaves tools lying about.' He nodded at the robin on
the spade handle. 'He always locks everything up in his shed.
I'll give him a ring, see where he is.'

'You've got his number?'

'Yeah, like I said, we're sort of mates now. Weird, isn't it,
how things turn out?'

Ant scrolled through his contacts and dialled, then held
his phone to his ear and waited. Bea could hear the faint sound
of a ringtone nearby. Her eyes met Ant's.

'Oh good, he *is* here somewhere,' said Ant. 'Must be talking to someone.'

Bea looked around, trying to identify the direction the
noise was coming from, scanning across the plots to see if she
could see which one Mr Bradley was on. Ant was looking, too.
He narrowed his eyes and lowered the phone, which was still
trying to connect.

He got up and started walking towards the top of the
plot. Bea followed. The ringtone was louder, but still muffled.

'I think it's coming from in there.' Bea pointed to the
shed on Dylan's plot. The uneasy feeling she'd been trying
to suppress was turning to something sharper, her stomach
twisting into knots.

'That's odd. It's locked up. He wouldn't leave his phone
behind, though. Let's have a look.'

Bea stood back. Sweat was prickling the skin under her
arms and across her forehead as she tried not to think about
being trapped in the dark with a gun pointed at her face.

There was one little window, with metal security bars across it, and Ant peered in.

'It's difficult to see anything. Hang on.'

He killed the call and the other phone stopped ringing. He switched on his phone's torch, then held it up to the window and squeezed his face as close to the glass as he could. Then he stepped back quickly.

'Oh no. Bea, don't come any closer. He's in there. He's on the floor. I think . . . I think he's dead.'

CHAPTER TWO

'What!' Bea gasped. 'Are you sure?'

'I think so. We need to get in there.' Ant went round to the door and tugged at the u-shaped bar on the lock. It didn't budge. He looked around wildly, then sprinted down Dylan's plot and yanked the spade out of the soil.

'Is something wrong?' Cyril called over.

'Dylan's in his shed. He's not moving. I think he's—'

'Oh, dear lord.' Cyril put down his watering can and started walking across the plot towards them, then changed direction and broke into an ungainly sort of run. 'I'll fetch Lionel.'

Bea was keeping her distance. She'd had a bad feeling as soon as she'd heard the distant phone. The few minutes since then had seemed like hours. The shed, just like the one which had featured in her nightmares for months, drew her eyes like a magnet.

She didn't want to believe this was happening. How *could* there be a body here? It was just too awful to be true. She didn't want to go inside, so what could she do to help?

She got out her phone and rang 999.

'Emergency, which service do you require?'

'Errr—'

Was Dylan past the point where an ambulance crew could help? The closed padlock was bothering her. Had someone shut him in, locked the door and walked away? Whatever had happened to Dylan, it looked like someone else was involved.

'Police,' she said, 'and maybe ambulance.'

She gave her details and the location and rang off.

Ant was back, clutching the spade. He lined up the blade with the top of the lock, raised the spade above his head and brought it down again with all the force he could muster. The wood around the fixing splintered but didn't give way. He tried again and smashed through it completely, shearing one side of the lock away from the doorframe. He threw the spade down and opened the door.

Bile gathered in Bea's throat as she saw a pair of feet splayed on the ground.

'Keep back, Bea.' Ant went inside and knelt down, holding his hand to Dylan's neck. He was saying something, too, but quietly. She edged a little closer and realised that he was talking to Dylan. Her stomach lurched with the thought that he might be alive after all.

'It's okay, mate, it's okay. I'm just checking what's going on. I can't feel a pulse. Ah, you're cold. I'll see if I can find a blanket for you. I'm so sorry you've been on your own. I'm so sorry, mate. I'll stay with you now.'

It was clear he was gone. Tears spilled out of Bea's eyes and she dashed them away.

Cyril and Lionel approached now, crowding around the door and blocking her view.

'What's happening?' Lionel said.

'Dylan's dead,' Ant said. 'I think he's been here a while.'

'Have you called an ambulance?'

'I have,' said Bea, and they all turned to look at her. 'Police and ambulance are on their way.'

'Good, good. Heart attack or something, I expect,' Lionel said.

'I don't think so,' said Ant. He shifted so that light from the doorway fell onto the body.

Cyril gasped and staggered backwards, bumping into Bea. She put her arms out to steady him.

'The door was locked, Lionel. And there's a hand trowel stuck in his head. He was murdered.'

CHAPTER THREE

It felt like the whole world was converging on the allotments. As all the allotment holders gathered around, and ambulances and police vans started arriving, Bea took a step back. What she really wanted to do was to slip away, to walk home to the safety of the little house she shared with Queenie, her mum, dive into bed and pull the covers over her head. She felt disconnected, an outside observer, as the scene unfolded in front of her.

Uniformed police were soon pushing the gathering crowd back from the epicentre, creating a cordon of crime-scene tape and ushering people further away. She went along with the herd as they were corralled just inside the main gates, from where she could see Ant being interviewed by Tom, one of her exes and now a fledgling police detective. After ten minutes or so, Tom let him go and Ant picked his way along the path, searching the crowd as he did. Bea raised her hand. He didn't smile, but he met her eyes with a look of relief and ducked under the tape to join her.

'Are you okay?' she asked.

He shook his head and she put her hand on his arm. 'Let's get out of here, Ant.'

'They might need to speak to you. You'd better ask.'

Bea approached the nearest officer in uniform. He took her name and contact details and agreed that she could leave.

'Come on, mate,' she said to Ant and linked her arm through his.

They walked out of the gates together. Vehicles were streaming through the normally quiet streets. There was practically a queue forming, including a van with a dish and aerial on top. The press had got wind of it.

They didn't speak until they were almost back at Bea's house.

'Do you want to come in, Ant, have a cup of tea?'

He nodded, and they walked to number twenty-three and then up the garden path and round the side to the back door. Bea's heart sank a little when she saw that the kitchen light was on and the door yielded when she tried it — her mum was home from work, as of course she would be at this time of day.

'Hello, love,' chirped Queenie. She had a metal tray bearing frozen chips in her hand.

'Hi, Mum,' Bea said. 'I've got Ant with me.'

'Oh, lovely! Come on in, then. Do you want some food? It's only egg and chips, but I can easily squeeze some more chips on my tray . . .' Her voice trailed off as she looked at Ant, and then at Bea. She cocked her head to one side. 'You look awful, both of you. What's happened?'

'There was a . . . we found a . . .' Bea realised that she couldn't actually say it. The words caught in her mouth.

'Someone's murdered my friend,' said Ant. 'We found his body at the allotment.'

'Oh my God! Sit down, both of you.'

Queenie put the tray on the countertop and headed to the kettle instead, filling it to the brim. Bea felt like she could weep. No amount of tea would make this better, she thought, but in fact, after a couple of mouthfuls of a brew so sweet she could have stood her spoon in it, she was able to speak again, and she slowly told her mum what had happened.

For the most part, Queenie listened without interrupting, but when Bea told her who had died, she gasped. 'Oh no. He was a lovely man. He was very kind when your father died, rang up a couple of times to check how things were at home and let me know if you'd been upset at school.'

Ant had stayed silent, staring at his undrunk tea, when Bea was talking, but now he spoke. 'Someone did that to him. And I'm going to find the bastard.' He glanced up. 'Sorry about the language, Mrs J.'

Queenie reached across the table and put her hand over his. 'That's quite all right. You're upset, love, of course you are. But you must leave all this to the police. Both of you.' She looked meaningfully at Bea. 'No investigating. Not this time.'

Bea drained the rest of her tea. 'Don't worry, Mum, I'm not getting involved. This isn't a game or a hobby. It's a terrible, terrible thing and I hope the police find whoever did it, lock them up and throw away the key.'

Then she realised what she'd said and clapped her hands to her mouth.

'What?' said Queenie.

'The key,' said Ant, dully. 'Dylan was locked in his shed and left to die.'

'I'm so sorry, love. Try not to think about it.'

'But where's the key? Has someone still got it or did they get rid?'

'If it's somewhere on-site, the police will find it, won't they?' said Bea. 'They'll brush it for fingerprints.'

'Bloody hell,' said Ant. 'They're probably trampling on Marvin right now with their size-nine feet.'

'Marvin?' said Queenie, looking confused. 'I thought you said it was Dylan Bradley that died.'

'Ant's marrow,' Bea whispered, and Queenie's mouth formed an 'o'.

Ant shook his head. 'Not that it matters anymore. It really doesn't, does it? Nothing really matters.'

Queenie squeezed his hand and gently took his mug of tea from him. 'This has gone a bit cold. Let me warm it up in the microwave, then I'll put the chips on.'

'I'm really not hungry, Mrs Jordan. I'd better go.' He braced his hands against the table as if he was about to get up.

'You're not going anywhere,' said Queenie. 'I'm doing some food for me, anyway. You can have some if you fancy it. Stay here for a little while. You've had a shock, love.'

Ant didn't take much persuading. He drank the reheated tea meekly, but couldn't manage any food. They took some more cups of tea into the lounge and watched the telly. Rather, the TV was on, but it was only Queenie who was watching the soaps, giving a running commentary as she normally did. Bea and Ant were lost in their own thoughts, each reliving the day and experiencing a series of shockwaves as they tried to process what had happened.

When the local news came on, there was already an item about Dylan's death. Queenie turned the sound up, unnecessarily. It was a fairly sparse item in terms of information, and no one was naming Dylan yet, but it included a live report from the allotments with a reporter standing in front of the police tape in the car park.

'. . . *The victim is believed to be a local man in his early sixties, and police say his death is being treated as suspicious.*'

'No kidding,' said Queenie. 'Locked in a shed with a trowel in the back of his head. More than a bit suspicious, I'd say.'

'Mum,' Bea frowned, 'can we not?'

'Not what?'

'Not talk about it like that, and can you please turn the sound down? It's deafening.'

'I'll do better than that.' She snapped the TV off, plunging the room into silence. 'It's time for bed, anyway. I'm sorry you had a horrible day, Ant. I'll see you in the morning, Bea.'

With that, she left them to it. Bea turned to Ant and rolled her eyes.

'Sorry about her,' she said.

'It's all right,' said Ant. 'She's lovely, your mum.'

'If you say so.'

'I do. You're lucky to have her. I haven't seen mine for ages.'

Ant's mum had lived in Cardiff with her sister, and two of Ant's siblings, since their family broke up.

'I should just go,' Ant said. 'Maybe I should try and get to Cardiff tonight. I can't face going back to Neville's.'

'Stay a bit longer. I don't mind talking about it with you. It was just Mum that was too much. I thought you were amazing today. You were so calm.'

'My first-aid training kicked in.'

'I heard you talking to him. That nearly broke me. You were so kind.'

'It just felt like the right thing to do. I knew he couldn't hear me, but I felt like he deserved to be treated like he was still with us, a real person, someone who mattered. It was a sort of respect thing. Does that sound mad?'

'Not mad at all. It was beautiful.'

He suddenly looked like he was going to cry. Bea moved closer to him on the sofa and put her arms round his waist. He leaned into her and wrapped his arms around her shoulders, and they sat together for a long time, not saying anything, just comforting each other.

When they drew apart, they looked at each other, eye to eye, so close that they could feel each other's breath on their faces.

Finally, Ant turned away. 'I'd better go.'

'You don't have to,' said Bea, and he looked at her again.

'Can I kip here, on the sofa?'

'You don't have to,' she repeated.

She stood up and held both his hands, gently pulling him up to join her.

'Are you sure?' he said.

'I'm sure.'

She led him through the room to the stairs, switching out the lights as they went.

CHAPTER FOUR

'Heard you get up in the night.'

Bea popped a couple of slices of bread into the toaster and kept her back turned so that Queenie wouldn't see her blushing.

'Yeah, I couldn't sleep so I got up and made a cuppa.'

'I thought I heard the back door go.'

Damn you and your bat-like ears, Bea thought, but said as smoothly as she could manage, 'I stepped out for a few minutes to get some fresh air. It was lovely out there, actually. Cold and clear. Lots of stars.'

Her mother sniffed loudly. Was she expressing scepticism? Bea still didn't turn round.

'Nice,' said Queenie. 'You'll be late for work, if you don't get a wriggle on.'

'I know. I'm going to get dressed in a minute.'

The toaster popped. Bea extracted her slices, put them on a plate, slathered them in butter, and grabbed her mug of tea. 'I'll take these upstairs.'

'All right, love. I'm nearly ready. I'll see you later.'

In her bedroom, Bea set the mug and plate on her bedside table. Yesterday's clothes were, uncharacteristically, in an untidy heap on the floor. She picked them up and put them in the little wicker clothes basket in the bottom of her wardrobe. The hems of her trousers were grubby with dust from the allotment. And suddenly she was back there, sitting in the sunshine, feeling the warmth on her face, and all the while only a few yards away a man lay on the floor of a shed with his head bashed in. She could hear his phone ringing now, the faint, muffled noise. She would never unhear it. And then she could see Ant bringing the spade down on the lock, smashing it away from the wood of the door. And there were Bradley's feet lying at such an odd angle, lifeless.

She found that she was staring into the soft darkness of the wardrobe. Her breathing was fast and shallow, and her chest felt tight as if she was being squeezed and squashed from the inside.

Come on, Bea, she told herself. *Get dressed and get yourself off to work.*

She looked along the rail and took out a shirt and some black trousers, held them up, then put them back. A stretchy top and leggings got the same treatment, then another outfit and another. The further she went along the rail, the more panicky she felt. Nothing was quite right. Nothing would do.

She started throwing rejected clothes onto the floor. When she got to the end of the rail, she was sweating profusely, and her legs felt like jelly. She was also furious that she hadn't got anything to wear. There must be *something* she could put on in all this mess.

But there wasn't. It was hopeless. She didn't want to go anywhere. No, that wasn't it. It wasn't that she didn't want to. She couldn't. What on earth was wrong with her?

This is silly, she told herself. She slowly made her way across the room and sat on her bed. Just those few steps took every ounce of energy, and she was shaking by the time she made it. She wondered if she was hungry but the sight of the cold toast on her plate turned her stomach and she started to heave. Perhaps she was coming down with something — you

23

couldn't always avoid catching the neighbourhood bugs working at somewhere like Costsave. That must be it.

She climbed into bed, curling up in a foetal position and pulling the covers up around her ears. She'd have five minutes here and then see how she felt. She pulled her duvet over her head and there, against her nose, was a slight mustiness and the twang of Lynx. She breathed it in, and her body started to relax.

At a quarter past eight, Queenie called out, 'I'm off now. See you later.'

Bea, who had been half-asleep, didn't reply.

Then she heard the door opening and Queenie coming in. 'What's up, love?'

'I'm not going in today,' she replied from the depths of her duvet cave.

'Are you ill?' The voice was close to her bed.

'Yeah. Stomach bug or something. Can you take that toast away?'

'Okay, are you going to be all right?'

'Yeah, I just need to sleep.'

'All right. I'm only five minutes away. I'll pop back at lunchtime.'

Bea grunted.

She listened as her mother left the room and pottered about the house. Finally, she heard her call out gently, 'Bye, love.' A click and the dull thud of the door closing announced that she was finally on her own, and instantly her panic started building again.

There was another murderer on the loose in Kingsleigh. Was the door locked? Was she safe? Would she ever feel safe again?

CHAPTER FIVE

Ant kept to the back of the staff room for the morning brief-ing, his thoughts switching restlessly between Dylan and Bea. He couldn't quite believe that Dylan was dead. Despite being a teacher, he was — had been — the nicest guy in the world. Who on earth would take a trowel to him like that? He may have kept calm when he'd discovered him, but now he was haunted by the memory. He liked a violent action film as much as the next person, but being confronted with the results of violence in real life was shocking and sickening. That moment, seeing Dylan's body, touching his cold neck to check for a pulse, would stay with him for the rest of his life.

As for Bea, he had an uneasy feeling that he'd just messed things up between them, big style. He loved her, had done so for quite a long time, but she'd always made it clear they existed in the friend zone, which was actually a pretty brilliant place to be. So he couldn't figure out what had happened between them last night. Had he taken advantage of her when she was upset and vulnerable? Was he a really bad person? Would she hate him now?

He'd fully expected Bea to be at work today but couldn't see her there. He scanned the room and his eyes met those of Neville, the deputy manager. Ant had been lodging with

Neville, his wife and two young daughters for several months. Neville was something of a mentor to Ant and saw it as his Christian duty to try and guide him through the troubled times he'd experienced since his family break-up. But, although grateful for a warm room and home-cooked food, Ant found the Parkin household a little oppressive.

He groaned inwardly. He hadn't told Neville he was staying out last night. By the look in Neville's eye, there were going to be consequences.

After the briefing, as Ant headed for the men's locker room, he could sense Neville following him and his heart sank. He pushed open the door and looked behind him. Sure enough, Neville was looming towards him in the corridor.

'Anthony—'

'Neville, if this is about my living arrangements, can we talk at break time?'

'Yes, of course. I just don't understand why you didn't ring or text. Carole and I were very worried. It was thoughtless and selfish behaviour.'

The thought of enduring a bollocking during his break, and then sitting through a frosty family dinner in the evening was too much.

'Neville,' Ant said, 'you and Carole have been amazing, you really have, but I think it's time to move on. I'll collect my stuff after work today.'

Without waiting for a reply, he dived into the locker room. He sent a quick text to Bea to ask if she was okay and then started getting changed into his Costsave outdoor gear. Neville didn't follow him in and by the time Ant went back out into the corridor he had gone. Ant's relief was tinged with guilt, but he tried to put both feelings behind him as he went out into the car park to tackle the trolleys.

At break time, Ant couldn't face the staff room. Instead, he checked his phone while he wandered into the stores. He frowned as he saw that there was no reply from Bea and, even though his first message was marked as delivered, he sent another one, just in case. He found Dean in the makeshift man cave he'd created in a quiet corner behind some stacks of boxes.

He unfolded a rickety garden chair and set it next to Dean's. 'Milk and two sugars, please, mate.'

'No can do,' said Dean. 'They've taken my kettle away. Said it was company policy. I've got to use the staff room like everyone else or have something cold.' He brandished a can of cherry-flavoured Coke.

'You're kidding. That's one of the perks of the job, isn't it? A cuppa to warm up in between deliveries.'

'Not anymore. The only perk now is measly staff discount like everyone else and the chance that you might be left alone for a few hours, if you're lucky.'

Ant was pondering the merits of a cold drink rather than the tea he'd been looking forward to when Tyler appeared. He was Costsave's newest and youngest recruit, and Ant had taken him under his wing.

'Tyler, mate,' said Ant. 'You don't fancy bringing me a cuppa from the staff room, do you?'

Tyler didn't hesitate. 'Sure. Do you want one, Dean?'

Dean held his can up in salute. 'No ta. You get one for yourself while you're there, though.'

'Will do. Milk and two sugars, Ant?'

Ant gave him two thumbs up. 'Just the job. Thanks, Tyler.'

Dean sniggered as Tyler walked away. 'Does he do everything you say?'

'Shut up. He's a good lad.'

'Yeah, I know. Anyway, what's the news about Mr Bradley? Word has it that you were the one who found him. Is it true?'

Ant would rather not have spoken about it, but he told Dean an edited version of the previous fifteen hours or so, deliberately omitting any mention of Bea. He hadn't always been friends with Dean, and although they got on fairly well nowadays, he wasn't someone Ant would confide in. But he had found himself opening up to Dylan these past few months, as they enjoyed the summer evenings, having a beer or a smoke. He could probably talk to his mate Saggy about

27

most things, but, come to think of it, the only person he would really trust was Bea herself.

He closed his eyes, remembering how she had felt in his arms, the smell of her skin, the delicacy of her touch. She was everything. His phone remained silent and motionless in his pocket. No new messages. He couldn't bear it if he'd messed things up with her. God damn it, why was everything so complicated?

'You all right, mate? You look like someone just kicked you in the kidneys.'

Ant opened his eyes, which had become screwed up, while his jaw muscles tensed and his nose wrinkled. 'Yeah, I'm fine.'

Dean shook his head. 'You're a terrible liar. Odd, when you've had so much practice.'

'What are you talking about? I don't lie.'

'You were famous for it at school. How many times did your granny die so you could bunk off PE or a Maths test?' He grinned.

'Oh yeah, well, school doesn't count, does it? You just do what you can to get by.'

Tyler reappeared, carefully carrying two mugs. He was followed by the more substantial figure of Bob.

'Is this a private club or can anyone join in?' he said.

'Pull up a pew.' Dean indicated the stack of folding chairs.

Bob took a chair, set one up for himself and one for Tyler, then lowered himself down rather tentatively. They all watched with delicious anticipation as the rickety chair shifted under his weight, the various hinges and joints squeaking in protest but staying intact.

'Just needed a bit of male company,' Bob said. 'The staff room is like a WI meeting. I looked around and realised I was the only bloke up there. Well, apart from Neville, but you know . . . Nothing wrong with the fair sex, but . . .'

'You could do with a rest from all the squeaky voices,' said Dean.

Ant winced and wondered whether to point out that Dean's own voice was at the higher end of the register, but he didn't want to rock the boat. 'How did you get on yesterday?' he asked Bob, hoping to change the subject. 'Frome, wasn't it?'

'Oh yeah, it was very nice — very nice indeed — but just a bit far from Kingsleigh. Most of our guests will be coming from here, so I think it's got to be somewhere a bit closer to home.'

Bob and Dot's wedding felt like a community event, with the staff room getting regular updates on colour themes, flowers, venues and catering options. Colleagues had even benefited from cake samples and had contributed to a poll on the whiteboard in which chocolate sponge had proved more popular than traditional fruitcake by a surprisingly large margin.

'I haven't had my invite yet,' said Dean.

Ant winced again. This could get awkward.

'Don't you worry,' Bob said. 'We haven't sent them out yet. All in good time.'

'Do you mean I'm getting one?' Dean's voice was incredulous.

'You're on the list, with Eileen as your plus one. That's all right, isn't it?'

Dean rolled his eyes. 'Yeah, I s'pose. Can't leave the old bird out.'

'You're on fire today, Dean,' said Ant. 'If your mum knew you called her that, you'd be in so much trouble.'

'Nah. I've called her worse to her face.'

'Somehow the wedding doesn't seem very important with everything else that's gone on.' Bob's face seemed to sag as he spoke. 'I can't believe what happened with Dylan. Such a nice bloke. It's really close to home, isn't it? I rang Lionel last night. He was pretty shaken up. I know they didn't see eye to eye on a lot of things but at the end of the day we're all growers, aren't we? We all love that place.'

'Did you know I found him?' said Ant.

'I did hear that, lad. I'm sorry you had to go through it. I can't imagine how awful that must have been.' Bob leaned across and put a weighty hand on Ant's shoulder, resting it there for a minute or two.

The group lapsed into silence.

'Why didn't they see eye to eye?' said Dean. 'What was the beef?'

'Well, the group running the allotments are a conservative lot — they like things done a certain way.'

Ant snorted his agreement.

'Dylan was always a bit different,' Bob went on. 'He was a no-dig, organic gardener. He left bits of carpet on top of the soil for ages to kill the weeds, which, to be fair, we'd done a few years before, so he wasn't the first. The others took exception, though, said it looked scruffy. A lot of them were secretly hoping that his veg would be rubbish, and the first couple of years he had patchy results, but this year his stuff was looking great. He had some fun winding his detractors up, saying he was going to beat them all at the flower and produce show. It didn't go down well.'

Dean rolled his eyes. 'Sounds like handbags at dawn to me.'

Bob frowned. 'It was a bit, but you'd be surprised how seriously everyone takes this stuff. When Cyril's tomatoes got nicked last week, there were accusations flying left, right and centre. It was getting nasty.'

'People thought Dylan was the tomato thief?'

'Cyril did. I don't think anyone else seriously entertained it. It was just something else to throw at him.'

'Messy.' Dean mimed lobbing an imaginary tomato and spread his hands out as it exploded on impact.

Bob ignored him. 'To be honest, it wasn't just gardening. He liked shaking things up a bit, getting under people's skin. He was doing it on the council, too.'

'He was on the front page of the *Bugle* again this week, wasn't he?' said Tyler.

Dean grunted. 'He should have known better than to try and change things. K-town's just not up for it.'

Ant, who had been quiet through all this, sat up. 'Trying to change things, do things better — that's a good thing, isn't it? It shouldn't get you killed.'

The others all looked at him. 'No one's saying it did, son,' said Bob. 'Chances are he surprised someone breaking into a shed or something.'

This was no comfort to Ant, whose father was currently serving the latest in a long line of jail stretches for burglary. 'Well, you don't deserve to get killed for that either. Most robbers wouldn't bash someone if they're challenged. Basic rule is if you're rumbled on a job, if you can make your way out, you scarper.'

Bob looked at Ant, searchingly. He was well aware of Ant's family history and, whether Ant knew it or not, he tried to fill in the gap left by Ant's dad, just like Neville. Ant had been doing very nicely at Costsave, and the way he'd taken to tending the allotment had been wonderful, but now Bob feared that losing Dylan, and leaving the safe haven of Neville's spare room, might send him off the rails. He needed a bit of support.

'You're right. No one deserves to die like that,' he said. 'It's a dark day for the town. A very dark day. Now—' he slapped his legs — 'back to the coalface! Let me buy you a pint after work, though. I reckon we could both do with one.'

'Oh,' said Dean, brightening up. 'That's very good of you, Bob.'

Bob sighed. 'Boys' trip to the pub it is.'

CHAPTER SIX

Dot glanced up at the growing queue of customers. She loved working on the tills at Costsave — it suited her down to the ground — but it was much more of a slog without Bea at the next checkout. She had come into work this morning bursting to tell Bea about her day out with Bob. Not only that, but there was a new murder case to pick over. She was sure that Bea would have some theories about it. Knowing her, she would have already started digging around to see what she could find out. So, she was rather crushed to find out Bea wasn't in, and, with no one to take her place on the tills, it had been non-stop all morning.

At break time, she sent Bea a quick text then found Eileen and Kirsty in the staff room. They were a willing audience for her tales of swanky Bablington Court and the lunch she and Bob had enjoyed there, but it wasn't the same without Bea. She noticed Bob slinking out of the room and wondered if he was getting a little weary of wedding talk. He'd seemed as keen as her yesterday, but perhaps it was all an act. She made a mental note to check in with him later.

After discussion of menus, décor and the reality TV star Dot thought she'd spotted at a nearby table, talk turned to the death of Dylan Bradley. Neither Eileen nor Kirsty had much to add to the information that was already public knowledge but that didn't stop either of them holding forth. Kingsleigh was a small town and Dylan's roles at the school and on the town council had made him high profile in local terms. Again, Dot thought that Bea, with her involvement in a few investigations into the seamier side of Kingsleigh, would have had something more interesting to say. In any case, she was sure Bea would want to hear all the gossip and spotted an opportunity to gather some more nuggets soon after lunch.

Just before two o'clock, Wendy Fox joined her queue. Wendy was a familiar figure in the town, having been the clerk to the council for fifteen years or so. Despite local councillors' fondness for a photo opportunity and a headline in the *Bugle*, Dot suspected that the fact that anything ran smoothly in the town was mostly down to Wendy and her staff. She was known for being a no-nonsense sort, always immaculately turned out, in smart office clothes and a statement necklace, with her hair dyed a silver blonde and styled into a neat bob. Today, she was waiting in line, holding a couple of items, and looking pensive.

With Wendy only buying a large jar of coffee and a box of a dozen iced doughnuts, Dot knew she would have to be quick to get anything out of her. As soon as she'd given the previous customer her receipt, she played her opening gambit.

'I was so sorry to hear about Councillor Bradley,' she said. 'It must have been an awful shock.'

She beeped Wendy's items through and rang up the total.

'Yes, it was,' Wendy said. 'Hence the doughnuts. A bit of a sugar boost to rally the troops.'

Dot smiled. 'That's a nice thought. I expect you've been busy.'

'We're cancelling tonight's Community Safety sub-committee, that took a bit of work, and we've opened a book of condolence — it's been steady with the public in and out. Plenty of councillors in, too.'

'Wanting to talk about him? Share their memories?'

Wendy grimaced. 'Wondering about his place on the council and how we're going to fill it. No room for sentiment in local politics, apparently.' Her pursed lips expressed her unspoken thoughts about her elected masters. She paid for her shopping with her personal debit card.

'I might pop down,' said Dot. 'Pay my respects. It's just awful.'

Wendy nodded. She put the coffee jar into a reusable shopping bag but held on to the doughnut box to keep the contents flat. 'Thank you,' she said and marched quickly out of the store.

As Dot greeted the next customer, she saw Ant sauntering along the front of the checkouts, doing his old trick of carrying an empty cardboard box, a sure sign that he was malingering. She carried on processing a rather large trolley full of shopping, but called out to him as he got nearer, 'Ant! Do you know how Bea is?'

Ant visibly flinched and veered away from her like he'd been prodded with a harpoon. 'No, why should I? Why are you asking me?'

Dot screwed up her eyes. 'Because you're her friend . . .' She said it with a hint of a question mark at the end.

He relaxed a bit. 'Oh, yeah. Sure. I don't know. I've texted her but she hasn't replied.'

'Mm, me too. I hope she's okay. Better get a move on. Bandit at eleven o'clock.'

Ant looked at her blankly. 'Huh?'

'Neville's coming.'

Ant didn't need telling a third time. He shot off, threading his way through two checkouts and heading for the back of the store.

Shopping processed, Dot helped her customer pack her bags.

Finally, there was a little lull and she was able to mull over the day so far. She may not have found out much about Dylan Bradley, but she had learned that Ant was being uncharacteristically touchy about Bea.

34

CHAPTER SEVEN

At half past five, Bea was back in bed. She had managed to get up for a couple of hours in the afternoon and watched a few episodes of her favourite property programme, but when she found herself shouting at another couple, who, after viewing three jaw-droppingly lovely cottages in pretty villages decided to 'keep looking', she took herself back to bed. If she was tired of *Escape to the Country*, she was clearly tired of life.

It wasn't the kind of weariness that would let her sleep, though, and she lay in bed wide-eyed, listening to the everyday sounds in the world outside — cars driving past, kids chattering on the way home, someone kicking a football. Nothing had changed. Everything was the same. Except her. She was the odd one out, the one who couldn't cope.

She pulled the duvet up a little more and got the faintest whiff of Lynx. She hadn't answered any of Ant's texts. She hadn't answered anybody's. The longer she didn't reply to him, though, the odder she felt. She wondered where he was now, how he was feeling. Would they ever be able to look each other in the eye again, let alone be friends?

Before too long she heard someone approaching the house. Her stomach gave a little flip thinking it might be Ant, but then she realised that she could hear two sets of footsteps, one of them a very distinctive click-clack of heels. She sat up in bed and was just fixing her hair in a ponytail when there was a sharp knock on her bedroom door and Queenie and Dot came barging in.

'Hello, doll,' said Dot.

'Um, hello,' said Bea. 'This is . . . unexpected.'

Dot had taken her heels off and padded over to Bea's bed in her stockinged feet. 'Do you mind if I come in?'

'Er, no. Make yourself at home.'

Dot perched on one side of the bed and Queenie on the other side. It was starting to feel quite crowded.

'How are you, love? I heard you were poorly.'

Bea looked at Queenie and wondered whether that was all she had told Dot.

'I'm okay,' she said. 'I'm just . . . I don't know. Tired.'

The two most important women in her life both looked at her sympathetically. There was an element of steel in her mum's eyes, though, which unsettled her.

'How's your tum?' said Queenie.

'My stomach?' For a moment Bea had forgotten her cover story. 'Oh, yes, I think it's better.'

'Want to get up for some tea?'

'Yeah, I might try something. What is it?'

'Soup and toast? Would that be nice?'

Bea nodded. 'How was Bablington Court, by the way?' she said to Dot. 'Did you book it?'

'It was amazing. Very posh but comfortable, and the staff were lovely. We think we saw a celeb in the dining room. One of those girls off that thing.'

Bea rolled her eyes. 'Oh yeah, I know. *Her.*'

Dot laughed. 'I've been trying to place her all day. Long hair, puffed up lips.'

'Well, that narrows it down.' Bea was laughing now too, but she noticed Queenie wasn't joining in. 'You all right, Mum?'

Queenie forced a smile, but she wasn't fooling anyone. 'I'm just worried about you.'

'I'm fine now. Soup and toast would be lovely. And a cuppa. You two go and put the kettle on and I'll come down.'

The women left her to it, and Bea hauled herself out of bed. It wasn't worth getting dressed, so she just reached for the dressing gown at the end of her bed and threaded her arms into it. Then her feet searched around for her slippers. One of her toes brushed against something hard.

She looked down and saw an orange plastic cigarette lighter on the carpet, half under her bed. She scooped it up and put it in her dressing gown pocket, thanking her lucky stars that neither Queenie nor Dot had spotted it.

CHAPTER EIGHT

In the Ship, the men of Costsave started their evening with a toast to Dylan Bradley. Ant, Bob, Dean and Tyler raised their glasses and said his name in unison. Then they each took a swig of their beer or cider and stayed silent for a while, remembering him in their own way.

'I just don't really get how you can be talking to someone one day and the next day they're gone,' said Ant. 'I can't take it in.'

Bob took a sip of his pint. 'It's one of life's mysteries, son. Even though I'm happy with Dot, obviously, I still miss my Babs, can't believe I'm never going to see her again. It's the only certainty we've got, though. We're all going to go that way one day.'

'True that. Gotta make the most of it, haven't we?' said Tyler. 'Try and get something good out of every day. That's what Scout says.' Scout was Tyler's girlfriend. She had lost one of her brothers earlier in the year, and everyone was amazed how well she was doing since then, working hard in the sixth form and helping her other brothers to run the family business.

'She's got an old head on young shoulders, that one,' said Bob, and they raised their glasses again and took another drink.

'Yesterday is history, tomorrow is a mystery, today is a gift — that's why we call it the present,' said Dean.

They all looked at him, with varying levels of incredulity.

'That's deep, man,' said Ant.

Dean shrugged. 'Mum's got it in cross-stitch, framed up in our downstairs bog.'

'Nice.' Ant made a mental note to tell Bea about it. It was just the sort of titbit she'd love. If she was still talking to him . . . He was unsettled by her non-appearance today and even more uneasy at her continuing radio silence. He surreptitiously checked his phone. She still hadn't replied to his messages.

'Uh-uh!' Bob wagged a sausage-like index finger at him. 'Phones away. Let's just have an hour talking. Like people used to in the old days.'

'I'll drink to that,' said Dean.

'The thing about Dylan,' Bob continued, 'is that he was a good example of how to live life — not everyone agreed with him, but he gave his all to everything he did. Threw himself into the school and politics, even his allotment and growing stuff. He was enthusiastic.'

'Yeah. And he'd help anyone who needed it,' said Ant. 'He certainly helped me.'

'As busy as he was, he always had time for you,' said Bob. 'That's something we can learn from him.'

They all took another swig.

'I just don't get who would hurt him,' said Ant.

'Well, Bob did just say not everyone agreed with him. I don't have a scooby about politics, but I do know it can get nasty,' said Dean.

'Not in a little place like Kingsleigh, surely,' said Ant.

Bob wiped a bit of froth off his top lip. 'You'd be surprised. Power goes to people's heads, whether it's a town like this or Westminster. It can be a nasty game and Dylan didn't mind stirring things up.'

'What did he do?' asked Tyler.

'Well, he was trying to change actual council meetings, so they were more open to everyone. He was arguing for a bigger childcare allowance for councillors who needed it, or a crèche, and more time for questions from the public.'

'Seems fair,' said Ant.

'The guy I was talking to called it "woke". What does that word even mean?' said Bob. 'Everyone bandies it about these days.'

'It means being considerate of other people's needs and feelings,' said Tyler. 'If you hear someone using it as a slur, they're a twat.'

'Hey,' said Dean. 'That's not fair. I use it all the time—'

The others started laughing.

'What? Shut up.'

'No offence, Dean,' said Tyler. 'I won't call people who use it twats in future. Each to their own and all that.'

Dean nodded and tipped his glass towards him. 'Cheers, mate. I appreciate that.'

'That's okay. I wouldn't want to deliberately hurt your feelings.'

Dean smiled. 'You're a gent . . .' Then he stopped and realised what Tyler was doing. 'And a twat.'

They all clinked glasses again and drank in amiable silence for a moment or two.

'He wasn't universally popular up at the allotments, either,' Bob continued. 'I mean, *we* liked him, didn't we Ant, but he ruffled the feathers of the older ones with his no-dig this and organic that. Some of them think they know it all and don't like new ideas.'

'Yeah, but come on, no one's going to kill someone over a row about growing stuff, are they?' said Dean.

'Aren't they? He was walloped with a trowel at the allotments,' said Tyler. 'Maybe that's a big fat clue.'

Ant rummaged in his pocket and drew out a notebook and biro.

'What are you doing?' said Dean.

'I'm going to write some stuff down. Do this properly.'

'Do what properly?'

'Try and find out who killed Dylan.'

Bob shook his head. 'Don't waste your time, son. Chances are the police have already found some prints on the handle of the trowel, run them through their computer and have someone in their sights. It'll all be over by tomorrow.'

'And if it isn't?'

'Then it won't take them long to find out who it was. That's their job.'

Ant grunted. 'You've got a lot more faith in them than I have.'

'Haven't you learned your lesson? Doing your own investigating is dangerous. People get hurt.' Bob glanced sideways at Tyler, who nodded.

'I know it's dangerous, but it's also important. And I *have* learned a lot, a hell of a lot. I've learned from the best. For example—' Ant opened the notebook and scribbled on one corner of a blank page to get the biro ink flowing — 'you start with the basics: motive, means and opportunity. Hang on.'

They all watched as he wrote the words out slowly. Bob couldn't help smiling to himself. Not only was Ant's handwriting beautifully neat, but the spelling was correct, too. He had come a long way since he'd started at Costsave, unable to read or write.

Ant clocked his expression. 'What? What have I done wrong?'

'Nothing, Ant. You've got it all spot on. You can fill in the "means" bit pretty easily, can't you? Anyone can hit anyone with a trowel. Could be male or female, old or young.'

'Well, whoever it was must have used a lot of force. They can't be ancient or a bit spindly. I think we can rule out Charles. And Dean.'

'Oi!'

'Ha! Yes. Okay, just put ninety-five per cent of Kingsleigh in that bit then.'

Ant duly wrote it down, and soon all four of them were making suggestions for the other categories and, after another round of drinks, the page was full.

'I'll need a bigger notebook at this rate,' said Ant.

41

'Why are you carrying one around anyway?' said Dean.

Ant blushed. 'Well, you know . . . It's um . . .'

Dean looked at him blankly.

'Okay, I use it to write down words I really like or words I want to find out more about or words that are difficult but useful, so I want to practise writing them.' He stopped, consumed with embarrassment.

'What sort of words?' Dean grinned. 'Let's have a look!' He made a grab for the notebook, but Ant swept it up with one hand and fended him off with the other.

'Gerroff, Deano!'

'Hey, boys, that's enough.' The sound of Bob's authoritative tones stopped their tussling. 'We're just having a nice drink, aren't we? No need for nonsense.'

'Sorry, Bob,' said Ant.

'Yeah, sorry,' said Dean. He paused. 'What words, though?'

'Silence.' He put the notebook back in his pocket.

'Rude,' said Dean.

'No, that's one of my words. S-i-l-e-n-c-e. It's got two ess sounds but they're different letters. I just write down stuff like that. I'm a word nerd now.'

'Fair play, mate. Fair play.' Dean held his hand up and he and Ant high-fived, while Bob looked on approvingly. They weren't a bad bunch of lads at Costsave, not bad at all. On the strength of that feeling, he stumped up for a third round and they chewed the fat for a bit longer then called it a day.

As they bundled out of the pub, agreeing that it had been a top evening and that they should do it again soon, Bob remembered why he'd suggested it in the first place.

'Ant!' he called out, as the three lads set off down the high street. 'Come here a minute.'

Ant told the others to go on ahead while he trotted back to Bob, carrying the small, tattered holdall that contained all the belongings that he'd collected from Neville's house on the way there.

'I heard you and Neville have parted ways. Where are you staying now?'

Ant shuffled his feet. 'I'm going to go to Saggy's for a bit. It's all right there. They've got a nice padded sun lounger and a couple of German shepherds to keep me warm.'

Bob pulled a face. 'Why don't you stay at mine? I've got a spare room and I'm at Dot's half the time anyway. Plus, there's a never-ending supply of sausages and bacon in the fridge. Always feels a bit sad doing a fry-up for one. What do you say?'

CHAPTER NINE

True to his word, Bob provided a breakfast fit for a king the next morning. By the time Ant wandered downstairs, after his best night's sleep for ages, Bob had two large frying pans on the go and the whole house smelled of bacon. Ant stood in the doorway, blinking. It was almost too much to take in.

'I didn't know if you like black pudding or not,' Bob called over, his voice competing with the sweet tones of Dolly Parton extolling the virtues of her Tennessee mountain home, 'so I've just put one slice in for you. Fried bread or toast?'

'Fried bread, please! If there's some going.'

'Coming up! It'll be ready in two minutes. Help yourself to tea. Turn the radio down if it's too loud for you.'

Ant shambled over to the breakfast bar, sloshed half an inch of milk into a mug and poured some tea. He looked around for a sugar bowl.

Bob spotted him and waved a spatula in the direction of one of the cupboards. 'Sugar? Up there, behind the stack of saucers. Dot thinks I've given up.'

Ant grinned, found the secret sugar bowl and added two generous spoonsful to his tea before replacing the bowl in its hiding place and then perching on a stool. He was feeling a

44

little thick-headed, and slightly queasy. Must be the unaccustomed solid eight hours' sleep, Ant thought. It wouldn't be anything to do with three pints of cider on an empty stomach . . .

Bob dished up and threw the pans into the sink, where they hissed and spluttered as hot metal met soapy water. Then he carried the plates over to the breakfast bar.

'He we are, sir. A proper full English. You won't see a hash brown in this house, although occasionally I'll fry up a potato cake if I've got some leftover mash. Not today, though.'

'Blimey, Bob, this is epic.' Ant added a good dollop of ketchup to his plate and tucked in. Any doubts about his physical robustness were banished as the hot food hit the spot. They ate without talking, concentrating on the job in hand, savouring every mouthful, while a succession of country songs washed over them in a warm and schmaltzy wave. When Ant had briefly stayed with Bob a year or two ago, it was the music that had driven him out. Now, though, he found himself liking it. It added to the feel-good vibe.

Eventually, Ant pushed his plate away a little and sat up on his stool to relieve the pressure on his stomach. 'Bloody hell, Bob, I'm never leaving, mate. That was spectacular. No wonder Dot said yes. I'd marry you, if you asked me.'

Bob worked at a bit of food stuck between his top teeth with his tongue, then resorted to digging at it with his fingernail. Mission accomplished, he replied, 'Dot must never know about this, son. She thinks I'm slimming down for the big day next year.'

Ant held his hands up. 'None of my business, but has she told you to lose weight, because that's a bit off, isn't it?'

Bob patted his large abdomen. 'No, she's not like that. It's coming from me. I want to look good on my wedding day. So does she. We're both trying to be our best selves for the photos.'

Ant nodded. 'I shouldn't encourage you, then, but seriously, Bob, that was the best breakfast I've ever eaten. After so long at Nev's I'd forgotten how normal people live. We went from cereals to porridge to weird grains. I honestly think he doesn't get his supplies from work anymore, he goes to the agricultural feed store. I feel sorry for their two girls. If they ever get their hands on a box of Coco Pops, they'd have to scrape the kids off the ceiling.'

Bob smiled. 'He's a good sort, though, Neville. In spite of it all.'

'Oh, I know,' he said hastily. 'I really owe him. I'm sorry it all ended the way it did. I'll have to make it up to him somehow. We're not really talking at the moment.'

He looked down at the table, remembering someone else who'd stopped communicating with him. It had been more than twenty-four hours since he'd heard from Bea. The longer the gap, the worse he felt. He resolved that if she wasn't in work today, he'd call round at her house afterwards and break the ice.

'By the way,' said Bob, 'word on the allotment WhatsApp group is that no one's been arrested yet and it's still all taped off. No access allowed at all. People are going mad. That's thirty-six hours without watering. I expect Marvin is okay, but I can't bear to think about the state of our dwarf beans. They were doing so well, too. Don't know if we'll have time to undo the damage before the show.'

Ant shrugged. 'Everyone will be in the same boat, though, won't they?'

'Except the back-garden growers. They'll all have the edge now. The police will have to open up the site today or there'll be a riot.'

Kingsleigh had experienced some social disorder earlier in the year and Ant doubted that anyone would want to go down that road again.

'That lot wouldn't take to the streets. It would all be behind the scenes. A word with the chief constable. A quiet chat in the local Rotary Club. A nod and a wink at the masonic lodge. You probably know better than me how all that stuff works.'

46

Bob looked offended. 'Not me, mate. I'm not part of that crew.'

'I bet they've asked you to join, though.'

He looked a bit shifty. 'Well, maybe, but it's not my thing.'

'Wouldn't have been Dylan's either, would it?'

'No, not at all. He wasn't a joiner like that. He was outside all the normal cliques and groups.' Bob stood up. 'Come on, lad, time we weren't here. Costsave awaits!'

They quickly dealt with the dishes. Ant washed while Bob dried and put everything neatly away. Five minutes later, they were in Bob's car and heading to work.

'Bob, can you add me to the allotment WhatsApp group?'

'I can't. That's Lionel's domain. You can text him to ask.'

'Oh. Mm, I dunno. I'm not his favourite person. I don't really need to be in the group. I just want to know who is.'

'That's easy, then. I can give you the list of names. Listen, if you and Bea are investigating, I want in. This one's personal, isn't it? You and I have lost a friend.'

'Thanks, Bob. I'll talk to Bea.' Ant checked his phone. No answer to his many messages. 'If she's in today.'

'You guys okay? You fallen out or something?'

'No, we're all right.' There must have been something in his tone that betrayed his doubt, because Bob glanced sideways at him. 'Actually, I haven't heard from her. It's all a bit weird. I don't honestly know.'

As if summoned by their conversation, Ant spotted a familiar figure walking along the pavement by the leisure centre in a leather-look jacket and black trousers, and hair in an artfully messy bun.

'Hey, there she is. Can you stop the car?'

Bob drew up alongside the kerb, let Ant out and drove off carefully. Bea was twenty metres or so ahead and Ant ran to catch up with her. He would normally have yelled something cheeky, maybe even sent an ironic wolf whistle her way, but he couldn't bring himself to do it today. He felt weirdly shy.

He didn't want to startle her, though, so he made as much noise as he could running along and then, when he was a few metres away, called her name.

She spun round. 'Oh, hi.' She smiled, but it was a tight, joyless effort, here one minute and gone the next, and her jaw was tense.

'Are you okay? Are you feeling better? I messaged yesterday.'

'Yeah, I just saw. I was having a day off from my phone. I'm fine.'

Fine, thought Ant. A word that can mean a million things, but rarely means what it says.

'Did your mum say anything about the other night?'

She shook her head. 'No, not really. I think she might suspect, though.'

'Did you find my lighter? It's gone walkabout somewhere.'

'Oh, yeah, it was on the floor. I'm sorry, I forgot to bring it.'

'No problem. It's not urgent. I've got another one. I should give up, really, shouldn't I?'

She shrugged. 'It's up to you, Ant. I mean, it's healthier not to.'

'Mm, something else to work on. Anyway, I've got loads to tell you.'

'Yeah?'

What he wanted to say was that he'd missed her, that he hadn't been able to stop thinking about her, that a day without her texts, without hearing her voice, had been agony. He wanted to tell her that he was starting to realise how important she was to him, whether it was as a friend or much more, that he needed her in his life on whatever terms she wanted . . . What came out of his mouth was different.

'The boys and I went to the pub. I've started writing a case file for Dylan. I'm pretty sure you'll think we've made a good start.' He started fumbling in his pocket for his notebook.

Her face clouded over. 'That's great, but I don't want to get involved.'

Involved? What? With him?

'What do you mean?'

'I can't do another investigation. It was fun for a while, but it all got too much, didn't it? Too much for me, anyway. Murder isn't a game, and it's not a business for amateurs like us. It's over, Ant. I'm done.'

CHAPTER TEN

'This place isn't the same without you. I'm so glad you're back.'
Dot linked her arm through Bea's and gave it a little squeeze.

'So am I,' said Bea.

'Tum all better?'

Bea hesitated, then lowered her voice. 'It wasn't really a
stomach bug. I had a bit of a . . . I don't know, funny turn
when I was getting ready. I reckon I just needed a day off.'

Dot frowned. 'Funny turn?'

'Just a bit wobbly. I went all hot and bothered and my
legs stopped working. I didn't tell Mum because she would
have panicked.' Bea's mum had suffered for years with agoraphobia, relying on Bea to be her link with the outside world.

'Sounds like that's what you had — a panic attack.'

Bea stopped walking. 'Do you think that's what it was?
It's happened a few times since February, actually. What happened at the allotments the day before yesterday has brought
it all back. It was properly grim.'

'I'd say it was natural to have some sort of reaction to
what you've been through.'

Dot squeezed her arm again and they walked on to their
tills, where they separated to start their respective opening-up

50

routines, adjusting their chairs, logging in, making sure everything was as it should be.

George strode past them with her big bunch of keys. 'Ready, ladies?' She didn't stop to hear their answers and was soon checking her watch and then unlocking the front door and activating the automatic mechanism. A few customers trickled in.

As Bea watched them, she realised she was still looking out for Reg, who always used to be there at eight o'clock on the dot, to buy his *Racing Post* and packet of cigarettes before spending the rest of the day in the betting shop. He'd come to a sticky end last year, behind the bus stop only a couple of hundred metres from where she was sitting now. She shivered.

A woman wearing a long coat that didn't quite cover up her pink pyjamas came trotting towards her till. She had half a dozen items in her basket, which she quickly unloaded onto the conveyor belt. Bea beeped a tin of sweetcorn, a jar of mixed herbs, a packet of vegetable stock cubes, one red onion and a bag of Costsave value-brand pasta shells through.

'Let me guess,' she said, although commenting on customers' shopping was a risky game, unless you were just saying how nice something was, 'someone's got Food Tech today and didn't mention it. Mediterranean pasta?'

The woman nodded grimly and bundled the ingredients into her bag. 'Spot on. Jaden only told me this morning. Why do they do this to us?'

Bea wasn't sure if she was referring to the school or her child. Both, probably.

'It never changes,' she said, having suffered that exact lesson at Kingsleigh Comp herself. 'Good luck! That's four pounds eleven pence, please.'

The woman looked stricken. 'I . . . um . . . haven't brought my card. I've only got cash. I've not got enough.'

She looked into her bag. 'You'd better take these back.' She handed Bea the pot of mixed herbs and the stock cubes. 'Someone will be able to give him a sprinkle and a spare cube, won't they? Silly everyone bringing in their own.'

Bea took the items off the bill and rang the total up again. This time the woman handed over three pound coins, collected her change, and sprinted out of the store clutching her shopping bag to her chest.

'Oh dear,' said Dot, who had witnessed the conversation. 'There's always someone worse off than yourself, isn't there?'

'Yeah. Who'd have kids, eh?'

'Well, it's not the worst thing in the world — I wouldn't be without my Sal for anything — but they are sent to try you. Not feeling broody, are you?'

'Christ, no. I only just managed to look after Charles's dog for a few weeks, I'm not ready for a kid. I'm only just getting started.'

'Good, plenty of time for that. Listen, Bea, I've had an idea about what you *could* do.'

'What is it?'

A trolley pulled up next to Dot's checkout and a woman started unloading an impressive amount of fruit and veg.

'I'll tell you later.'

Bea had another customer, too, and the tempo of the day soon picked up, with a steady stream of shoppers. Bea tried to focus on what she did best, working efficiently, offering a friendly word if it looked like it might be welcome, having a chat and a laugh with some of her regulars, and keeping an eye out for opportunities for her customers to get better value.

'Actually, two of the eight packs work out cheaper than this twelveser,' she said to a woman with a tired toddler perched in the seat of her trolley, indicating a bundle of plastic-wrapped toilet rolls. 'Shall I get someone to fetch you a couple?'

When the woman agreed, Bea switched on her call light and before long Ant came shambling along to her till. He wasn't normally on the shop floor, and Bea was surprised to see him there.

'Can you fetch two eight packs of these, please?' she asked. 'And put this one back?'

'Yeah, sure,' he said, and Bea started to help pack the rest of the shopping into bags.

Ant took so long that all the shopping was bagged and ready to go, the toddler, Callum, had started to whine and the woman looked like she was on the verge of giving up.

'I could have fetched it myself,' she said.

'It's better this way,' said Bea, trying to smile. 'He needs to get his step count up.'

'Don't we all? This is the first time I've been out of the house for two days. It's just me, him and four walls.'

Now Bea noticed the rings under her eyes and the unbrushed hair. 'He your first?'

'Yeah. My partner works away. I didn't know it would be this hard.'

Bea smiled sympathetically. 'Do you know about the baby and toddler group at Saint Swithin's? They run it in the church hall. I think it's on Wednesday mornings.'

'Oh, I'm not a churchgoer.'

'You don't have to be. It's for everyone. My friend used to go — she said it was really friendly, you get a cup of tea and there's loads of toys for the kids. You should give it a try, see how you get on. Have you got your phone there? We could check which day.'

'Um, okay.'

The woman got her phone out of her bag and fired it up. She frowned. 'I'm so tired I can't think straight.' She typed for a little while, then, 'Oh, here it is. Wednesday morning at ten thirty. All welcome. I'll add it to my diary, so I don't forget. Thank you.'

'Let me know how you get on, next time you're in, yeah?'

'I will.'

Ant finally reappeared with the two packs of loo roll. He stayed on after the woman had left and helped to pack Dot's customer's shopping. Bea wondered if it was a ruse to hang around by their checkouts. Their earlier conversation had ended awkwardly, but this wasn't the time or place to resolve anything.

'Indoors today?' she said, neutrally. 'That's unusual.'

'Yeah, Neville's got me working for Eileen, filling shelves and generally being her slave. Reckon it's his way of punishing me.'

'Punishing you? What for?'

Ant looked left and right, shiftily. 'I'll tell you later.'

She beckoned him closer. 'I'm sorry if I was a bit snippy earlier.'

'That's okay,' he said. 'You feeling all right?'

At that moment, Eileen herself hove into view. 'Ant! There you are! One of the freezers is leaking. I need you to fetch the mop and get some cones out!'

Ant rolled his eyes.

She clapped her hands together like a primary school teacher dealing with an unruly five-year-old. 'Quickly, Ant! Before someone slips over!' Ant sighed deeply and started walking slowly towards the back of the store and the cleaning cupboard.

'He's someone who needs close supervision, if you ask me,' said Eileen. 'They cut him far too much slack when he's outdoors doing the trolleys. I'll soon lick him into shape.' With a satisfied smile, she marched back to the freezer aisle.

There was a lull now and Bea watched Ant disappear from view. When she swivelled round in her chair, Dot was watching her.

'What?'

'Nothing, love. Want to hear my idea?'

'Go on, then.'

'You were so good with that woman just now. She opened up to you, you listened, and you found a solution.'

Bea shrugged. 'It's just my job, isn't it?'

'You do far more than most people. Wendy Fox was in yesterday. Dylan Bradley's death means that there's a vacancy on the town council.'

Bea pulled a face. 'So what? You going for it, are you?'

'No, not me, Bea. You should, though.'

CHAPTER ELEVEN

Eileen insisted that Ant should completely restock the crisp aisle before he took his morning break. When he had finally finished to her satisfaction, he raced up to the staff room, hoping to find a quiet corner in which to talk to Bea. He was too late, though, and she was just coming out as he clattered along the corridor.

'Shall we grab lunch together?' he said. 'Corner café. My treat.'

'I'd like that,' she said, and he felt a surge of pleasure, 'but I've brought some sandwiches in and I'm going to eat them with Dot. She's got a crazy idea about me being a councillor or something. Sorry.'

'Oh, right. Sounds random. Maybe catch you later . . .'

And just like that, she was gone, heading down the stairs and back to her till. Ant stood there for a moment or two, feeling numb. She'd said sorry, but had she meant it? Or was the thing with Dot another way of avoiding him? Perhaps he could just join in anyway. They never normally minded if he sat with them at lunchtime.

He loped into the staff room and went straight to the kettle. He needed an extra spoonful of sugar in his tea this morning.

Dean bounced up off the sofa and came over to him. 'Me and Tyler have been working on the case all morning — we've got loads of ideas. We're calling a meeting at lunchtime in the stores. You're coming.'

'I dunno about that,' Ant said. 'I spoke to Bea earlier and she said that we should keep away and leave it to the cops. She didn't want anything to do with it.'

'We don't need her! We can do it ourselves. We can be the three amigos! Find out who killed Dylan and nail the bastard.' Dean's eyes were shining brightly, and he was bobbing up and down on the spot. If Ant didn't know better, he would have thought he'd taken something.

'All right, all right, calm down. If you want to do this, you should invite Bob, too. He told me he wants to be involved.'

'Bob? Really?' He exhaled noisily. 'All right, then. That means we can't be the three amigos, though. How about the four musketeers? That could work . . .'

'We don't need a name, Dean.' Ant couldn't help remembering Bea's words this morning. *Murder isn't a game.* 'It's about what we do, not what we call ourselves.'

Dean looked a little crestfallen. 'Yeah, sure. I know that. You're in, though, aren't you?'

Ant thought about it for a moment. 'Yes, mate. I'm in.'

When lunchtime came around, Ant was impressed to see that Dean's den in the stores now looked less like a man cave and more like a CID office, with yellow sticky notes on the wall and bits of red string trailing from one to another. The four of them arranged their garden chairs in a semi-circle, facing the display.

'Bloody hell, boys,' said Ant. 'You're not messing around, are you?'

Dean and Tyler exchanged pleased grins. They had spent a happy morning, in between deliveries, writing on notes and placing them carefully. Dylan Bradley was at the centre with the things he was connected to arranged round the edge. It all echoed what Ant had written in his notebook the previous evening, but it was easier to take in like this.

'The obvious place to start is the allotments,' said Bob. 'That's where he was found, after all. I sent Ant a list of all the allotment holders.'

'It's not just them, though, is it?' said Tyler. 'It could have been someone nicking stuff.'

'Or anyone could have arranged to meet him up there — it's nice and quiet and out of the way, if you don't want to be seen,' said Dean.

'So, if he could have been meeting anyone, we need to think about the other parts of his life — school and the council,' said Tyler.

'Good point,' said Bob. 'What do we actually do?'

They all looked at Ant and he realised that, as a veteran of four investigations with Bea, they were assuming he would be their leader. But, faced with so much expectation, he felt at a loss. He'd always accepted that Bea was the brains of their outfit — he provided contacts and another pair of eyes, ears and feet. He was a drone to her queen. Now, the spotlight was on him. It was a bit much.

'Um . . .' *Come on, Ant. What have you learned over the last couple of years?* 'We need to do the stuff that the police can't.'

Dean wrinkled his nose. 'Huh?'

'Use our contacts. Talk to people. Colleagues, mates, people who knew him. We can build up a picture of what he was like, what he was interested in. Who he got on with and who he didn't. Anyone who might have had a grudge against him.'

'Ooh,' said Dean. 'That's good.'

'Plus—' Ant was warming to the subject now — 'We can find out who saw him over the last twenty-four hours or so of his life. Trace his movements.'

'Yes!' said Tyler.

'I reckon we could start with you, then, Ant,' said Bob. 'You said you spoke to him the night before he was found.'

'Yeah, I was up at the allotment on Monday evening, doing some watering and tying up the tomato trusses.'

'Ooh, er,' said Dean. 'Sounds kinky.'

Bob tutted loudly. 'Ignore him, Ant. Carry on.'

'I got there about six. Dylan was working on his plot, next to ours. We said hello and then got on with what we were doing. Later, maybe half six, we stopped and had a chat.'

'What did you talk about?'

Ant shrugged. 'All sorts, like normal. He told me a bit about his day, the meetings and stuff he'd been to. He was chuffed, too, because he'd bought a second-hand strimmer off eBay and it was just the job. He was telling me you can buy and sell anything on there, like I wouldn't already know.'

'That's boomers for you,' said Dean. 'Bless.'

'He wanted to show me something he'd found earlier, too. We're always digging up stuff there — coins, rubbish, bits of pottery. Dylan had a little collection on a shelf in his shed. This time he'd found a ring, a plain band with a little stone in it. Looked to me like something that had come out of a Christmas cracker, but he said it was metal. He wasn't sure what the stone was. I reckoned it was plastic or glass, but he thought it might be a little ruby. Could be someone's family heirloom.'

'What was he going to do with it?'

'He didn't know whether to post about it on the "Found in Kingsleigh" page on Facebook or somewhere, or hand it in to the cops. I don't know if he got round to doing anything. After he showed it to me, we sat and had a beer, watched the sunset . . .'

As he said the words, Ant realised that he would never do that again and a wave of grief started to build inside him. He had a lump in his throat and stopped talking.

'You all right, mate?' said Bob.

Ant blinked rapidly and swallowed hard. 'Yeah,' he said, but his voice broke halfway through the word. He shook his head and a couple of tears trickled down his face.

'It's okay.' Bob placed a large hand on Ant's back. 'I know it's hard.'

Ant nodded.

While he composed himself, Dean added a new sticky note to the board, in a column under the heading 'Allotment'.

'We need to find out what happened to that ring,' he said. 'It's a new line of inquiry.'

Tyler high-fived him as he sat down again.

'Was there anyone else up there that evening?' asked Bob.

'There were quite a few to start with,' said Ant. 'I didn't talk to them, but I saw them.' He reeled off a few names. 'Lionel was up there, and Cyril. Dylan said Cyril had even slept up there a couple of times since his tomatoes were nicked, trying to catch the thief. He's become obsessed.'

Tyler and Dean looked at each other and Dean started scribbling on another note.

'I left at about quarter to eight. It was getting pretty dark and a bit chilly. Dylan said he wouldn't be long. He wanted to put his tools away and lock up. He said he wouldn't be there the next evening because he had a meeting.'

Bob's phone pinged, and he took it out of his pocket and examined the screen.

'Shall we go back to the Ship after work?' said Dean. 'Carry on investigating?'

'We can do better than that,' said Bob. 'That message was from Lionel on the allotment WhatsApp group. The police have opened up the site again, so that's where I'm going as soon as I've finished here. You with me, Ant?'

'Yeah, sure. Could we pick up Charles on the way? I bet he's keen to get up there and check on Marv.'

'What about us?' said Dean. 'Are we invited?'

'Best not,' said Bob. 'It might look a bit ghoulish if we turn up mob-handed. Perhaps you two could look into his council work. Find out what committees he was on, whether he had any allies or enemies.'

'Boring,' Dean muttered under his breath.

'We need to get back to work, anyway.' Bob heaved himself to his feet and picked up two mugs. 'I'll take these mugs back to the staff room.'

Ant scooped up the other two. As they walked up to the staff area, Ant was quiet.

'You all right, mate?' Bob said at the top of the stairs.

Ant sighed. 'Yeah. Sort of. The thing is, I'm not sure I want to go back to the allotments. Bea said it was cursed, and I'm starting to think she was right.'

CHAPTER TWELVE

'If you're interested, you should go and talk to Wendy Fox,' said Dot. 'She can tell you more about what's involved.'

'I don't know,' said Bea. 'I've never even considered it before. I'm not really sure what the council does, apart from look after the parks and the bins in the high street.'

'There's loads more to it than that. Have a look on the website. The council is stuffed full of old fuddy-duddies — you'd be a breath of fresh air! You could represent the rest of us, like that young mum you just helped. At least talk to Wendy.'

Bea sighed. 'I'll think about it. Can we talk about something else now? There's only five minutes till we're due back.'

But it seemed as if fate wouldn't let her change the subject. As they returned to their checkouts, Bea noticed the Chair of the council, Malcolm Sillitoe, deep in conversation with Bob at the meat counter. There was a little queue of carnivores building up behind him, some of them showing signs of impatience.

Bea had seen Malcolm at various town events. If there was even a wafer-thin chance of a speech being made, he would be front and centre, usually wearing his gold chain of office. Clearly convinced that there was nothing sweeter in the world than the sound of his own voice, if he was meant to speak for five minutes, it was guaranteed he would drawl on for ten.

Within a few minutes of Bea opening up her till, she saw Malcolm heading towards her and shrivelled inside. That was one thing about working on the checkouts, you didn't get to choose your customers. As soon as Bea saw him bearing down on her, she imagined spending her evenings sitting in endless meetings with him and realised that she couldn't think of anything worse. In a way it was a relief. Although she'd been intrigued by Dot's suggestion, it was a non-runner. She was not going to put her name forward to be a local councillor.

Malcolm unloaded his shopping — three newspapers, including two nationals and a copy of the *Bugle*, a couple of chops from Bob and a box of paracetamol. The *Bugle* was face up, with a photograph of Dylan Bradley edged in black on the front page.

'I'm so sorry about Councillor Bradley,' she said.

The muscles at the hinge of his jaw worked and he winced a little. 'Thank you,' he said. 'It's a tragic loss.'

Dot swivelled round in her chair.

No, Dot, keep out of it, Bea thought, but it was too late.

'Bea here was thinking of applying to be a councillor. Can you tell her what she needs to do?'

Malcolm looked at her blankly. 'I'm sorry?'

'Shh, Dot,' Bea said, but there was no stopping her.

'Bea wants to know how to apply for the vacant seat. Does she need to fill in a form or something?'

He looked from Dot to Bea and back again. 'That's what I thought you said.' A staccato burst of mirthless laughter escaped his thin lips. 'Oh, no, that's all taken care of, or will be soon. We've got someone in mind.'

Bea shot Dot a furious look and drew her finger across her throat in the universal 'for God's sake, shut up' gesture.

'Oh, that's interesting. Can you say who?' Dot enquired sweetly.

He shook his head. 'I need to discuss it further with my colleagues, but he's an excellent candidate. Born and bred here. Community-minded. Just what we need.'

He, thought Bea. *Of course it's a he.*

Malcolm paid for his shopping and started to walk away.

'Mr Sillitoe,' Bea called after him.

He stopped and turned to face her.

'What happens if more than one person wants the job?'

'Well, if that was to happen, then there would have to be an election, but we try to avoid that. Elections are expensive and time-consuming. We have to think about how the rate-payers want us to use their money.'

Bea frowned. 'Aren't elections the most important thing of all, though? Aren't they what local democracy is all about?'

He looked at her like a wise old owl looking at the smallest, feeblest owlet, or possibly a mouse. 'Of course, and we have elections every four years no matter what, but what you don't understand about local politics is that it's very much about consensus. We try and agree what's best for the town, whatever our party allegiances — or lack of them. It's politics with a small 'p', you might say. Politics as it should be.'

'I see,' said Bea. 'Thank you.'

'You're very welcome—' he leaned forward and squinted at her name badge — 'Bea.'

She watched him walk away, past the customer service desk and through the double doors.

'Nice man,' said Dot, sarcastically, under her breath. She looked at Bea. 'Are you going to tell me off for sticking my oar in now? Go on, get it over with.' Dot held her hand out for Bea to slap and then looked away dramatically, waiting for Bea's admonishment.

Bea tipped her head to one side. 'I *was* going to, but actually I'm not now. I'm going to thank you instead and I'm *definitely* going to talk to Wendy Fox, find out a bit more about it.' She grabbed Dot's hand, stood up and did a little twirl underneath it.

Dot stood up, too, and squealed in delight. 'Attagirl!'

'What on earth is going on here, ladies?'

Suddenly, Neville was standing next to their tills, his Adam's apple bobbing up and down. 'This is a shop floor not a dance floor.'

'Ooh, good one, Neville,' said Dot.

He tried to hide his pleasure at her appreciation of his wordplay, but two little spots of colour in his cheeks gave him away.

Dot pressed her advantage. 'Perhaps we should do a charity thing? *Strictly Come Costsave.*'

'That discussion is for another time. Put it in the staff suggestion box, if you must. But for now, you both need to calm down and sit down. I mean it.' He tugged on the hem of his jacket and struck a tone that reasserted his authority. 'This isn't the sort of behaviour I can tolerate.'

Bea fought the urge to offer commiserations to his wife. She took her chair again. 'No, Neville. Sorry, Neville.'

Despite Neville's efforts to squash them, she and Dot were in high spirits for the rest of the afternoon, although they restricted them to a bit of banter and a few quiet bursts of song. As the end of their shift approached, Bea was feeling almost normal again. It was like the last couple of days had been a bad dream.

At the end of their shift, they walked towards the staff door. Bob joined them from behind the meat counter.

'Ant and I are going straight to the allotments,' he said. 'The police have opened them up again.'

'Oh,' said Dot, 'I was hoping to talk with you. Will you be back for tea?'

'I don't know. Depends what state it's in up there. We're taking Charles. I imagine he'll be a bit upset — I'll need to take him home again and make sure he's okay. Probably best not to wait for me. You go ahead and eat when you're ready.'

'But, Bob . . .' She hesitated. 'Oh, never mind. I'll see you when I see you.'

In fact, Bob had overtaken them now and was hurtling towards the stairs.

'Hey, Bob,' Dot called out, 'Bea's going to apply to be on the town council.'

His step faltered and he turned round. 'Oh, is she?' He looked about to say something else but stopped himself.

'Well, I'm going to look into it,' said Bea. 'We had a very interesting chat with Malcolm Sillitoe just now. I'm not sure I'm his ideal candidate. It sounded like he was looking for someone pale, male and stale.'

'Just like you, Bob!' said Dot.

Bob seemed not to notice the slight, or at least his mind was elsewhere.

'Dot!' said Bea. 'Play nice. She doesn't mean it, Bob. Bob?'

The butcher's face had coloured up, red blotches blossoming on his hamster-like cheeks. 'Actually,' he said, 'I *have* been approached . . . They want to coopt me. Malcolm said I'd fit right in.'

CHAPTER THIRTEEN

Outside the allotments, the little car park was almost full. Bob let Ant and Charles get out of his car before he eased it into the last space. They waited for him, watching as he squeezed out of the driver's seat. Ant looked apprehensively towards the gates. Beside him, Charles was holding his walking stick so tightly his knuckles were white.

'Come on, then,' said Bob. 'Let's see what the damage is.'

The grassy paths that criss-crossed the site had been well trampled but most of the plots themselves looked like they had been more or less left alone. Numerous allotment holders were busy inspecting and watering their plants, and it almost felt like an ordinary day until they got nearer to their plot, where there was no disguising the fact that things were far from normal.

The top ten metres or so of Dylan's plot were still sealed off with yellow tape, including the shed and the area in front of it. A uniformed police officer stood outside the tape, near the path, while Ant spotted Tom a little distance away, talking with Cyril and Lionel.

'It must be hard on Lionel,' said Bob. 'He runs a very tight ship up here. Has done for years. And now this has happened, together with that other business earlier in the year.'

He looked to Charles for a sympathetic comment, but Charles just muttered, 'Wouldn't waste my sympathy on him.'

'What do you mean?'

'You say "tight ship". I say little Hitler.'

Bob's eyes widened and he looked at Ant, who mirrored his expression and blew air out through pursed lips.

'All right, Charles.' Bob put a gentle hand on the older man's shoulder. 'Let's go and see how Marv's getting on.' He shepherded him down the path.

To everyone's relief, Marvin was still there, glossy and intact.

'Hang on,' said Bob. 'Look at these leaves. Do you think the police have trampled them?'

'Oh no,' said Ant. 'They were like that on Monday night. Bea and I spotted it. Someone had been there on Sunday or Monday, unless it was one of you.'

'It wasn't us,' said Bob. 'Bloody hell, do you think someone's eyeing him up?'

Ant shrugged. 'That's what it looks like. Maybe we should start keeping watch overnight like Cyril.'

'Let's give him a good drenching. Can you fetch the watering can, mate? It should be in our shed.'

'Yeah, sure.' Ant swung into action, walking back to the top of the plot while reaching for the padlock key in his pocket. When he got there, though, he couldn't help looking across to Dylan's and remembering the moment when he unlocked that door and revealed his friend lying on the floor. What the hell had gone on that had ended so catastrophically?

The police officer moved into his line of sight, breaking the spell. Ant had an innate aversion to anyone in authority but, by the look of him, this guy had been standing there a very long time. He felt a stirring of empathy for someone clearly at the bottom of the police pecking order.

'Do you want a brew?' he called over. 'I've got a little camping stove in here. Could heat up some water.'

The copper's face brightened instantly. 'Cheers, that would be great.'

'It'll take a while.'

The guy gave him the thumbs up.

Ant unlocked the shed and held his breath as he opened the door. There was no reason for there to be anything untoward in there, but it was still nerve-wracking. He half closed his eyes, as if squinting at the scene would lessen the impact of seeing any horrors.

Everything inside was as it should be. He fetched the little camping stove out and the aluminium saucepan, then filled the pan with water from a five-litre bottle of drinking water and lit the stove. While it was heating up, he went back and forth between the communal tap and Marvin, giving him a good soaking.

He made tea for everyone, adding powdered milk and sugar, for good measure, and carried a cup over to the officer, who took it gratefully.

'Been here long?' said Ant.

'All day,' said the officer, trying to stifle a yawn. 'Got another couple of hours. We're just here to reassure the public, really, and take statements from anyone who saw anything on Monday.'

'I've given mine already. I was the one who found him.'

The officer's expression softened, and Ant realised that they were probably about the same age.

'I'm sorry. That must have been a shock.'

'Yeah,' said Ant. 'I suppose you see stuff like that all the time.'

'Not in Kingsleigh. I've only seen one body, and that was the lad down by the river earlier this year. I'll never forget it.' He took a slurp of tea.

Ant did, too. 'Sorry the tea's not up to much.'

'No, it's grand. I appreciate it.'

Tom walked over to them. 'Ant,' he said, 'we need to take a fuller statement from you. I need to catch a few more people while they're here. Can I fix a time to come and see you?'

'Yeah, sure. I don't think there's anything else to tell you, though.'

'We need to talk to anyone who saw him on Monday. We're building up a picture of what happened that night.'

Ant shrugged. 'Of course. We can talk any time you like.'

'Sometime this evening would be good. Could I call round at eight?'

'Yeah, sure. I'm staying at Bob's.' Ant gave him the address and went back to see Bob and Charles.

He handed Bob a cup of tea. 'What will happen to Dylan's plot now?'

'Occasionally, they let relatives take on a plot, but I don't think Dylan had anyone who'd be interested. He was divorced and his two boys are grown up and have left Kingsleigh. The plot will pass to whoever's next on the waiting list.'

'And they'll get all this stuff? Look at his tomatoes! They're amazing.'

'Yeah, someone will hit the jackpot, won't they? It probably won't happen for a few weeks, though.'

'Perhaps we should look after it until someone else takes it on. We could enter his best stuff into the show, in his name.'

'That's a great idea,' said Bob. 'I'd have to check with Lionel, see if there are any precedents.'

'And we could put any spare produce by the noticeboard for people to help themselves,' said Ant. 'Or take it to the food bank. That's the kind of thing Dylan would have done.'

Bob slapped his heavy arm onto Ant's shoulders. 'That's just what he would have wanted. Let's pack up here and go and tell Charles.'

Charles was standing at the far end of the plot, which was the only area he gave over to flowers. In front of the fence, there were a few ancient rosebushes and a buddleia. A colourful butterfly was flitting about in the evening sun, occasionally coming to rest, then taking off again.

'Red admiral,' said Charles, as Ant and Bob joined him. 'My Catherine loved butterflies. I like to keep this little area as somewhere I can remember her.'

'That's lovely,' said Ant. He told Charles about their idea to enter Dylan's produce into the show.

'I don't think anyone would object to that.'

'Would you mind if I cut one of your roses?' said Ant.

'What for?'

'I want to put it down as a tribute, you know, near Dylan's shed.'

Charles nodded his assent. 'That's fitting. I've had this plot for nearly thirty years, seen people come and go, but Dylan was a good neighbour. I'll miss him. I'll choose him a rose.'

Bob produced some secateurs from his pocket and handed them to Charles, who took a couple of steps forward, examined the blooms on one of the bushes, and snipped the stem of a particularly fine red rose.

'Perfect,' said Ant. 'Shall we all go?'

'Yes,' said Bob. 'Pay our respects. I think we're done here. Do you agree, Charles? Time to go home?'

Charles nodded again and they set off, at his pace, towards the top of the plot. Lionel and Cyril were still talking on Cyril's plot. They watched as the three of them walked up to the tape marking the edge of the crime scene.

'Is it okay to put a flower down here?' Ant said to the constable.

'Could you do it the other side of the shed, by the path? This is still a crime scene,' he said.

'Okay.' They made their way to the path. Lionel came bustling over. Charles didn't say anything, but Ant could sense him bristling.

'All right, Lionel?' Bob said. 'We just want to put this here. For Dylan.'

Ant stepped forward, carrying the rose. Lionel looked at it as if he was carrying a large turd instead of a beautiful flower.

'Oh, no,' he said. 'I can't allow that. We don't want everyone putting stuff here, making it untidy.'

'But it's what people do,' said Ant.

'Not here.'

Ant felt Charles's hand on his. He plucked the rose from Ant's fingers. Leaning heavily on his stick, he bent forward a little. He couldn't make it all the way to the ground, so instead let the rose drop, right by Lionel's feet. He stood, head bowed, for a moment, then retreated.

'I can't let that stay there.' Lionel's voice was low and even, but he was breathing hard and Ant could tell he was seething.

Charles looked at him full in the face. 'If you touch it, Lionel, I won't be answerable for my actions.'

'Is that a threat, Charles?'

'Not a threat, old boy. A statement of fact. The rose stays as a mark of respect.'

And, with that, he turned and started walking towards the gate. Ant and Bob looked at each other and then at Lionel. His mouth was slightly agape as he watched Charles's back.

'Excuse me, Lionel, I brought these for Dylan. Where can I put them?'

They all turned to see Lisa, in her mud-stained dungarees, approaching them. She was carrying a bunch of flowers tied into an attractive bunch with some hairy string.

'Not here,' said Lionel.

'But—' She looked at the rose on the ground.

'I said no!' he barked, the force of his words making her flinch.

'I just thought—'

'You thought wrong.' He crouched down and picked up the rose, walked along the side of the hut and threw it onto the compost heap.

CHAPTER FOURTEEN

'Nice place,' said Tom, looking around Bob's lounge-diner.

'Yeah. Bob's been very good to me. It's only temporary
. . .' Ant was acutely aware that all his arrangements were
temporary. 'Are you still in your flat?'

'I've just moved into one of the new houses on the
Kingsmead estate. Two bedrooms and a little garden. It's good
for Noah when he stays with me.' Noah was Tom's son from
a previous relationship. He had been a baby when Tom first
invited Bea on a date, the start of an ill-fated, but brief, episode. Ant had never understood what she had seen in Tom,
and the thought of them together still rankled.

'It suits me for now.' Tom looked down at his notebook.
'Anyway, we need to talk about Dylan Bradley.'

'Of course,' said Ant, sitting up a little straighter.

'The other day you said you saw him on Monday evening.
Tell me about that.'

Ant had gone over and over the memory repeatedly in the
last few days, but now he found that he was nervous, almost
tongue-tied. He didn't know where to start.

'I was there on Monday, at the allotments. We . . . we
talked.'

Tom waited for him to say more, then had to prompt him. 'What time did you get there?'

'About quarter to six, something like that. Dylan was already there, pottering about. We said hi and I did all the usual stuff, then when we'd finished, we sat and had a chat.'

'What did you talk about?'

'This and that. How our plants were getting on. What sort of day we'd had.'

'What sort of day had Dylan had?'

'Just normal, I think. He said he'd had a meeting about council stuff earlier — he'd got a bee in his bonnet about opening a museum here — and then he'd come up to the allotments after lunch sometime.'

Tom wrote in his little notebook. 'What sort of mood was he in?'

'He was a pretty cheerful sort of bloke. Actually, on Monday he was quite excited because he'd found a ring when he was digging. It didn't look like anything to me, like something out of a cracker, but he thought it was proper.'

'Proper?'

'You know, gold with a stone, a little red stone. Did you find it in his belongings?'

Tom stopped writing. 'I can't tell you that.'

'Why not?'

Tom looked at him evenly. 'That's part of our investigation, Ant. I'm here to ask you questions.'

Ant snorted. 'I know that, but it's just you and me, Tom. We both want to find out who killed Dylan.'

'Of course, but I'm the investigating officer and you're . . . not. There are rules about disclosure of evidence, confidentiality, professional competence.'

Ant wondered if he was quoting a rule book or talking like this deliberately to put him in his place. Either way, he didn't like it.

'I get that,' he said, 'but the ring could be important. Even if it's nothing to do with what happened to Dylan, it might mean something to someone. Someone might be missing it.'

'Let's move on.'

'Have you written it down?'

'Seriously?' Tom couldn't disguise his irritation. 'Yes, I have written it down. So, Ant, after you talked, what happened then? Did you see him leave the allotments?'

'No, I left first. It was probably about seven. He was starting to pack up too. I just said I'd see him tomorrow and left.'

'Were there other people around?'

'Yeah, Cyril was there, who has the plot the other side of Dylan's, and Lisa — she grows the flowers. Lionel, who's in charge of everything, was there too. I can't remember anyone else.'

'And did you see anyone approaching the allotments as you were leaving?'

'I don't think so. Actually, no, the council van was coming into the car park.'

Tom nodded and made another note. 'Okay. So, the next day, talk me through how you found him.'

Ant looked down at his hands, which were starting to sweat. He swallowed and licked his lips.

'I'm sorry,' said Tom. 'I know it might be difficult.'

Ant raised his eyes and was surprised to see how genuine Tom seemed. He was sitting back in the chair, patiently waiting.

'Thanks, mate,' Ant said. 'It really is.'

'Take your time.'

He took a deep breath. 'Okay, so I'd persuaded Bea to go up to the allotments. She hadn't been there since February and I wanted to convince her it was okay and show her why I liked it up there.' A bitter laugh escaped from his lips. 'I mean, that went well, didn't it?'

Tom clamped his lips together in an expression of sympathy.

'Anyway, we went up there after work, and took a picnic.'

'Did you notice anything out of the ordinary when you got there?'

Ant shook his head. 'Not really. Someone had trampled on my marrow patch, broken a couple of leaves. That was the only thing.'

'Go on.'

'It was a lovely evening. It was just nice and chilled. Good vibes, you know? I wanted to ask Dylan something. I saw that there were some tools out on his plot, so I thought he must be around cos he never leaves things — left things — overnight. So, I rang him. And we both heard the phone. It was coming from inside his shed. I looked in the window and could see him lying there.'

'And you broke in?'

'The door was padlocked. I smashed it off with a spade. It took a couple of goes.'

'When you opened the door, what did you see?'

Ant closed his eyes for a moment and the scene was as vivid as if it had just happened. When he opened them again, Tom was staring at him, unblinking.

'Dylan was on the floor, lying on his front in a pool of blood with a . . .' Ant took a breath. 'A little trowel stuck in his head.'

'Did you touch anything in the shed?'

'I touched him. I mean, it was obvious he was dead, but I held my fingers to his neck to check for a pulse. Maybe it was silly, but it felt like the right thing to do. There was no pulse, obviously, and he was cold.'

'You didn't touch anything else in the shed?'

'I don't think so. Not then. I mean, I've been in Dylan's shed. I've carried his fold-up chairs in and out and stuff like that.'

'I'm going to need to take your fingerprints.'

'Sure. I mean, my prints are probably in the shed some-where. That doesn't mean anything, does it?'

Ant felt a sudden sense of unease, which wasn't helped by Tom's next question.

'Going back to Monday evening. Did you and Dylan argue?'

A nervous laugh escaped from Ant's mouth. The suggestion had come out of nowhere and taken him by surprise. 'No! Of course not. What would we argue about?'

'You tell me.'

'We didn't argue. End of.'

Tom looked down at his notebook and flipped back a few pages, then said, 'Did you at any point tell him to "Fuck off, you bellend, I'll batter you"?'

The unease that Ant had started to feel dissipated instantly. He knew what was going on now. 'Okay. I see what's happened. Yeah, I might have said it, but I was only having a laugh. We were talking about playing pool in the Ship. He thought he stood a chance against me, which, of course, he wouldn't.'

'You told a man forty years your senior and your former teacher to "fuck off", but it was just a laugh?'

'Yes. Banter. That's all . . . Wait a minute? What is this?' Ant sat forward, ready to spring up. 'I thought you were just taking a statement. Feels like I should have a lawyer or something.'

'Calm down, I'm just trying to establish the sequence of events on Monday.'

There was a knock on the door and Bob peered round. 'Everything all right in here?'

Ant got to his feet. 'No, it isn't. I'm being questioned like a suspect. You might not believe me,' he said to Tom, 'but Dylan was my friend. Finding him was one of the worst things that's ever happened to me, and now you — you're trying to make out that I was threatening him. I've had enough of this.'

'Ant—'

'No, it's out of order. I didn't sign up for this. I'm out of here.'

'Ant!'

He pushed past Bob and stormed out of the front door. Tom's car was parked in the road outside and he kicked its back tyre as he passed, swearing under his breath. He wasn't just cursing Tom, though, he was aiming it at himself. How had he been so stupid? Why hadn't he realised what was happening earlier?

He jogged through the quiet streets, trying to put as much distance as possible between him and Tom until his lungs gave out, which wasn't very far. He stopped near a block of garages, resting his hands on his thighs for a minute, and realised that he was in the network of streets, alleys and yards that was close to his old family home. He hadn't stayed away deliberately but he didn't make a habit of coming here — there were too many memories.

His feet took him down a narrow path between high brick walls and then out and across a scrappy little green. He stood by the trunk of a cherry tree, scarred and scratched with names and dates and doodles of genitalia. He remembered his eldest brother, Stevo, carving a heart and the initials of his first girlfriend with a penknife. She'd dumped him a couple of weeks later, but the heart remained — it was probably still here. He looked across to number fifteen, and in his mind's eye saw a snotty-nosed toddler pedalling a tricycle around the front garden, while a smaller child crawled on the ground picking up stones and putting them in her mouth. A woman came out of the front door and swooped down on the baby, putting her finger into her mouth, scooping out stones. Next, he saw a boy in a royal blue hand-me-down jumper and grey shorts having his picture taken on the front step. After a snap or two he was joined by two older boys. They stood behind him, in the same uniform, like guardians. Now, it was night-time, and a figure emerged from the side of the house, dressed in black from head to toe. Ant knew he had a balaclava in his pocket and the tools of his trade in the bag he was carrying — 'going equipped'. There was someone scuttling along next to him, a shoulder-height shadow wearing joggers and a black hoodie. He watched them walk silently along the road. When he looked back at the house, a word was daubed with red paint across the front of it, '*SCUM*'.

He heard a noise and was jerked out of his memories. A dog was scratching at the ground beneath the next tree along, then it cocked its leg. The man holding its lead squinted at Ant suspiciously. He yanked at the dog to pull him away then looked again and hesitated. 'Ant? Ant Thompson?'

'Yeah, that's me.' Ant recognised him as his former next-door neighbour.

'Haven't seen you for years. How's your mum getting on? She still in Cardiff?'

'Yeah, she's still there. She's fine.'

'Your dad still in . . . ?' He didn't need to say the final word. Prison.

'Yeah.'

'Are you waiting for someone? We've got a neighbour-hood watch thing going now, after we had some trouble down here.'

'No, I was just taking a walk.'

'Ah well, nice to see you again. I'll call the WhatsApp dogs off if they report a strange man on the green. You take care now.'

'Thanks. I'm off now anyway. See ya.'

Ant turned and walked back the way he'd come. He was calmer now, but sadder. Something about his memories had set alarm bells ringing too. Tom had mentioned fingerprints. Ant was sure they'd find his in Dylan's shed, but he had left Dylan alive and well. Other people would have seen him leave. Tom might view him as a suspect, but there was no way he could ever charge him, could he?

CHAPTER FIFTEEN

'Do you think I look all right?' Bea asked Dot, as she applied an extra layer of neutral pink lipstick.

'You look bloody lovely, as always,' said Dot. 'I like your hair like that. Suits you.'

Bea had spent quite some time putting her hair into a sleek, low bun, pinned at the nape of her neck and was rather pleased with how it had turned out. 'Jacket or not?'

Dot laughed. 'I don't think it matters, you're just going for a chat, but jacket, babe. You look like you mean business.'

Bea straightened the jacket and experimented with the buttons, decided that having one button done up was less 'try-hard' than all three.

Dot put her hands on Bea's shoulders and spun her gently round so they were face to face. 'Stop messing. You'll be fine. Do you want me to walk down with you?'

'No, I'm a big girl.' Bea ran her hands down her ample curves.

'I know you are, but it's nice to have a bit of moral support and I need to nip into the printers down that end of the high street and have a look at their wedding invitation samples. I was going to order online, but Bob said it would be nicer to use a local business.'

'Go on, then. If you're going that way.'

Bea was squeezing a visit to the town council office into her lunch break, having rung ahead and booked half an hour with Wendy Fox. Even though this was just an exploratory chat to find out more about being a councillor, Bea felt as nervous as if she was going for a job interview and she was desperate to make a good impression.

She and Dot walked arm in arm along the high street, Dot's heels click-clacking in her trademark style. The town council office was in the civic centre, near to the library and the indoor swimming pool. They parted ways near the municipal clock and agreed to meet back at Costsave. Bea checked her appearance again in her phone camera and took a deep breath. She walked the last few metres to the office door, pressed a large button to one side of it and waited as it swung open automatically.

Inside, she was faced with a reception desk. She recognised the woman behind it, who often popped into Costsave in her lunch hour or after work and whose name badge identified her as Jackie. Bea introduced herself and Jackie asked her to sign the visitors' book. As she was doing so, Wendy Fox appeared round the corner and greeted her.

'Come on in.' She ushered Bea into a small, glass-fronted office next to a larger meeting room. 'Do you want a tea or coffee?'

'Oh no, thank you.' Bea could picture herself spilling hot tea down the front of her jacket or swallowing some air and having a choking fit. Better not.

Wendy settled back behind her desk. 'So, you're interested in being a town councillor?'

Bea felt the heat rising in her neck, up towards her face. Why on earth had she thought this might be a good idea?

'Yes. I mean, I don't know. I'd like to . . . you know . . .'

Wendy smiled kindly. 'Why don't you tell me why you rang? What prompted you to pick up the phone?'

Bea sat forward. 'The thing is, I work on the tills at Costsave and I see all sorts of people every day. And so many of them are having trouble, things that really grind them down. Lack of money is the big one and I try and help by pointing out special offers or if they've got an expensive product, but I know our own-brand one is just as good. But there are other things that I can't help with. I keep all sorts of cards by my till — advice line numbers — and sometimes I've got just the right one to give to someone, you know, domestic abuse or housing or whatever. But I can't do much. The best I can do is be cheerful and efficient and not add any more stress to their lives . . . God, sorry, I'm going on.'

She paused. 'Where was I? Oh yes, the reason I rang was that I was able to tell a young mum, who was really lonely and struggling, about the baby and toddler group at Saint Swithin's. I felt that I made a difference to her. But there's only so much you can do working on the checkouts at a supermarket. That's why I rang. I want to make a difference. Sorry, I've burbled on and on. That's me, though. I like talking to people and listening, and helping.'

She stopped and the silence in the room seemed deafening. She wished the ground would open up and swallow her. She also regretted not saying yes to a drink, as she'd talked herself hoarse. 'Sorry,' she murmured again, hardly daring to meet Wendy's eye.

But she needn't have worried.

'No need to apologise,' Wendy said. 'I only wish more people could have heard you. This town council — *any* town council — needs people who care.'

'Oh, do you really think so?'

'I do, but, in fairness, I also need to make you aware of what the town council does and doesn't do, as well as tell you how it works here and how many meetings you'd need to go to, and what the time commitment might be. Is that okay?'

'Of course,' said Bea. 'That's why I'm here. I don't know much about it, to be honest.'

'Why don't I ask Jackie to bring us both a cup of tea and I'll talk you through it?'

By the time Wendy had explained about the responsibilities of the town council, its committee structures and working parties, Bea's mind was boggling. Kingsleigh was just a small, ordinary town. Did it really need all these meetings to make it function? And did she have to know about everything the council dealt with in order to be a councillor?

'I haven't got the first clue about stuff like planning,' she said.

'That's okay,' Wendy explained. 'We have an induction and training package for all new councillors. It can be daunting at first, but you'd soon get the hang of it. Have I put you off?'

'No. Well, I'm not sure. There's a lot to think about, isn't there?'

Wendy nodded. 'Yes, and it's not something to enter into lightly. But it *is* worth thinking about. If you want to put your name forward, there's an online form, or I can print one out for you. In fact, let me do that, so you'll have it, just in case.'

She typed something into her keyboard and swivelled round in her chair to collect the pages feeding out of the printer behind her.

Bea took the form. 'One thing,' she said. 'If there was someone else in the frame, would there be an election?'

'Only if someone calls one. Otherwise, councillors just decide between the candidates themselves. I know some existing councillors would like to avoid it, but it's not a big deal. Don't let that put you off.'

'Okay,' said Bea. 'Lots to think about. I'd better get back to work now, though.'

'The deadline for nominations is the twenty-ninth, so you've got a week or two to decide. Do ring or email if you've got any questions. Anything at all.'

'Thank you. I will.' Bea stood up, then stopped. 'Was Dylan Bradley a good councillor? I only knew him from school. He taught me History — I liked him.'

A copy of the *Bugle* was lying on Wendy's desk. Wendy glanced at Dylan's photo.

'Dylan was a one-off, like you. He challenged the way we did things. He wanted to open everything up, make it more accessible to ordinary members of the public. Some councillors would rather the public let them get on with things and didn't . . . I was going to say interfere, but that's not quite fair.'

'So he rubbed people here up the wrong way?'

'Some people. Not all.' Wendy was looking at Dylan's photograph on the front page of the *Bugle*. Bea wondered if there was a glitter of emotion in her eyes, but she soon switched on a businesslike smile and showed Bea to the door. 'Lovely to meet you, Bea,' she said, extending her hand.

Bea shook it. 'Likewise. Thank you.'

She tottered out to the high street. The sun had come out while she was inside, and Kingsleigh was looking at its best. She walked back towards Costsave, her mind reeling. It had been a good meeting, and she certainly hadn't been made to feel stupid for going there, but it would be a lot to take on. She shouldn't do it just to spite Malcolm or prove a point. She should only put her name forward if she really believed she could make a difference. And could she?

CHAPTER SIXTEEN

As she rounded the corner into the Costsave car park, Bea recognised a familiar figure leaning on the wall. As soon as he saw her, Ant stood up, threw his cigarette to the ground, and extinguished it with his foot.

'There you are!' he said. 'Blimey, you look nice.'

Bea gave a little twirl in the street. 'Do you think so? I was trying to look businesslike.'

'You look amazing. Dot said you had an appointment. I thought you were at the doc's or somewhere.' She could see his expression change as her words sunk in. 'Hang on, businesslike? Have you been for a job interview? Are you leaving?'

They started walking along the rows of parked cars.

'It wasn't really an interview. More like a fact-finding mission. And I won't have to leave Costsave. I went to the town council office to learn about being a councillor. Reckon I might put my name forward.'

'Really?'

With Dot being so enthusiastic, she'd expected something a little less lukewarm from Ant.

'What?' She stopped walking. 'Don't you think I could do it?'

A driver wanting to turn his green van into a space they were blocking beeped his horn rather aggressively. Bea glanced up, waved an apology to the bearded man, who flailed his hands in exasperation, and walked on, with Ant scurrying after her.

'Yes, of course I think you could. I don't know why you would *want* to. Sitting round in meetings. Do you really want to do that?'

'I don't know. But the meetings are just a means to an end. They're a way of getting people to agree to stuff, to get things done.'

He puffed his cheeks out and exhaled. 'S'pose so. That's evenings, though. And then in the day you're here.'

'And?'

They walked round the side of the building towards the staff door.

'Well, I just thought we would be doing more things together . . . I mean, I've hardly seen you since Monday night.'

Bea had expected him to be completely supportive of her new venture. Was he really objecting to her at least having a go at it? Did he think one night together gave him some sort of right over her? She wasn't having that.

He held the door open for her.

She didn't go through. 'And whose fault is that? You've been up at the allotment or in the pub with your mates. Where were you last night, for example?'

'I went up to the allotment and then Tom came to Bob's and interviewed me.' He thought he noticed a change in her at the mention of his name. 'He's treating me like a suspect, Bea. He's got me in his sights. I couldn't handle it, so I went out after that, walked around for a bit.'

'A suspect? That's ridiculous. You didn't think of ringing me?'

'I did, but I was pretty het up and you'd said you didn't want anything to do with the case, and—'

'I don't want to do any investigating. I didn't mean I don't care about what happens to you. Something like that is huge. You could've, *should've*, rung me.'

'Sorry. I got it wrong again. I thought—'

'That's just it, Ant. I'm not sure you always *do* think.'

Ant was still holding the door open and Neville emerged through it. He did a double take at Ant and Bea lurking outside, then checked his watch.

'I know, I know,' said Bea, to pre-empt a telling-off about timekeeping. 'We're back. We've still got three minutes.'

Neville sniffed and looked her up and down.

'You're very smart today, Bea.' She could see the cogs turning in his brain, but professional scruples stopped him asking her straight out why she had dressed up.

'You know me, I like to look nice for the customers, Neville.' She ducked past him to go into the building.

Ant was left holding the door, eye to eye with his former landlord. There was a moment's silence, when Ant imagined he caught a ball of tumbleweed blowing across the car park in his peripheral vision, then Neville turned his head and marched away. Ant stayed for a few seconds longer, feeling emotionally battered and bruised by the last few minutes. He shook his head. He couldn't do anything right, could he?

'How did you get on?' Dot asked as Bea slunk into her seat at checkout six.

'Good,' said Bea. 'There's a lot to think about. I don't know if it's really "me" or not. Ant doesn't seem to think so.' She said the last bit under her breath.

'What was that?'

'Nothing. Nothing worth hearing anyway. Is Bob going to go for it?'

Dot shrugged. 'I don't think so. We haven't really discussed it. He's being a bit evasive at the moment. We're having a quiet night in this evening — I promised him stew and dumplings — so I'll ask him then. I mean, I'll be a bit peeved if he does go for it. He's overcommitted already and we've got a wedding to plan.'

'If he really wanted to, though, you wouldn't put him off, would you?'

Dot looked at her quizzically. 'No, course not. If he was really set on it, I'd back him all the way. That's what you do, isn't it? Back your partner up? Be their biggest cheerleader.'

Her words made Bea even more uneasy about her last interaction with Ant, but she covered it up with a smile. 'He's lucky to have you.'

'He bloody is! And I don't let him forget it!'

They both started laughing.

'How were the invitations? Did you like any of the samples?'

'Yes, there are a couple I really like. They're twice the price of the online ones, though. I'm seeing a florist on Sunday — young lass called Lisa. She said she'd come to the house and talk through my ideas. I need to make sure Bob's there. It's his wedding too.'

Outside, Ant slunk along the front of the store, pushing a train of trolleys towards their fellows by the main entrance. He glanced in through the plate glass as he was passing the checkouts, half raised his hand then seemed to think better of it and carried on slinking.

'Everything all right between you two?' said Dot.

'Yeah, of course. What do you mean?' Bea was aware of a slight snappiness in her voice.

'Nothing. You just don't seem quite as matey as usual.'

'We just had a bit of an argument. Well, not an argument. I dunno, Dot, it's . . . complicated.' She turned gratefully to her next customer.

Dot didn't react, but she noted the word 'complicated' and stored it carefully away. She was pretty sure she knew what that meant. Ant and Bea weren't the only amateur investigators in Costsave. What with that and Ant's orange lighter on the floor of Bea's bedroom the other day, she was building up a pretty watertight case of her own.

CHAPTER SEVENTEEN

As Ant approached the allotment gates, he heard a bell ping and a tricycle towing a little open trailer drew up beside him. Lisa Bloomfield dismounted and greeted him with a cheerful, 'Hiya.' Her long blonde hair was tied back in a plait and she was wearing dungarees with patches all over them, with a pink long-sleeved top underneath.

She wheeled her trike over to the fence and he waited while she padlocked it to the railing and picked up a couple of buckets from her trailer.

'Be better if I could take this on-site, but you-know-who doesn't approve,' she said with a grimace.

They both glanced towards the central hut. The door was open, which meant that Lionel was somewhere about, but they couldn't see him.

'He was such a dick the other day, wasn't he?' said Ant.

Lisa looked at the ground and opened her eyes wide, so they were bulging in exaggerated agreement. 'You could say that. I hate confrontation — it's just not me — and that was *mean*. I used to love it here, it's my happy place, but I'm not sure now.'

'You're not going to pack it in, are you?'

She shook her head. 'No. I couldn't manage without it. I can grow nearly everything I need for my summer weddings. I've hardly had to buy in anything for the past few months.'

'I like your plot,' said Ant. 'It's so beautiful.'

She sent a broad smile his way. 'Thanks, I do my best. Yours is looking good. That marrow's insane!'

They had reached the side path that led to Charles's plot now.

'Yeah, he's a big boy, all right. Just fattening him up for the show . . . not that that seems to matter so much now.'

'Hmm,' said Lisa, 'I kind of feel the opposite, like the things that bring us joy are even more important. You know, raindrops on roses, the scent of sweet peas, or . . . an absolutely mahoosive marrow. Whatever floats your boat.'

'That's a good way of looking at it.' He started to walk down the side path, noticing that Cyril was busy on his plot the other side of Dylan's, then stopped and turned back. 'You were here on Monday evening, weren't you? Did you see Dylan?'

'Yes, I got here late and left late. I was doing some cutting. I had a little weekday wedding at Kingsleigh Grange on Tuesday — just the bridal bouquet, and a couple of buttonholes. Dylan was still here as I was leaving.'

'Was anyone else still here then?'

'There were a few people around. Cyril and Lionel were having a chat at the top of Cyril's plot. I remember saying goodnight to them. Dylan was packing up when I saw him.'

'I wish I'd stayed later,' said Ant. 'I wish I'd been there. Everything might have been different.'

Lisa shook her head. 'You can't think like that, Ant. We don't know what happened, or why, but it wasn't your fault.'

'Maybe not, but at least one person knows what happened. Until we find out who, we should be very careful up here. I'll stick around until you're done today, shall I? Safety in numbers.'

'Thanks, Ant, but I'm only going to be half an hour or so.' She set off across the site towards her colourful plot and

Ant got stuck into his daily checks and chores. Marvin was sitting pretty. There was no sign of any further damage to the plants around him.

Ant glanced up and found Cyril looking at him then looking away quickly. Suddenly he knew who had reported his words to Dylan from Monday night. Interfering old busybody.

He walked over to the far side of the plot and then crossed Dylan's too.

'Cyril, mate,' he said.

Cyril looked around as if checking for backup. There were plenty of other people about.

'Anthony.' Behind his metal-framed glasses he was blinking hard.

'Did you tell the police that I threatened to batter Dylan?'

Ant took another step forward, and Cyril stepped back.

'I did,' he said, with a hint of defiance. 'Because it was true.'

'We were having a laugh, that's all. Did you tell them that, too?'

'I reported what I heard. It was my duty. I don't think you should be talking to me about this.' He looked around again and, spotting Lionel at the central hut, waved in his direction. Lionel started heading towards them.

'He was my friend, Cyril. I'd never have hurt him.' Ant didn't really know why he was even bothering, except that the truth mattered. And it stung to think that people might suspect him of having something to do with Dylan's death.

'Everything all right here?' Lionel said.

'Yes, it's fine,' said Ant. 'We're just talking. I was telling Cyril that I don't like people snitching on me, that's all.'

'I'm sure we all want to help the police in their investigation,' said Lionel. 'Recriminations and threats won't help and won't be tolerated here. There are rules about conduct.'

'I'm sure there are, but I'm not threatening anyone.' Ant held his hands out wide, palms up. 'I didn't threaten you, did I, Cyril?'

Cyril was licking his lips nervously, making Ant think that maybe he was intimidated by him. That hadn't been his intention. He took a couple of steps back. 'I didn't mean to sound threatening. I'm sorry if that's how it came across.'

He caught Lionel and Cyril exchanging a look. 'Are you going to ring the cops and report me again? If you do, I'm sure you'll tell them that I can't have had anything to do with Dylan's death. He was definitely still alive when you saw me leave.'

'I didn't actually notice you leaving,' said Cyril. 'I mean, I accept that you left, but I didn't see you going.'

Ant rolled his eyes. 'What is this? Are you trying to frame me? Is that what's going on? He was my *friend*. I had no beef with him. Not like you. He told me you thought he'd nicked your tomatoes. He was laughing about it, but you weren't laughing, were you, Cyril?'

'There haven't been any thefts since Monday,' said Cyril. 'You work it out.'

Ant shook his head in disbelief. 'Because the site's been closed off and swarming with cops, and then every single allotmenteer has been up here. It's been like Piccadilly Circus. I think it's better if I don't talk to you. I think . . . Never mind.' He turned away.

As Ant walked back across Dylan's plot, he bent down a little and cradled a truss of glossy red tomatoes in the palm of his hand. These were a different variety to Cyril's, smaller fruit but in larger clusters.

'Cyril,' he called out, 'look at these, just look at them. Why on earth would he nick yours?'

Cyril didn't move and didn't answer. Instead, Lionel clapped him on the shoulder and they turned and walked towards the communal shed. They looked like a pair of harmless old buffers, but there was more than that under the surface. There was resentment, jealousy — venom even. And that got Ant thinking, had Cyril disliked Dylan enough to kill him?

CHAPTER EIGHTEEN

'Shall we start the second layer?'

Bea and Queenie were sitting in their usual places in front of the TV, sharing a box of Costsave own-brand milk chocolates that Queenie had dug out of a cupboard. They were watching the late-night local news bulletin, in which a short item about Dylan's death had focused on an appeal for information by Dylan's two grown-up sons.

'Rude not to.' Queenie lifted the empty plastic tray out of the top of the box to reveal the tempting selection below. 'No wife, then, if his sons are doing the appeal. Doesn't sound like the police have got much further with the case, does it?'

'Divorced, by all accounts,' said Bea. 'They interviewed Ant yesterday. Well, Tom did.'

'Your Tom?'

'He's not mine. Never was really.' From time to time, Bea wondered what would have happened if she and Tom had made a go of things, but then she remembered his penchant for going behind his partners' backs. If he'd been willing to cheat *with* her, then surely he would have cheated *on* her eventually. 'I wonder why he hasn't got in touch with me? I only gave a very brief statement on Tuesday evening.'

'I expect he will eventually, love. They'll be more interested in people who were there on Monday.'

'Yeah. Like Ant. It's got him rattled. He'll be all right,
though. I mean, from what he told me he wasn't the last one
to see Mr Bradley. There will be plenty of witnesses that saw
him leave. Anyway—' she shifted a little in her seat with her
hand hovering over the pristine layer of chocolates — 'I'm
not going to get involved in all that. Leave it to the experts,
that's what I say.'

'Finally!' said Queenie. 'I've been telling you that for years.'

'Well, turns out you had a point. It's like they say, even
a stopped clock is right twice a day.'

Queenie picked up the box and withdrew it from Bea's
reach.

'It's a joke, Mum. Just a harmless little joke.' She grinned
and waggled her fingers indicating Queenie should put the
box back. 'You know I value your opinion.'

'As if!'

'I do! Actually, I want to pick your brains on something.'

'Go on, then.' Queenie placed the box back on the sofa
between them.

'What do you think people in Kingsleigh really want?'

'Money, sex, an easy life . . . a big win on the lottery.'

Bea sighed. 'I can't fix any of that, can I? Let me rephrase
it, what do people want from their council? What are the local
issues I should try and help with?'

'Oh, I can tell you that!' said Queenie, popping a noisette
twirl into her mouth. 'Car parking charges — they don't want
any — and dog poo — they want people to pick up after
their pets. If you could provide free parking and clean streets,
everyone would be happy.'

'That can't be it. Car parking and *dog poo*?'

'I guarantee it is, love. What do *you* think the problems
are?'

'Lack of affordable housing? Not enough for young people
to do since the youth club shut down? Epidemic of loneliness

93

— young people and old. Then there's all the sustainability stuff — energy and clean water and saving our bees.'

Her words stopped Queenie in her tracks. She gazed at Bea. 'You really are remarkable, you know, Bea. How many people your age would come up with a list like that?'

Bea shrugged. 'Lots of them would. I think most young people think about that sort of thing these days. It's not all TikTok and vaping.'

'Well, I'm impressed. You really should go for it, but don't forget to mention parking and poo, that's my advice. If you don't believe me, why don't you ask people?' Queenie chose a second almond chocolate, knowing that Bea didn't like the nutty ones, then nudged the selection box in Bea's direction.

'What, stand in the high street with a clipboard? I don't think I fancy that.'

'No, just ask your customers. Everybody comes through Costsave, apart from the ones who only shop in Waitrose, and I don't think we need to worry about them. Pretty sure they can afford to pay a quid for an hour's parking behind the civic centre and their dog walkers pick up their pooches' poo for them.'

Bea laughed at her mum's rather prejudiced summary. 'Haha, lots of people go to Waitrose, Mum, not just poshos. *We* like going there for a few treats and a latte in the café. But I take your point. I could ask people what they want. That's a really good idea.'

'I'm not just a pretty face, love. Do you want these strawberry kisses? They're too sweet for me.'

Bea took a heart-shaped chocolate and bit into it. 'Think these might be my favourites,' she said with her mouth full. 'I like how compatible our chocolate preferences are.'

'Jack Sprat and his wife,' said Queenie.

'What?'

Queenie smiled. 'Never mind. Are you going to put your form in then?'

'Yeah, after a bit of customer research and a mooch through the town council website, I reckon I will.'

94

CHAPTER NINETEEN

'Blimey, talk about peas in a pod,' said Ant. He was watching two young men walk through the allotment gates. They both had unruly mops of dark hair and walked with a particular round-shouldered gait, which was so familiar that it gave him a jolt.

'They couldn't be anyone else's boys, could they?' agreed Bob.

Ant had been contacted by Tom, who told him that Dylan's sons wanted to visit the place where he died and talk to the person who found him. Ant had asked Bea if she wanted to come along, but had got a rather sharp 'no' in response. Bob had been more than happy to be there as moral support, though.

The 'boys' were accompanied by Tom and a middle-aged woman, presumably their mother, and the three of them were met by Lionel in the car park, who was now showing them towards the plot. Ant felt ill at ease as they approached. He didn't know what to do with his hands, putting them behind his back, then clutching them in front and finally ramming them into his pockets, where his fingers found his cigarette packet and his second-best lighter. Would it be rude to have a smoke now? He had an inkling that Bob and Lionel would disapprove even if Dylan's lads were cool with it. He joggled one of his legs, unable now to think of anything except a nicotine hit.

'Here we go.' Bob wiped his hand across a rather sweaty forehead, and Ant realised that he was nervous, too.

'Hello, I'm Miles,' the oldest son said, reaching a hand towards Bob. Bob shook it and introduced himself and Ant. Miles introduced his brother, Sean, and his mum, Rosie, and a rather complicated session of handshaking ensued.

'I'm so sorry for your loss,' Bob said. 'He was a good neighbour here and a good man.'

'Thank you,' said Miles.

'I'm sorry, too,' said Ant. 'He was a top bloke, even though he was a teacher.'

The two boys laughed, but Bob cleared his throat and there was an audible intake of breath from Lionel, and Ant was suddenly mortified. 'Sorry, um, that came out wrong.'

'It's all right. We know what you mean. We both went through Kingsleigh Comp with him on the staff. Bit awkward sometimes.'

The two brothers looked at each other. 'Do you want to do this?' said Miles.

Sean took a deep breath. 'Yeah.'

They looked towards Dylan's shed. After the police had examined and recorded the scene, they had arranged for a handyman to patch up the door and fix a new lock.

Tom stepped forward, holding a couple of keys on a plain ring. 'Would you like me to do the honours?'

The boys nodded.

Tom unlocked the new padlock. As he opened the door and stepped back to give Miles and Sean some space, Ant felt a rush of horror surging through him. The door, the dark space, the metallic smell of blood . . . and his friend. Already gone. Beyond any help he could offer. He turned away and walked down towards the marrow plants. Bob followed him but gave him some space, while Dylan's sons paid their respects.

After a minute or two, they had emerged from the shed and were looking at the rest of Dylan's plot. Miles and Rosie went ahead, while Sean fell behind. When he was parallel with Ant, he looked across and smiled. Ant read it as in invitation to go over and talk.

'It's nice up here, isn't it? Peaceful,' said Sean. They made their way slowly towards the far end, stopping to examine the rows of beans, tomatoes and flowers.

'Did you used to come up here with your dad?' Ant asked.

'No, he didn't have it when we were at home. I reckon it was his way of settling down a bit after his mid-life crisis, along with going on the council.'

'What was his mid-life crisis?' He checked himself. 'Sorry, you don't have to answer.'

'No, it's okay. Normal stuff — going out on long cycle rides in neon Lycra and, er . . .' Miles looked at his mum, who was several metres ahead of them, deep in conversation with Lionel, and lowered his voice. 'Shagging our next-door neighbour.'

'Oh,' said Ant, not knowing what the correct response would be. He rejected 'sly old dog' in favour of silence. Dylan hadn't talked about his love life and Ant hadn't ever given it a second thought. Was it possible that Dylan's death had been a crime of passion? He decided to make a note in his book when everyone had gone.

'Mum kicked him out and they separated there and then. Now she's in Gloucester, I'm in Sheffield and Miles is working in London. Feels weird being back in K-town, to be honest.'

'I bet.' Ant was going to tell him about his family being scattered, too, but then thought better of it. This wasn't about him, after all.

'I don't think Dad would ever have moved, even though he'd retired. He loved this town. I'm glad he had a plot here. It looks very well cared for, like he spent a lot of time in this place.'

'Yeah, he did. He put the hours in. I think he was happy here.'

'That's good to know. It's so peaceful. I can't get my head around someone attacking him here.' Sean shook his head and looked down at the ground.

'Me neither. I'm so sorry,' Ant said, letting Sean collect himself. 'Are you staying in K-town until the funeral?'

'Probably not. It depends. We can start looking at dates now that the post-mortem has been done.'

Ant's ears pricked up. 'Do you know what it found?'

'No surprises. He died from a blow to the head sometime on Monday evening.'

'God,' said Ant. 'I don't like to think of him out here all night. I'm sorry I didn't find him sooner.' To his embarrassment, tears welled up in his eyes.

'I'd been thinking the same,' Sean said, 'but then I remembered Dad telling me how he'd sit here sometimes in the summer, looking at the stars. That makes me feel a bit better. The sky above him. His happy place.'

'Oh, man,' said Ant. There was some comfort in the thought, but it was still overwhelmingly sad.

By now, the others had clustered around them, making sympathetic noises.

'I'm so sorry.' Ant wiped his eyes. 'I should be comforting you, not the other way around.'

'It's okay,' said Rosie. 'It's hard for everyone. It's been a terrible shock.'

Ant, Bob and Lionel retreated to let the family have some time on their own. The Bradleys only spent a few minutes together and then started making their way back to towards the car park. They stopped to say goodbye and to thank Ant and Bob for looking after Dylan's plot.

'We thought we could enter one or two of your dad's things into the flower and produce show, if you agreed,' said Bob.

Beside them, Ant could hear Lionel making low growling noises in his throat. He glanced sideways and saw colour flushing his cheeks.

98

'Everyone here thinks it's a good idea,' Bob continued.

'That would be a nice touch. Thank you,' said Miles. The boys and their mum looked at Lionel, who went a deeper shade of red.

'It hasn't happened before, but it feels a fitting tribute,' he managed to say through gritted teeth.

'Thank you,' said Miles. 'We appreciate that.'

'And we'd like to take the rest of the produce to the food bank, if that's okay,' said Ant. Again, this was met with approval.

'What will happen to the plot now?' asked Miles.

'Assuming you don't wish to take it on, we'll be offering it to the next person on the waiting list,' said Lionel.

'Of course, that's fine,' said Miles. 'Do we need to clear out his stuff?'

'Ideally, yes,' said Lionel. 'But there's no particular hurry.'

The boys shrugged at each other.

'We don't need any of this. Could someone else do it? Share the stuff out among the people here or take it to the tip? Could you do it?' Miles was looking at Ant and Bob now.

'Yes,' said Bob. 'We can take care of that. Do you want us to try and sell anything?'

Miles shook his head. 'No, just give it away to anyone who would use it.'

Bob nodded.

'Shall I let you know how we get on with the show?' said Ant.

'Oh, yeah, that'd be great,' said Sean, and they swapped phone numbers.

Then they all shook hands again and Lionel escorted the Bradleys to the car park.

'Nice lads,' said Bob, as they watched them get into their car and drive off.

'Yeah,' said Ant. 'Good job putting Lionel on the spot about the show. I saw what you did there.'

Bob tipped his head in acknowledgement. 'How could he say no to the bereaved family?'

'You're good at dealing with people,' said Ant. 'I reckon you'd make a decent town councillor. Are you going to go for it?'

Bob shook his head. 'My life wouldn't be worth living if I took something else on at the moment. I think I'd better concentrate on the Wedding of the Year. Besides, I'm not a great one for meetings. I'm more of a doer.'

'Bea's got her eye on it, you know,' said Ant. 'I think she's barking. Doesn't seem like much fun for someone our age.'

Bob turned to face Ant. 'Bea's not your typical young woman, though, is she? She's something special, that one. Give her twenty years and she'll either be managing Costsave or running the country. Neither would surprise me.'

Ant found himself glowing vicariously at Bob's words. It was heartwarming to hear such praise. 'You're not wrong, Bob. She *is* something special.'

'Are you two . . . you know?' Bob looked at him quizzically.

Ant shuffled his feet a bit in the loose surface of the path. 'No. Yes. Maybe.'

Bob pulled a sympathetic face. 'Come on, lad. Let's get this lot tidied away and go and have a pint. I think we could both do with one.'

As they were packing up, Lionel approached them. Any hope that the boys' visit might have mellowed him was quickly dashed.

'The shed,' he said. 'There's no rush.'

'Oh, good,' said Bob.

'I'll give you a week, then anything left will go to the tip.'

CHAPTER TWENTY

'So, you and Bea,' said Bob, leaning back in his chair. 'What's the story?'

Ant sighed and stared into his pint of cider, not knowing where to start. Bob waited patiently.

'I really like her,' Ant said eventually.

He glanced up to see Bob smothering a smile. 'Spoken like a man facing the gallows. Has she given you the brush-off?' Bob slurped his pint of bitter, gaining a thin frothy moustache for his trouble, which he wiped off with a large cotton hanky.

'No, it's more . . . complicated. Everything's complicated, Bob, and I don't really understand why.'

'Have you told her you like her?'

'Yes. Like and . . . the other one. You know, the other L word.'

Bob's eyebrows shot up and he put his glass down. 'Blimey, Ant. I didn't realise it was so serious.'

'Well, it is and it isn't. It is for me, but I don't know if it is for her, and we've hardly done anything. I mean we've done something but—'

Bob put his hands up. 'Whoa, whoa, whoa, I don't need to know the gruesome details. That's between you two. Sounds like you just need to have a proper talk with her.'

'I've tried.'

'Well, I can see it's not easy with her living at home and you living with me. If you want to ask her over, just let me know and I'll make myself scarce.'

'She said she wanted to be left alone this weekend.'

'Fair enough. Give her some space. Then, maybe take her somewhere neutral. Make her feel special. Ask her on an actual date.'

'Do you reckon?'

Bob shrugged. 'Can't hurt, can it?'

'I guess not. Where would you suggest?'

At that moment, the door opened and Dean and Tyler came in. They were laughing and jostling as they went through the door and Dean gave a shout when he spotted Ant and Bob sitting in the corner. Ant felt his heart sink. It wasn't that he didn't want to spend time with his friends, just not *now*.

After a quick detour to the bar, Dean and Tyler came over.

'Mind if we join you, gents?' Of course, it wasn't a real question and Dean had already put his lager down on the table and was lifting a spare chair round from nearby. Tyler did the same, although his drink was a half-pint of orange juice.

'A little bird told me you were here,' said Dean. 'It's time the Four Amigos had a bit of a catch-up. We've been busy, haven't we, Tyler? And we need to hear all about what's gone down at the allotments. You got your notebook ready, Ant?'

Ant sighed but got his notebook out from his coat pocket. Bob sensed his reluctance and took the lead.

'I can tell you about the allotment stuff,' he said to Dean and Tyler, 'but why don't you start with what you've been up to?'

'You asked us to look at his council work,' said Dean, 'but fuck me, it's as dull as it gets! Trust me, nothing interesting goes on in Kingsleigh Town Council. Nothing at all. So, I trawled through the local chat forums instead, looking for gossip.'

'Anything?' said Ant.

'Lots of tributes to him. Some funny stories from school. Do you remember when he and some of the other teachers dressed up as the Spice Girls for the end-of-term concert?'

Ant and Tyler grinned.

'Blimey,' said Bob. 'Which one was he?'

'Think ginger wig and Union Jack minidress.'

'I don't think I want to. Press on, Dean. What else did you find out?'

'Not much. He lived on his own in a flat in Chewton Road. People seemed to like him, to be honest.'

'What about you, Tyler?'

'I found a little book he published,' said Tyler, looking rather pleased with himself. He produced a slim paperback book from his rucksack. 'It's called *Somerset's Hidden Jewel: The History of Kingsleigh*.'

'Sounds riveting.'

Dean did a sort of snort-laugh and had to dab at his nose with a hastily grabbed serviette from the next table.

'I've started reading it — it's quite good, actually,' said Tyler. 'You can buy it online, but they've got copies in the newsagents and the second-hand bookshop in the Stables courtyard.'

'Let's have a look,' said Ant. Tyler passed it over and Ant flicked through the pages. The text was illustrated with black-and-white photographs, maps and line drawings. 'Can I borrow it after you've finished?'

'Sure. He definitely knew his stuff.'

'So, what's been happening at the allotments?' said Dean, clearly not impressed with Dylan's literary work. 'That's where all the action's been.'

Ant set out what he knew about the timeline on the fateful Monday evening and who was still there when he left, and Bob told them about the visit from Dylan's sons and being asked to clear out his shed.

'That Lionel sounds like a twerp,' said Dean.

'You're not wrong,' said Ant. 'I can see why Charles doesn't like him. I don't see the rush about getting the plot ready to pass on either — he's only given us a few days.'

'Why don't we do it tomorrow?' said Dean. 'I've been itching to go up there. I've never been to an actual murder scene before. What do you say, boys?'

Ant and Bob looked at each other doubtfully.

'Well,' said Bob, 'it would be good to get on with it, and many hands make light work. Shall we meet there tomorrow at eleven?'

They raised their glasses to the middle of the table and chinked them together. The Four Amigos were back in the saddle.

CHAPTER TWENTY-ONE

Ant and Bob were at the allotments well before eleven the next day.

'Do you want me to do the honours?' Bob's solemn face reflected how Ant was feeling, too.

'Yes. I don't think I could.'

Bob undid the padlock, pulled at the door and it creaked open. Feeling sick, Ant forced himself to look inside. The logical part of his brain knew that Dylan wasn't there, yet he still half expected to see a heap on the floor. He found himself narrowing his eyes and squinting into the relative darkness.

Bob opened the door as far as it would go, letting in light and air. He looked back at Ant. 'All right?'

Ant swallowed and nodded, not trusting himself to speak.

'Do you want a minute or two to yourself in there? It's okay if you don't.'

'Actually, yeah.'

Bob stepped aside. Ant looked at the open doorway, took a deep breath and went to the threshold. He felt a rush of relief as he realised that the space felt different from the last time he was in there. The morning sunshine had transformed it into somewhere neutral, almost benign. When he'd found Dylan, the sun had been setting, the light leeching away. The inside of the shed had been gloomy, the air growing cold and carrying the metallic taint of blood. Now, motes of dust danced in the light and the contents — the tools and pots and string and netting — that Dylan had used and loved seemed to sit in silent tribute to him.

And then he looked down.

Although someone had obviously made an effort to clean up, there was still a dark patch on the floor where Dylan's blood had spilled. Ant crouched down. He put his hand in the middle of the stain, and remembered feeling for a pulse, talking to the body even though he knew that's all it was — a body. The person who had been Dylan, his life, his spark, hadn't been there anymore.

He heard footsteps behind him and then a voice.

'So this is where it . . . actually happened? Oh, sorry, mate. Were you . . . ?'

Ant stood and turned to face Dean. Tyler was standing behind him.

'I was just . . . you know . . .'

'Is that where he—' Dean tipped his head towards the dark patch on the floor.

'Yeah.'

They all fell silent. Bob joined them and they stood, hands at their sides, heads bowed, in a spontaneous act of respect. After a minute or two, Bob said gently, 'Okay, lads, let's do this.'

It didn't take the four of them long to take the contents out and put them on display along the side of the shed. Bob had put a message on the allotment WhatsApp group and people started gathering around and staking a claim on things that they could use. What started as a sober, muted and hesitant event turned into something rather glorious — a shared celebration of growing and gardening. As Ant watched people carrying forks and spades, earthenware pots and bamboo poles back to their plots, he felt that Dylan's devotion to his little patch of earth would somehow live on in the work of the other allotmenteers.

One thing that Ant couldn't bear to give away was Dylan's collection of finds. They had been displayed on a shelf, and Ant carefully put them in a shoebox: fragments of pottery, a couple of old glass bottles, three coins and a belt buckle. Tucked at the back there was also a copy of Dylan's own local history book, looking a bit dusty and scruffy.

'Nobody will mind if I have this, will they?' said Ant.

'Course not. You don't need to borrow mine now,' said Tyler. 'What are you going to do with all his finds?'

'Bung them in Charles's shed or take them back to Bob's,' said Ant. 'I don't suppose they're worth anything, but they just seem too personal to chuck away. They were his own little museum.'

They all gathered up the remaining bits and bobs and put them in the back of Charles's shed for the time being. Ant put the book in his bag and had a last look round. He didn't want to give Lionel any chance to find fault. It felt better now that it was empty. It was a blank canvas, stripped of all personality and ready for the next person. Ant felt a surge of satisfaction at a job well done.

'Is it too early for a drink?' said Dean. 'It is the weekend, after all.'

'I'm ahead of you.' Bob opened up the cool box he'd brought with him to reveal a heap of cellophane-wrapped rolls and some cans of cider and pop. 'A thank you for turning out today.'

They set up some chairs and sat in a huddle, tucking into the ham rolls and enjoying the sunshine.

'I've been thinking,' said Dean. 'You know Dylan told you he'd found a ring, where was that exactly?'

'I'm not sure,' said Ant, 'but he said he'd dug it up and the only part of his plot he'd been digging recently was his potato patch down the bottom there.'

'Hmm.'

'What's on your mind, Dean?' said Bob.

'Just that if someone had nicked some stuff and buried it, there might be more.'

'Which would have to be handed in to the police, if anyone found it,' said Bob.

'Yeah, sure. Course they would,' said Dean.

'Why, do you fancy digging over that whole patch on the off chance? I might pay good money to see that,' said Ant.

'No. I think we could be cleverer than that,' said Dean. 'We could use a metal detector.'

'Saggy's got one of those!' said Ant. 'It's sitting around in his lean-to, by the dog beds.'

'Now, wait a minute,' said Bob, shifting forward in his chair. 'You can't go around detecting and digging wherever you fancy, willy-nilly. There are all sorts of rules about using those things. You need to get permission from the landowner for a start. I think this is council land, rented to the Allotment Association, so you'd have to ask both of those. It's a non-starter, as far as I can see.'

'Ah, that's a shame.' Dean reached for another sandwich. 'It was a good idea.'

'Not one of your better ones . . .'

When all the food was gone and the cans emptied, they packed up and prepared to go their separate ways.

As they trailed towards the gates, Dean took Ant aside. 'What do you reckon, mate?'

'I reckon we don't need permission if we come up here when no one's about.'

Dean tapped the side of his head. 'My thinking exactly. Do you think Saggy would be up for it?'

'I've already texted him.'

'Do you want a lift home, Ant?' Bob called from the car park.

'No, it's okay. I'll see you later.'

'All right, son. I'm in tonight but at Dot's tomorrow, remember?'

108

Ant gave him the thumbs up.

'Perfect,' he said to Dean.

Tyler came up behind them. 'What's perfect?'

'Fancy a moonlight expedition?' said Ant.

Tyler looked worried. 'Back here, in the middle of the night? Um, I don't think my mum would like that . . . Do you really need me?'

Ant shook his head. 'No, you're all right. One to detect, one to dig, one to hold the torch. We'll be fine with three. Don't tell anyone, though, okay?'

'Of course not.'

Ant's phone pinged and he examined it, then grinned. 'Saggy's in. He wants to go tomorrow night.'

CHAPTER TWENTY-TWO

Usually, Bea loved watching Saturday night TV with her mum, but this evening she was head down, studying her laptop and making notes in her notebook. She was vaguely aware of Queenie commenting on *The Masked Singer* as usual but didn't join in the guesswork or banter. Eventually, she heard her mum say, 'Might as well be sitting here on my own,' followed by an exaggerated sigh.

'What's that, Mum?' she said, without looking up.

In her peripheral vision she saw Queenie get up from her armchair and perch on the arm of the sofa, so she could peer at Bea's laptop screen.

'I said, I might as well be sitting here on my own. What are you doing? Please don't tell me you're looking for Mr Bradley's murderer.'

Bea paused her note-taking and looked up. It was only half past seven, but Queenie had already got changed into her pyjamas and a big fluffy dressing gown.

'No, Mum. I told you I'm done with all that.'

'So, what are you doing?' Queenie screwed up her eyes to try and work out what the table of figures in Bea's open tab was showing.

'I'm researching. Trying to understand what being a councillor is all about. There's loads of information on the town council website when you dig into it. I'm having a look at the accounts, seeing where the money's spent. It's fascinating.'

Queenie sniffed and rose from her perch. 'It doesn't sound fascinating to me. You're a strange girl. Sometimes I can't believe I gave birth to you. I'm going to the kitchen. Do you want a cuppa or a *drink* drink?

'Cup of coffee, please.'

'Coffee? In the evening?' In the Jordan household, coffee was a morning-only drink. 'You'll be up all night.'

'A little bit of caffeine to sharpen my brain.'

'Crikey, you are taking this seriously.'

'I've got to, Mum. If I'm going to give it a go, I need to know what I'm getting into. Plus, I don't want to be a useless councillor. I want to be the best one I can be.'

'So, what have you found out?' Queenie called through from the other room.

'Well, I've found out that the staff costs are the biggest expense. As well as the people in the council office, there's the street cleaner and a team of two groundsmen who look after the parks, play areas, sports pitches and cemetery. Who knew?'

'What was that?' By now, the kettle was hissing and Bea knew that she had no chance of Queenie hearing her, even if she yelled. She waited until her mum came back, bearing two steaming cups and a packet of chocolate biscuits. Then she repeated what she'd said.

'Well, we all know Ivan, the street cleaner, don't we? And I've seen the two men down at the cemetery, when I've been visiting your dad. One of them's Ed Sillitoe, Malcolm Sillitoe's son.'

'Really?' Bea sipped gingerly at her hot coffee. 'When you hear "nepo baby", you don't automatically think of a life grave-digging and emptying dog bins.'

'What's a nepo baby?'

'You know, kids who are successful or famous because of their parents.'

111

'I don't think Ed Sillitoe is one of them. He's a decent groundsman. He does building repairs and tree work, all sorts. He's pretty handy.'

'I was only joking, Mum. Trying to. To be honest, if you have to spend five minutes explaining it, it's not the best gag in the world.'

Queenie flapped her hand in Bea's direction. 'That was just me being dim. What else have you found out?'

'Not much yet. I don't understand a lot of it. I might ask Anna about some of this on Monday.' Anna was the power behind the throne at Costsave, taking care of the admin in the office. Bea had filled in for her briefly, enjoying the work but missing the day-to-day contact with her customers.

'That's a good idea. But put it away now and watch the telly with me. It's a double reveal tonight, but it's no fun if you're not joining in.'

Bea was starting to get a headache anyway and was ready for a bit of a rest, so she shut the laptop and helped herself to a biscuit. She'd have another session later.

'Talking about the cemetery, shall we go and visit Dad tomorrow?' she said.

Her mum smiled. 'Yeah, if we went early perhaps we could stop off for lunch somewhere on the way back, maybe the diner, save ourselves cooking.'

'Nice idea.'

Later, after a giant chipmunk had been revealed as a former England footballer, and a mobile phone turned out to be one of Queenie and Bea's favourite soap stars, Bea said goodnight and took her laptop up to bed.

She was going to examine the accounts again but got distracted by a section titled 'Meetings'. She guessed that these would be the meat and bones of being a councillor, so she'd better find out what they involved. There was a bewildering array of categories — committees, sub-committees, working parties and full council meetings — with agendas and minutes for all. For a moment or two, Bea just looked at the list, not knowing where to start, but then she thought she'd begin at the top and try the most recent full council meeting. That should give her a flavour of things.

The minutes were written in a very formal style, recording who was there and what was agreed. Bea read them from start to finish, not allowing herself to skip a word, making notes as she went. By the end, she felt she'd lived the whole, rather dull experience. The minutes recorded that the meeting had taken just under two and a half hours and her notes told her they'd concluded the following:

Raising car park charges — no decision.
Extra money for Christmas lights — agreed.
Museum for Kingsleigh — feasibility study agreed.

The last item had clearly been a pet project of Dylan Bradley. Reading between the lines, he had delivered the same speech to the town council as the one he used to roll out at school at regular intervals. However, on this occasion, his proposal had been agreed, with twelve councillors voting for the engagement of consultants to plan the development of a town museum, and three against.

'Good for you, Dylan,' Bea murmured. Perhaps if she got onto the council, she could follow this up and help to make sure it happened, as a tribute to him.

She clicked on a few more links, but soon tired of it. Her brain was tired now but the caffeine from her evening coffee was still buzzing away in her veins. She reached for her phone.

There was a text from Ant. *Goodnight, Bea. Love you.*

It had been sent over an hour ago. Was it too late to reply? Would it be even worse not to reply at all? For the life of her she didn't know *how* to reply. Was it 'love you' as in a casual 'K bye, love you,' sort of sense, or was it a declaration of something more meaningful? He'd sent it at 10.43, pub turning-out time. Probably just a case of the cider talking, then. Oh, Ant.

She tapped a reply, deleted it and tried again. Not the L word. Kisses? Nothing seemed quite right.

Night. Xx

She looked at it for a while, added another 'x', then pressed send.

CHAPTER TWENTY-THREE

Bea and Queenie didn't visit the cemetery every Sunday, but it wasn't unusual to go there, like a lot of widows and widowers, bereaved children and parents. Despite most of the shops being open in the high street, Sundays were rather quiet and flat in Kingsleigh and it was easy to get the feeling that the town was full of happy families enjoying roast dinners, each in their own homes, turning their backs on those around them who didn't have such a cosy set-up.

As Bea walked slowly down the long, sweeping entrance road, arm in arm with her mum, the sound of shouts and whistles drifting across from the nearby playing fields seemed to emphasise the feeling that life was going on without them. They'd been a family of two for seven years, which was fine and they enjoyed each other's company, but Bea wondered if they were making the most of things. Was this how Sundays were going to be until it was just her making a solo pilgrimage and visiting two graves? The sun had broken out and it was surprisingly warm, but she shivered anyway.

'What's up, love?' said Queenie. 'Someone walked over your grave.'

Bea started, worried that she had said her thoughts out loud by mistake, or that Queenie could somehow read her mind.

'Mum, that's a horrible saying. Especially here.'

Queenie pulled a face. 'Not the best, was it? Sorry, love. I was only asking if you were all right, really.'

'I'm all right.'

Her mum looked at her, waiting for more, but Bea wasn't in the mood. She was rather wishing they hadn't come. It might have been a good day to spend some time with Ant and work out what was going on between them . . . She winced as she thought of the text she'd sent him last night. The three kisses at the end wouldn't have made up for the missing 'Love'. But did it matter? What sort of love had Ant meant?

After spending a few minutes standing at the grave, Queenie knelt and tidied up the little lavender sprigs she had planted at the start of the summer, which had bushed out nicely, picking off brown leaves and plucking out the odd stray weed, while Bea walked over to their normal bench. It was a good spot to rest their legs, enjoy some dappled sunshine and think. Today, though, it was already occupied.

Bea's initial resentment melted away when she realised that it was Charles on the bench, with Goldie lying on the ground near his feet. Although he was facing her as she approached, he didn't seem to see her. She understood — it was the sort of place to get lost in your own thoughts. Goldie recognised her, though. She didn't bother getting to her feet but her tail thumped enthusiastically.

'Room for a little one?' Bea said.

Charles looked up at her and his preoccupied expression gave way to a genuine smile. 'Bea! Of course there is.' He shuffled sideways and patted the bench next to him.

'You two have walked a long way this morning.'

'Yes, too far. To be honest, I'm not sure how I'm going to get back. You haven't got a car, have you?'

'No, but I'm sure we can ring someone who has.' Bea ran through the options in her mind. 'We'll sort something out. What brought you here?'

He blinked rapidly behind his glasses. 'Sometimes you just want to sit and think, don't you? And this seemed like the right place. I still talk to her, you know. Tell her what I've been doing or what's doing well in the allotment.'

Bea didn't need to ask who he was talking about. Nearly forty years on, Catherine was still a big part of his life.

'And you feel closer to her here,' she said. 'I get that. It's the same with my dad.'

He nodded sympathetically. 'It's silly, isn't it? The place shouldn't matter because they're always with you, in here—' he patted his chest — 'but somehow it helps.'

Queenie joined them, easing herself onto the bench the other side of Charles.

'A rose between two thorns,' he said, enjoying the women's expressions of mock offence. 'Or a thorn between two roses, more like.'

'Let's call it three roses, shall we?' said Queenie.

'Charles can't face the walk home,' said Bea. 'I'm going to try ringing Bob. See if he'll give Charles a lift.'

'Maybe us, too,' said Queenie. 'I'm quite tired today.'

Bob's mobile number went to his messaging service, so Bea tried Dot.

'Hiya, love.'

'Hi, Dot. Is Bob about?'

'He's up at that flippin' allotment again polishing that flaming marrow. Sometimes I think he loves it more than me.'

'Charles will be pleased, anyway. We found him at the cemetery, and he could do with a lift home.'

'Oh, that's no problem,' said Dot. 'I'll get the Micra out. She could do with a run out. Give me five minutes and I'll be there.'

'Thanks. That would be great,' said Bea. Then, 'Oh, she's gone. I didn't have a chance to ask if she minded squeezing Goldie in, too.' Dot's car was compact, to say the least. The last time Bea had had a lift in it, she and Ant had decided to make their own way home instead of suffering squashed limbs on the trip back.

'She's coming to our rescue, is she? I'm sure Goldie will be fine in Dot's car,' said Charles.

116

Bea wasn't so confident, and her doubts were confirmed when they spotted the little purple car coming down the access road. They walked up to the parking area and Dot wound down the window.

'Morning, all!' she said, chirpily. 'Ooh, Goldie too. That's going to be cosy in the back!'

'Actually, I think I'll walk Goldie back to Charles's,' said Bea. 'The exercise will do us both good.'

'Are you sure?' said Queenie. 'What about going out for lunch?'

'I'm so sorry,' said Charles. 'I'm causing trouble and messing up your plans.'

'What about us all going for lunch at the diner?' said Dot. 'Do they take dogs there?'

'I . . . I think I just want to go home,' said Charles.

'Have you got some food in?' said Queenie.

'Yes, I'm fine.'

This was all getting too complicated for Bea.

'I'm going to set off with Goldie,' she said firmly. 'And I'll pick up some sausage rolls on the way through town. I'll drop a couple in to Charles when I take Goldie back and then bring the rest home. If you bung some oven chips in, Mum, in about ten minutes, then we should be ready for lunch when I get back.'

'Sausage rolls and chips?' Dot frowned. 'I'm on a diet.'

'I've got some tins of soup in,' said Queenie.

'Well, one sausage roll and maybe a few chips wouldn't hurt, would they? It is Sunday, after all.'

Bea wasn't sure what Sunday had to do with it, but didn't question the logic. She started walking, leaving her mum climbing inelegantly over the tipped-forward passenger seat to get into the back of the Micra. The little car passed her as she was nearing the gate and she nearly jumped out of her skin as Dot beeped the horn. She responded with a cheerful two-fingered salute, extremely grateful that she was out in the fresh air and not crammed into the small metal box full of dog's breath.

'You and me, Goldie,' she said.

The dog looked up at her.

As the Micra pulled away and out of the site, another vehicle turned in — a green van with the Kingsleigh Town Council logo on the side. It drew level with Bea and pulled up in the road. The driver wound down the window. It was the man who had beeped, rather rudely, at Ant and Bea in the Costsave car park earlier in the week.

'No dogs on-site,' he said bluntly. 'Didn't you see the signs?'

'Um, no, and I didn't actually bring her here.'

He raised his eyebrows. 'You obviously did.'

She tried an appeasing smile. 'She's not my dog, you see. My friend brought her down here and I'm walking her home. Long story. It doesn't matter. We're going now, anyway.'

'It does matter, and I could report you.' He looked her up and down. 'I'll let you off with a warning this time.'

His manner was so officious that Bea could feel her hackles rising but it wasn't her dog or her battle, really, so she swallowed her anger and smiled sweetly. 'Thank you!'

She started walking away. The van's engine fired up again and she breathed a sigh of relief that the unpleasant encounter was over. It was then that she remembered what Queenie had said. Malcolm Sillitoe's son worked for the council. Of course, she could see the family resemblance now and not just in the set of the eyes and prominent forehead.

'Like father, like son,' she muttered. She wondered if either of them would have a different attitude to her if she became a councillor herself. It would be rather fun to find out.

CHAPTER TWENTY-FOUR

True to his word, Bob had gone to Dot's for Sunday evening, so Ant had the house to himself while he killed time before meeting up with Saggy and the others. He'd got a reduced-price pizza in the fridge that wasn't too far past its use-by date, so he cooked it in Bob's oven and ate it in front of the telly, luxuriating in the novelty of having sole control of the remote. But it was difficult finding something he actually wanted to watch. He couldn't settle on anything, endlessly flicking through the channels, switching to different streaming platforms, and even checking the programmes saved on Bob's list.

'Really, mate?' he muttered, as he discovered that Bob's preferred viewing included *The Great British Bake Off*, *Say Yes to the Dress*, *Nashville* and *The Kardashians*. He wondered if Dot had been adding programmes when she was here.

He finally settled on a thriller series. After one episode, though, he gave up, took his plate back to the kitchen and put it in the dishwasher, then, still hungry, started idly looking through Bob's cupboards. For a moment, he imagined what it would be like to have a place of his own — his own kitchen, bedroom, sitting room. Back when his mum and dad were still in Kingsleigh, the house had always been full of life and noise and chaos. All he could hear now was the odd creak from the central heating system, the sound of a car going past, and then quiet. It was odd. He didn't know if he liked it or not. After months — years now — of sleeping in people's spare rooms or worse, he wasn't even sure he wanted this. He thought he did, but maybe what he really wanted was his family back together. It was never going to happen. They were scattered to the four winds now.

He was being silly. *Come on, Ant*, he told himself. *Don't be a twat*. He should appreciate what he had — a quiet evening in on his own in a nice, safe, warm house.

He was going to crack open a can, then thought better of it — he needed to be alert for this evening's expedition — so he made a mug of tea and raided Bob's biscuit barrel, hidden at the back of the cupboard near the sugar bowl. Really, he thought, as he took a handful, he was saving Bob from himself.

He went upstairs, propped himself up on his pillows and picked up Dylan's book, which he'd left on the bedside table. He smiled as his fingers felt the dust on the cover, then started to wonder why Dylan had kept a copy in his shed. Surely he had copies of his own book at home. Why did he need one there?

He opened the front cover. On the back of the title page, some information was printed. *Bradley Books, 2013. Copyright Dylan Bradley. All rights reserved.* There was also a dedication, 'For all those who have been and all those to come, and for my boys.'

Ant turned the page and started reading the introduction, but soon the words were swimming in front of his eyes. He did want to read it, but he'd have a better chance of taking it in when he wasn't so tired. He flicked through the pages and looked at the photos and illustrations. Some of the corners of the pages were folded over at the top. With his newfound reading skills, Ant had started to value, almost revere, books and he felt a little bit shocked. Was it okay to do this? He'd have to remember to ask Bea. He looked at the first page that had been marked in this way. There was a pencil asterisk against one paragraph and a circle around a couple of words: '*Roman coins*'. Ant started to read the page from the top, tracing the words with his index finger.

* * *

He woke up in a panic and checked his phone. Twenty past nine. Okay, he hadn't missed anything. He sat up, rubbed his eyes, picked up the book, which had fallen onto the floor, put it on his bedside table, and then wandered along to the bathroom. He ran a bath, adding jasmine-scented bubbles and filling it nearly to the top, and left the door open just because he could. He was so busy dunking his head, getting Bob's shampoo into a good lather and showering it off, that he didn't hear the front door going or the tread on the stairs. The first time he knew that he wasn't alone anymore was when he was replacing the hand shower in its holster by the taps and saw a shadow in the bathroom doorway.

He emitted a high-pitched shriek and, for some bizarre reason, covered his bare chest with his hands, then thought better of it and plunged his hands into the water to hide his crotch.

'All right, mate?' said Bob. 'Didn't mean to disturb. Dot was dyeing her hair and then she said she was going to ring her Sal, so I thought I'd come home and see how you were getting on. All right, it seems.' He grinned.

'Oh, okay. Sweet,' said Ant.

'Make sure you dry the floor when you're done, will you?'

Ant peered over the side of the bath to see an impressive pool of bubbles and water on the lino, along with his discarded clothes, now in a soggy heap.

'Yes, Bob. Sorry, Bob.'

'It's not a problem. You make yourself at home, son. Shall I close this?' He indicated the door.

'Yes, please.'

Bob grinned again and shut the door behind him, leaving Ant to ponder how he was going to sneak out of the house later without prompting too many questions.

At ten to eleven, they were both in the lounge watching the football highlights. Ant had got dressed in black jeans and a long-sleeved tee. He was going to layer up with a hoodie and jacket on top before going out. He messaged Dean and Saggy so they wouldn't knock on the door and raise Bob's suspicions and his phone pinged twice as he received a thumbs up emoji in response, and then, *ETA, 11.03 outside yours*.

Ant stood up.

'You off to bed?' said Bob.

'Um, no,' said Ant. 'I'm going out.' He waved his phone in Bob's direction. 'I've just got a match. Looks like my luck's in.'

Bob's eyebrows shot up.

'I thought you and Bea were . . . Never mind,' he said. 'Just be careful, okay. And respectful.'

Ant grinned. 'If you're going to give me "the talk" about the birds and the bees and using protection, can we do it tomorrow? Don't want to keep her waiting.'

Bob held his hands up. 'I wasn't . . . Okay, maybe I was . . . Sorry, son. I know I'm not your dad.'

'And I'm twenty, but I do appreciate that you care.'

'I do, mate. I do. Off you go. I'll leave the hall light on.'

Ant sped upstairs to fetch his things and then let himself out of the front door. Saggy and Dean were waiting outside, also dressed in black.

'All right?' said Saggy. 'Did you get out without Bob seeing?'

'No, I had to tell him I was on a booty call.'

Dean snorted. 'Sorry, Ant. You're not my type. You might be in with Saggy, though.'

Saggy punched him in the arm and Ant worried that a scuffle was going to break out, but Dean took it in good part.

'I've got the metal detector, some head torches, a spade and a couple of trowels. I'll hand them out when we get there,' said Saggy, who Ant now saw was carrying a large black bin bag, which didn't wholly disguise its contents.

'Bloody hell,' said Ant. 'We look well dodgy. Did anyone see you walking up here?'

'Not really. The odd dog walker, some lads coming home from the pub. It was fine.'

Ant puffed his cheeks out and exhaled. It would have to be. 'Okay, lads. Let's get on with it.'

Operation Detectorists was go.

CHAPTER TWENTY-FIVE

Once inside the allotment gates, they switched on their head
torches and Ant led them towards Dylan's plot. He picked his
way along the path to the far end, where the rows of potato
plants shone palely in his torchlight.

'Here?' Saggy started taking his detector out of the bin
bag.

'Yeah,' said Ant. 'Start here. Do the area which is already
dug up, nearest the plants — that's the bit that Dylan will
have harvested most recently.'

The breath caught in Ant's throat as he realised that Dylan
would never tend this plot again. He was gone. *Murdered*. The
finality of it hit him again.

Saggy switched his detector on. It wasn't the most sophis-
ticated model. Ant had thought that these days they came
with headsets so that only the operator heard the results, but
Saggy's had no such accessories, and as he swept from side
to side in front of him, slowly walking along the first row of
disturbed soil, it emitted little squeaks and pips.

'What does that mean? Have you got something?' Dean
was unable to keep the excitement out of his voice.

'No, it's got different tones. Stuff like tin cans or ring
pulls make that sort of noise.'

He stopped at one area and went over it a couple of times. 'Maybe something here.'

Ant and Dean drew closer and they all listened. The machine's noise was higher pitched and clear. They looked at one another.

'Who's got the spade?' said Saggy.

Dean scampered back to the bin bags. He was just about to plunge the blade into the soil, when Ant saw something else — a light bobbing around in the distance. 'Hang on, fellas. I think we've got company. Kill your torches. Saggy, switch that off.'

They stood together in the dark and, yes, there was a light and it was getting closer.

'Shit, what do we do now?' hissed Dean. 'Shall we leg it?'

'It's coming down the main path, I think,' said Ant. 'By the time we got to the gate, they'd spot us. We'd better stay put and find somewhere to hide.'

'Go on, then,' said Saggy. 'You know this place. Show us where.'

Ant thought hard. 'This way. Keep your torches off.'

They walked slowly in the inky darkness, feeling their way with their feet on the uneven ground. Ant took them onto Charles's plot and behind the rosebushes at the end. He traced the line of the perimeter fence with one hand. The bushes on his left provided a bit of resistance, but he pushed through, thorns scratching his face and neck.

'Ow!' said Dean.

'Shh, get in here. Now crouch down,' Ant whispered.

They huddled together. Ant could only see the light intermittently now, through the cover provided by the shrubs. If he couldn't see it, then they, in turn, wouldn't be seen, he thought, but it was definitely getting closer. When it did shine through, the light was so bright that it dazzled him. It was impossible to see who was behind it.

The light stopped moving. It was playing along the rows of plants on the plot beyond Dylan's. Ant wondered if it was Cyril himself on one of his rumoured night patrols. He thought he heard rustling, like the sound of a plastic sheet or bag. He felt in front of him and gently moved some branches apart to create more of a gap.

The light suddenly fell a couple of feet, and Ant guessed someone had dropped their torch.

'Shit!' The voice that swore was relatively high-pitched and youthful. Definitely not Cyril, then. There was more rummaging about as the torch was retrieved. The light played on the foliage of the plants, and a hand moved through them.

Caught in the act, Ant thought. *The tomato thief!*

His heart was thudding in his chest. Or was this Dylan's murderer revisiting the scene of the crime? You'd have to have some brass neck to come back to nick a few vegetables at the place where you'd killed someone. It didn't make sense to Ant, but it was possible . . . wasn't it?

The light moved a little closer. The thief was examining all sorts of plants but hadn't picked anything yet.

Beside him, Dean let out a little whimper. 'They're going to find us,' he whispered.

'Shh.' Ant squeezed his shoulder. 'I think it's the thief.'

He kept watching through the leaves of the shrub, trying to see the torch-holder's face, but all that showed up in the little pool of light was their hands and a bag. Now there was something else — the glint of a knife.

'Shit,' Dean whispered. 'Can you see that?'

'I see it. Shh.'

'What? I can't see anything,' whispered Saggy.

'He's got a fucking knife.' Dean was unable to keep a rising hysteria out of his voice, even at a whisper.

The thief bent over and reached forward. Ant tried to remember what Dylan had been growing in that part of the plot. His stomach flipped when he thought of Marvin, but Dylan hadn't grown any marrows. He couldn't see what was happening until the figure stood up again, placing something large into the bag. The light caught a circle of fresh green leaves with a glimpse of something white in the middle.

'A cauliflower,' Ant breathed. 'He's nicking a cauliflower!'

But the thief wasn't done yet, and when they started walking down the side of Charles's plot, Ant had a vision of them slicing through Marvin's stalk and he couldn't bear it. It was time to act.

'Okay. On a count of three, boys, we're going to jump up and shine our torches at them,' he hissed.

'Have you lost your tiny mind?' Saggy hissed back, while Dean only managed a terrified squeak at a bat-like pitch.

'Just do it. Trust me. Here we go. Torches on. One, two, three!'

Trusting that they would follow his lead, Ant stood up, trained his torch beam at the intruder and shouted, 'Hey, you!'

For a moment, he thought that it was going to be one against one. He had surprise on his side, but the other guy had the knife. He breathed a sigh of relief as Dean and Saggy sprung up beside him and trained their torch beams on the intruder, too.

The thief froze in the spotlight, face turned towards them, eyes narrowed against the glare. It was a young lad. He held one hand up to shield his eyes, then turned and started running, taking the bag with him.

They tracked him with their torches as he stumbled and flailed away, eventually throwing the bag over the fence and scrambling after it.

'Bloody hell,' said Dean. 'I thought we were for it then, but he was more scared of us.'

'Only young, wasn't he?' said Saggy.

'Yeah,' said Ant. 'Still at school, I should think.'

'Nicking food from here in the middle of the night? That's a bit desperate, innit?'

Ant shrugged sadly. 'Desperate times, mate, for a lot of people.' He turned back to Dylan's plot, his heart slowing down, no longer afraid. 'Come on, let's get back to the spot we were at before. See if it makes your machine beep again.'

CHAPTER TWENTY-SIX

Ant, Dean and Saggy struggled out of the bushes and picked their way back to Dylan's potato rows.

'We were just up here, weren't we?' Saggy switched the detector back on and moved it gently from side to side. It soon beeped again.

He stood back a little, allowing Dean the space to dig. He used the spade to start with, pressing it into the soil with his foot, then turning the earth over a couple of times. The spade didn't hit anything solid and nothing came to the surface.

'Do the machine again,' Dean said.

Saggy obliged and held the device directly over the place where it beeped. 'Just there.'

Dean handed the spade to Ant and crouched down with the hand trowel. 'Ha!' he cried, triumphantly, holding something between his index finger and thumb. He put the trowel down and placed the object on his other palm while the Ant shone his torch on it.

It was a five pence piece. Despite its humbleness, Ant felt a little thrill. Saggy's machine actually worked.

Saggy carried on, walking forwards slowly and sweeping the detector from side to side. Nothing. He got to the end of the row, turned round and came back the other way. Eventually, he had covered almost the entire dug-up portion of Dylan's plot with no further discoveries.

'Reckon we've drawn a blank,' said Dean. 'Five pence three ways isn't much of a haul. I'll stick it in the charity tin at work. Should we try somewhere else?'

'Nah, this place is huge. I reckon it's time for some kip,' said Ant. 'Saggy, are you ready to pack up now?'

'Wait a minute.' Saggy was at the far end of the plot, running his detector over a section of undug soil between the last potato row and the hedge. The machine was beeping. 'There's something here.'

Ant and Dean joined him. This time Ant dug at the unturned soil with the spade and Dean stepped forward with the hand trowel. He sifted through the soil and picked out something small.

'We're in, boys! This is more like it!' He rubbed the soil off with his thumb to reveal a delicate earring. Still crouching down, he held it up to the light for the others to see. Even cleaned roughly, its gold stud gleamed and the teardrop opal dangling beneath glittered in the torchlight.

'Nice,' Saggy whistled. 'Very nice.'

'What's that in the hole?' said Ant. He directed his torch beam to a paler patch in the soil, near to where Dean had picked out the earring.

Dean reached forward and touched the white patch. It was solid, like a stone. He rubbed the soil away, revealing more. With some of the dirt removed, the shape of it emerged. It wasn't one solid object. There were two of them, close together, joined with a sort of hinge.

'Oh shit,' said Saggy. 'Get away from it, Dean!'

'What?' Dean looked round, shining his torch into Saggy's face and then Ant's.

Ant squinted into the beam. 'What is it, Saggy? What's wrong?'

Dean directed his torch back to the hole in the ground. One of the stones seemed to have some smaller ones sticking into it. He rubbed at the soil again with his thumb and gasped as he realised what he was touching.

He'd cleaned the mud off somebody's teeth. It was a jaw-bone, a jawbone attached to a skull.

CHAPTER TWENTY-SEVEN

Dean jerked backwards and ended up sitting on his backside in the dirt. 'Holy crap!' His hands were shaking and he'd broken into a sweat.

'Oh no,' said Ant. 'Oh God, no.'

Dean leaned towards the hedge bottom and threw up noisily. He stayed on his hands and knees until Ant helped him up. Then they all stood near the hole and stared in horror.

'W-what do we do now?' said Saggy.

'We'll have to call the police,' said Ant.

'But we shouldn't be here out of hours. We're going to be in a whole lot of trouble.'

'Saggy, we can't dodge this one. It's a body. We haven't got a choice. I'm calling it in.'

He reached for his phone and dialled 999. He asked for the police and was put through instantly. He gave his details and where he was calling from and when he reported what they'd found, the operator told him to stay put and not to touch anything else. Someone would be with them soon.

They stood, side by side, waiting. In the torchlight, Dean's face was as white as a sheet. Ant noticed that his hands were shaking as he took out his phone. But his sympathy

131

turned to disbelief when Dean started to take photographs of their find.

'What are you doing?' Saggy asked.

'Recording it. It's a once-in-a-lifetime thing, isn't it?' said Dean.

While it was true, Ant still felt queasy about it. 'Don't post them anywhere, mate,' he said. 'I don't think the police would like it.'

'I'm not an idiot.' Dean moved round the edge of the hole, crouched down and took a few more. He looked up at them. 'Shall we get one of the three of us?'

'No, Dean, you sicko!' Saggy screeched.

'For God's sake, Dean, have some respect,' said Ant. 'That's a real person. Somebody who used to be somebody. You don't take selfies at a time like this.'

'All right, all right, keep your hair on, both of you. It was only a joke,' Dean said, but Ant knew that it hadn't been. If they'd been up for it, he would have snapped the three of them grinning in front of their gruesome discovery. Dean might be less of a muppet than he used to be, but he was still definitely a work in progress.

'My mum's going to kill me when she finds out what we've been doing,' said Saggy, then added hastily, 'Not literally, but, you know . . .'

'Yeah, mine too,' said Dean.

'I don't think Bob's going to be impressed, either, although we weren't technically doing anything wrong,' said Ant.

'Digging up a dead man's allotment in the middle of the night?' said Dean. 'It doesn't look legit, does it?'

'No, but we'll only be in trouble with Lionel and his mates cos we didn't ask them for permission. I don't *think* we've broken any actual law.'

'I could just go . . . take the metal detector with me,' said Saggy, 'if you think that would look better.'

'How would that look better for anyone, except you?' said Dean. 'Ant and me would just be weirdos digging up a random allotment in the middle of the night then.'

'You could just say you were guarding your tomatoes or something,' said Saggy, 'tell them about the thief we scared off.'

'They're not gonna believe that. They'll think *we're* the tomato thieves unless we tell them about the ring and the metal detector. Sorry, mate, you've gotta stay. Where the hell are the cops?'

They seemed to have been waiting for hours, but it had actually only been a few minutes, and soon they heard the wail of a siren and saw blue lights playing on the nearest rows of houses. The others stayed put while Ant set off to meet them at the gate. By the time he got there, Tom, in jeans and a puffer jacket, together with a uniformed officer Ant didn't recognise, were standing outside, examining the keypad.

'Can you turn your head torch off, please, sir?' said Tom. Then, as Ant extinguished the light, 'Bloody hell, it's you, Ant. I might have known. Please don't tell me Bea is here, too.'

'She isn't. It's just me and a couple of mates.'

Tom shook his head in disbelief. 'What's the code for this lock?'

'I'm not allowed to tell anyone.'

Tom snorted in disbelief. 'I'm the police. You've found a body. Tell me the number now.'

Ant relented and Tom undid the lock. He and his colleague entered the site.

'Okay, lead on,' said Tom.

Ant switched his torch back on and set off down the path.

'What were you three doing up here, anyway?' said Tom.

Ant pretended he hadn't heard to give himself a bit of thinking time. Tom repeated the question, a little louder this time.

'We were giving Saggy's metal detector a go,' Ant admitted, finally.

'And?'

'And what?'

'That's not the whole story, is it? This isn't the most obvious time or place to test out a new toy. Come on, mate. Spill the beans.'

They were at the start of Dylan's plot now. Saggy and Dean's torches were clearly visible in the gloom at the far end.

'Like I told you, the day he died, Dylan found a ring somewhere on his plot. We were just using Saggy's detector where he most likely found it to see if anything else turned up. We thought it might be someone's stash of stolen goods, or something like that.'

'You took things into your own hands, like you and Bea have done before.' Tom couldn't keep the irritation out of his voice. 'It won't do, Ant. It really won't. We'll talk about it later.' They had joined the others now. 'All right, lads? Is this it? Give me a bit of space.'

Ant, Saggy and Dean stood well away from the hole, while Tom approached and knelt down. He shone his torch over the soil.

'Okay, what are we looking at here?' he asked. Then, 'Oh, shit.'

'We found the earring first. That's what set the detector off. Then we found the . . . other thing,' said Dean.

'Okay.' Tom stood again. 'Don't move while I radio this in.' He turned away from them, which had no effect at all as they could all hear everything he was saying as he requested urgent support. When he'd finished, he turned back to the subdued group. 'Right, we need to preserve this area as much as possible. Seb, take these guys back to the gate, but don't let them leave. We're going to need statements from all of you. I'll look after the remains until the SOCO guys get here. Bring them down when they get here.'

'You sure you want to stay here on your own?' Ant said.

Tom looked at him witheringly. 'This isn't my first body, you know.'

'Okay, if you say so. Should I ring Lionel Gittins?'

'The guy in charge of the site? Yes, please.'

Ant rang Lionel's number. It took a long time for him to pick up. Finally, a voice that managed to be both bleary and tetchy said, 'Gittins.'

'Lionel, it's me. Ant.'

'Ant, who?'

'Ant Thompson, Bob and Charles's friend.'

'Oh, *Ant*.'

'I'm at the allotments. The police are here too. I think you'd better get down here.'

'Why? It's . . . half past two in the morning. What's going on?'

Ant looked at Tom to check if he was allowed to tell Lionel the news. Tom held out his hand to indicate that Ant should hand over his phone.

'Mr Gittins, this is Detective Constable Tom Barnes. We're dealing with another serious incident here. We'll be sealing the whole site off.'

Ant couldn't hear Lionel's reply but Tom soon rang off, so he assumed Lionel was on his way. The three friends picked their way back along the grassy path, with Seb, the uniformed officer, trailing behind them.

'I wouldn't want to be there on my own,' said Saggy.

'Me neither.' Dean shuddered. 'It was bad enough the two of us just now.'

Soon after they got back to the gate, Lionel arrived. Ant was amused to see he was wearing a winter coat over his pyjamas, which were a surprisingly flamboyant paisley pattern. Ant and Dean helped him open both gates wide as a second police car drew up and then another unmarked vehicle. Soon the whole place was floodlit, taped off and full of people in various uniforms and crinkly white all-in-one suits.

Ant, Dean and Saggy stood to one side. Ant was actively trying to avoid Lionel, who was busy supervising for a while, but all too soon he fixed Ant in his sights and made a beeline for him.

'You owe me an explanation,' he said.

'I can't explain, Lionel. I can only say sorry, that's all.'

'Poking around here in the middle of the night? Using a metal detector? Digging up someone else's plot? You're banned, Ant. For ever.'

Ant knew that the three of them had been in the wrong, of course, but he suddenly saw red. He was so tired of authority figures yelling at him. School, work and now the allotments. A lifetime of resentment bubbled up to the surface, and before he knew what he was doing, he heard himself saying, 'Can you do that? Just ban me? Don't you have to get your committee to agree?'

Lionel tipped his head to one side, as if he was unsure of what he just heard. 'Oh yes, I can do it, all right. The committee will back me up. What you did tonight was beyond the pale.'

Ant held his ground. 'I want to see it in writing. Official like.'

Lionel narrowed his eyes. 'Of course. To be honest, I'll be writing several letters in the morning. I've been turning a blind eye to all sorts of infractions for far too long, including Charles's clear incapacity to maintain his plot. I know that Bob's been tending it for him for years, and now they've brought you into it. So, I'll be writing to you and I'll be writing to Charles, informing him that he's broken the terms of his agreement and forfeited the right to the plot.'

It felt like the ground was dropping away from beneath Ant's feet. Lionel was deliberately going to make Charles suffer for something that he, Ant, had done. It was vindictive.

'You can't do that! He's had his allotment for ever!'

'I'm sorry it's come to this, but you've brought the spotlight onto a situation that clearly breaks our rules,' Lionel snapped. 'I can do it and I will. You will both hear from me in the morning.' He checked his watch. 'Well, in a few hours' time, actually.'

'But it's crazy! Just think about it. Some poor sod is lying dead in there, and you're firing out letters about rules and regulations. Please, I know what I did was wrong. I apologise. I'll grovel, if you want me to. Tonight's been mad. Let the dust settle a bit. Talk to your committee — I'll come and apologise to them, if you want me to. Please don't take this out on Charles.'

Lionel looked at him coldly. 'It's been a long time coming. You've been breaking the rules for too long and now it's time to reap what you have sown.'

CHAPTER TWENTY-EIGHT

While people in crinkly boiler suits picked their way around the end of Dylan's allotment and a white tent was put up, Ant, Dean and Saggy were taken to a quieter area in the car park and interviewed in turn.

To Ant, the whole thing seemed unreal. He badly wanted to wake up on Bob's sofa with a cricked neck and dried dribble on his chin to realise that it had all been a bad dream, so he pinched himself hard on the wrist. If this was a dream, the pain would wake him up. But the pain was real, and so was this macabre scene. And in front of him stood the officer, Seb, who had arrived with Tom, peering at him and waiting, as if he was expecting an answer to a question.

'I'm sorry, mate,' said Ant. 'What did you say?'

'I was asking you to talk me through what happened, from arriving here to ringing us.'

'Yeah, right, of course.'

Ant recounted the events as best he could. He left out seeing the tomato thief, but felt uneasy, not knowing if the others were doing the same. They hadn't thought to coordinate their stories.

'And why did you decide to come here tonight?'

Ant dug his hands into his pockets. 'Strike while the iron was hot. Just had the idea in the pub at lunchtime and decided to get on with it.'

After the officer had run out of questions, Ant waited with the others. He checked, but neither Dean nor Saggy had mentioned the thief. It seemed they had all had the same instinctive feeling that it would be more trouble than it was worth. Someone came to photograph the soles of their shoes and record their size and make.

'I bet our footprints are all over the place,' said Dean.

'I suppose they have to do that, but it's a bit daft, innit?' said Ant. 'Whoever buried that body probably did it years ago.'

'Do you reckon?'

'Well, I don't think things . . . people . . . rot down to just their bones in days or weeks. It takes ages, doesn't it?'

Dean shivered. 'I don't want to think about it. I can't believe I touched it.'

The bravado he'd shown when he was taking photographs had seeped away and he was looking pasty and fragile.

'Have you rung your mum?' asked Ant. 'I think she should come and fetch you.'

Dean turned even paler.

'Are you kidding? I'm going to be in enough trouble without waking her up at—' he checked his phone — 'half past three in the morning.'

'What about you, Saggy?'

'Same. I'll go home and face the music in the morning, well, hopefully afternoon. I'm knackered.'

Ant thought about ringing Bob. He was sure he would want to know about the events of the night and Lionel's catastrophic decision, but it would wait. And there was someone he needed to tell first. It was the right thing to do.

CHAPTER TWENTY-NINE

When the police told them that they were free to go, the boys walked through the dark, empty streets together.

'That was . . . a lot,' said Ant. 'I can't really believe what just happened. Shall we meet up tomorrow and talk it through?'

'I'll see you at Costsave in four hours, mate.' Dean rubbed his hand across his eyes. 'Unless I pull a sickie. I don't feel great right now.'

'Why don't I walk you home?' Ant's first-aid training was kicking in and he suspected Dean had gone into mild shock. 'I don't want you keeling over round the back of the high street. It'd make the place look untidy.'

'It's not on your way,' Dean protested, half-heartedly.

'I'm not going back to Bob's right now.'

'Bea's isn't my way, either,' Dean said, as he and Saggy exchanged winks.

'What do you mean?' said Ant. 'We're not a thing, okay? Well, not officially.'

'Shame,' said Dean. 'Does that mean I can have a crack?'

In Dean's current state, it wouldn't take much to deck him, Ant thought, and it was a tempting prospect, but he decided to rise above it and take the better way. 'That's not for me to say, is it? If you do have a go at work, though, I'll be there with a bucket and sponge to mop up what's left when she's finished with you.'

'You don't think I'm in with a chance, then?'

Ant looked at him and realised he was serious. 'I think this is a conversation for another day, mate.'

They were at the point where their route and Saggy's diverged. They all exchanged weary high fives.

'I'll be in touch,' said Ant.

'I don't think I want to be in your gang anymore, mate,' said Saggy. 'That wasn't quite what I was hoping for.'

Ant sighed. 'Yeah, sorry about that. It's been a weird one, hasn't it?'

'You can say that again.'

Saggy peeled off and Ant and Dean continued to Kingfisher Drive. When they reached number forty-one, Ant gently patted Dean on the back. 'Have a cup of sweet tea before you go to bed, get some sugar into you, then tuck in with a hot water bottle.'

Dean managed a smile. 'Thanks, Mum.'

'No problem.'

'Sorry if I offended you, talking about Bea. For what it's worth, I think you two would be great together.'

Dean walked up the garden path and let himself in. He raised his hand in salute before closing the door very gently. Ant set off back the way they'd come. He checked his phone. It was nearly twenty past four now. He didn't know how long he'd have to wait, but it would only be an hour or two. No point going back to Bob's.

As he walked through the streets, his mind was trying to process the night's development. A second body, but one that looked like it had been there a while. Were the two deaths connected? Could they be? It would be a hell of a coincidence if they weren't, but stranger things had happened.

They had only found the remains today because of the metal detector. If they hadn't used that, it might never have

140

come to light. He wished, more than anything, that he could tell Bea about it. She wouldn't thank him to be woken early, though, especially when she'd made it crystal clear that she didn't want to know about their latest investigation.

He sighed and walked on until he came to the old people's bungalows. He didn't want to alarm anyone if they happened to look outside during a sleepless moment, so found a spot twenty metres or so further along and parked himself on a low wall.

He knew Charles was an early riser, but wasn't sure just how early. He kept an eye on number three and after maybe half an hour, a light came on. Ant shifted from his perch. His legs were stiff and he was light-headed from lack of sleep, but he focused on what he needed to do.

He approached Charles's and gently tapped on the front door. Wary of waking the neighbours, he was just wondering if he needed to increase the volume a little when he heard Goldie scratching at the other side of the door. *Clever girl*, he thought, hoping that Charles would have noticed what she was doing. Soon, he heard another sound — a chain rattling and a lock being turned — and the door opened to reveal a sliver of light blocked halfway up by Charles's anxious face.

'Hello?' he said. 'Is somebody out there?'

'Charles, it's me. Ant.'

'Ant?'

'I'm sorry it's so early. I need to talk to you.'

'Yes, son, of course. Hang on.'

The door closed again, there was more rattling and rummaging about and then it opened wide. Charles stood there in his striped pyjamas and slippers, a dressing gown tied loosely around his middle. Beside him, Goldie wagged her tail enthusiastically. Ant was one of her favourite people. Well, in truth, everyone she met was her favourite person — she was that kind of dog.

Charles shepherded Ant inside and showed him into the lounge. Ant sat on the sofa at the front of the cushion and leaned forward, his right leg jiggling uncontrollably. Charles eased himself into the armchair opposite and Goldie flopped down between them.

'Do you want some tea?' said Charles. 'I just put the kettle on before you knocked. I have a cuppa around this time every morning. I let Goldie out for a tinkle and then we go back to bed, don't we, girl?'

'Um, no, not yet, thank you. I need to tell you something and I don't want you to hear it from someone else.'

'Have you been up all night? It must be important. Spit it out.'

'I have and it is.' Despite having had hours to prepare what to say, Ant was rather lost for words. 'The thing is, I . . . I did something silly.'

'Go on.'

'I went up to the allotments at night with my mates and a metal detector. We found a . . . we found another body there and called the police, and Lionel. Lionel was really angry. He's mad with me and is going to ban me, which is fair enough, but he also says that you aren't looking after your plot anymore and he's going to take it off you.'

Charles was silent. He kept looking at Ant, like he was trying to take in what he had just told him.

'I'm sorry,' said Ant. 'It's a lot. Basically, I stuffed up and he's taking it out on you. I know how much the allotment means to you and I'm sorry you're going to lose it now.'

Charles blinked rapidly. 'Well,' he said, taking a deep breath, 'it was going to happen sometime. I hoped Lionel would keep turning a blind eye, but he can be a spiteful bugger. It's not your fault, Ant. He would have done it anyway at some point.'

Ant breathed a sigh of relief. He'd been expecting a much more emotional reaction — anger or even tears. This was going better than he could possibly have hoped.

'Tell me about the other thing,' said Charles. 'Did you say you found another body? That can't be right.'

Ant sat back a little bit and ran his hands over the top of his head. 'I know. It just seems unreal, but it *is* real. We uncovered part of a . . . a skull. It was buried fairly deep.'

Charles shook his head. 'A skull,' he repeated. 'And the metal detector found it?'

'It found an earring. A gold stud with a little opal dangling beneath it.'

Charles suddenly gripped the arms of his chair, his knuckles white as he clung on for dear life.

'Charles? Are you all right?'

'Was that the only thing you found?' Charles asked, faintly.

'Yeah, but before he died Dylan had found a ring, gold with a red stone. That's why we were looking there.'

'Oh no,' said Charles, so faintly Ant could only just hear him. Then he started trying and failing to get to his feet, breathing hard as he struggled. 'Ant, I need you to take me up there. I need to see it for myself.'

CHAPTER THIRTY

By the time Ant and Charles got to the allotments it was light and there was a growing crowd of locals and press. Whatever Ant had said, Charles couldn't be dissuaded — he had been adamant that he had to go to the allotments. In the end, Ant had rung Bob, explained everything as quickly as he could, and asked for a lift. While they were waiting, Charles had got dressed and Ant had made some tea, nice and sweet, for both of them.

Now, as he and Bob tried to shepherd Charles through the crowd safely, Ant could feel adrenaline adding to the sugar surge in his bloodstream. Charles hadn't told them why he wanted to speak to the police, but had been so agitated that he was sure it was something important.

'Scuse me—' Ant lightly placed his hand on the shoulder of the man in front of him — 'Can we just get through?'

The man looked round and smiled in recognition. It was Dan Knibbs, a reporter for the *Bugle*. 'Oh, hi. Ant, isn't it?'

'Hi, can you let us through?'

'Sure.'

Ant could see Dan's curiosity had been piqued and he hoped that whatever Charles was going to do or say, he would be afforded a bit of privacy. He checked around. He couldn't

144

see any TV cameras, but his spirits slumped when he spotted Kevin, the *Bugle*'s photographer. He was snapping away, his long lens focused in on people in the crowd.

They reached the front of the crowd and came up against a line of police tape cordoning off the front half of the car park, which was occupied by a range of official-looking vehicles. Various people, some in uniform, others in plain clothes, were milling around. Charles was worryingly breathless.

Bob spoke to the uniformed officer guarding the tape. 'My friend here would like to speak to someone. He has some information.'

The officer looked doubtfully at Charles, who looked every one of his eighty-three years. 'We're very busy securing the scene,' he said. 'It would be better to ring up. We can log your call and—'

'I need to talk to someone now!' Charles was trying to shout, but his voice was weak and husky.

The officer looked again. 'It's important to keep calm, sir. I'll do what I—'

At that moment, Ant spotted Tom at the far side, near the gates. 'Tom! Tom! Over here!' he bellowed, causing the officer and everyone else within earshot to wince.

Tom looked round and Ant could swear he rolled his eyes. Having got his attention, though, Ant pressed his advantage. 'Tom! I've got something for you!'

Tom made a great show of holding his hand up, as if he was stopping the traffic, and finishing talking to another man in plain clothes, before walking between a couple of vans and making his way over.

'Morning, Ant,' he said. 'Didn't think I'd see you again so soon.' From his tone and expression, it was perfectly clear that it wasn't a pleasant surprise.

'Tom, Charles here has the plot next to Dylan's that we help him look after. He's got something he wants to tell you.'

A hush fell over the crowd, as people strained to hear what was being said. Some of them were holding up mobile phones.

Tom looked at Charles. 'Yes, sir.' He had one eye on the eager faces around them. 'Would you like to step through the cordon and I'll try and find somewhere a bit quieter?'

'Can I go and see her?' said Charles. 'The . . . body. Can I see her?'

Her, thought Ant. Of course, the earring indicated a woman, but somehow Charles made it sound more personal. Ant's nerve endings were tingling now and he felt slightly sick.

'I'm afraid that's not possible, sir. Why don't we go and sit in a van?'

The uniformed officer had undone one end of the tape and was holding it open for Charles. Tom held his arm out, inviting him in.

'I need to see where she is! I need to see her!' Charles was getting increasingly upset.

'Let's just go this way . . .' Tom had his arm round Charles's shoulder now.

'No! Get off me. You don't understand.'

'Let's go and have a chat and you can tell me about it.'

'But I need to see her. The body . . . the woman you've found.' His voice was breaking now and Ant was horrified to see tears trickling down his cheeks. 'It's Catherine. It's my wife.'

CHAPTER THIRTY-ONE

'Thin on the ground today.' Bea looked round the staff room. The gathering for the Monday-morning briefing was noticeably depleted and she started counting the missing faces on her fingers — Ant, Dean, Bob.

Everyone was buzzing about the discovery of the second body. Bea had seen a wobbly video clip online of Charles appearing to say, 'It's Catherine. It's my wife.' In fact, she'd viewed it four or five times, trying to take it in. She had recognised a sleeve just in shot as Ant's, and seen the back of Bob's head, and she had a strong suspicion that they wouldn't be seeing either of them today.

'Bob went to the police station with Charles,' said Dot, standing close to her. 'He wasn't allowed to go in with him but he said he'd wait there until he could take him home.'

'My Dean's at home in bed. He's a nervous wreck,' Eileen chipped in. She was standing behind them and they drew apart to hear more. 'He found the body — you know, actually touched it. I don't know how he'll ever get over it. He's such a sensitive boy.'

Bea tried to maintain a neutral but concerned expression on her face, and not give in to the urge to laugh at this description of Dean. 'Sensitive' wasn't the first thing that sprang to her mind, although, to be fair, anyone would be shaken up by what he had experienced.

'I'm going to have a few words with Ant when I next see him,' Eileen continued. 'My Dean would never normally get involved in anything like this — he's been led astray.'

'Have you heard from Ant?' Dot directed the question to Bea.

'I texted him,' Bea said. 'He just said he was okay and would tell me about it later. I don't think he'll be in. Oh—'

At that moment the room went quiet and there was an audible intake of breath from several people nearby. Ant had appeared in the doorway, looking distinctly worse for wear. He spotted Bea across the room and made his way towards her.

As he reached their little cluster, George and Neville swept into the room and took up their usual positions. They made no reference to the news that was at the front of everyone's mind, and concentrated on the weekly sales report, new lines coming in, and targets to meet. The staff listened in silence, with none of the usual comments, questions or banter, and, when dismissed, started to file out meekly to their posts. Bea wondered if she could grab a couple of minutes with Ant, but George beat her to it.

'A word, Anthony,' she said.

Ant visibly flinched. 'I wasn't late. I'm here, aren't I?'

Bea put her hand on his arm and noticed a couple of little tears in the fabric of his black jacket. 'Steady, Ant,' she said.

Neville sniffed. 'It's not your timekeeping, Ant, it's your appearance. We have certain standards to maintain.'

Ant looked down at himself. His shoes were in a state. His trousers were muddy. His jacket was torn. He felt something itchy, put his hand up to his hair and pulled out a small twig, studded with thorns.

'I haven't had time to go home and clean up,' he said, somewhat stating the obvious.

148

'What you do in your private time is your business,' Neville said, stiffly, 'but we have rules here, one of which is turning up in a fit state to work.'

'I was up at the allotments — maybe you've heard, there was another body.' The tail end of the queue of people filing out of the staff room stopped moving as those within earshot lingered to hear more.

'Which, interesting as it may be—' Neville flapped his hands at the lurkers, trying to shoo them out of the room — 'is not relevant to your role here. My former statement stands. You must turn up for your shift ready to work, which is clearly not the case.'

Bea had a feeling of impending doom. With at least one warning already on his records, Ant was on extremely thin ice now. It wasn't her battle, but he looked so spaced out and broken that she couldn't help stepping in.

'I think what Ant is saying,' she said, speaking slowly and firmly, 'is that he's had a very trying and traumatic experience, but that he didn't want to let you down. In his single-minded determination to be here and honour his commitment to you, to Costsave, he powered through his exhaustion and judged that the state of his own clothes would not matter too much since he mostly wears Costsave gear for the heavy work that he does. That's right, isn't it?' She tipped her head towards Ant, her eyes bulging meaningfully.

Taking the hint, Ant stood up a little straighter, like a soldier on parade. 'Yes. That's exactly it. I absolutely, one hundred per cent, did not want to let you down.'

Careful, thought Bea. A simple 'yes' would have been better. They both looked at George and Neville, who seemed a bit nonplussed by her speech and Ant's reaction. Bea pressed on. 'Given the extreme and unusual circumstances, might I suggest that Ant is allowed an hour to have a wash and brush up before starting his shift today?'

'Half an hour,' Ant chipped in. 'I can just go in the leisure centre and use their showers.' Bea remembered that this had been one of his practices when he was sleeping rough and it tweaked her heartstrings to realise how far he'd come since then.

'Well . . . um . . .' Neville looked at George.

'Yes,' she said, with a surprising and welcome warmth in her eyes. 'I'm glad that you did come to work today, Ant, which some others haven't managed.'

'My Dean is sick!' Eileen squawked from the doorway. 'He's not fit for work!'

George held up a hand. 'Okay, okay, I'm not saying that he isn't. But, Ant, well done for coming in. Please take an hour to tidy yourself up, maybe have some breakfast, and return here at nine o'clock sharp, ready to work.'

'Yes, George. Thank you, George.'

Ant didn't need telling twice. He shot towards the door before George could change her mind. His colleagues let him through, pleased that what seemed like an inevitable firing hadn't happened. Ant was popular in the store, and they also appreciated evidence of a human touch from management. Who knew when any of them might need a bit of leeway?

Bea trotted after him to find that he was waiting for her at the top of the stairs.

'Thank you,' he said. 'You saved my bacon.'

'You're welcome. I couldn't bear it if you'd lost your job over this.'

'You were magnificent.'

She blushed. 'Thanks.'

'I'd better go, but shall we catch up later? Can I buy you lunch to say thank you?'

'Yes and yes,' said Bea. 'I think you'd better tell me what you've been up to.'

He put his hands gently on her shoulders and she sensed he was about to lean in and kiss her when he stopped and looked behind to where Dot, Eileen, George and Neville were waiting in the corridor, taking the scene in.

He let go. 'See ya later,' he said and clattered down the stairs.

150

CHAPTER THIRTY-TWO

Bea had difficulty maintaining concentration through the morning. She was pleased to see Ant returning to the store at ten to nine, looking well-scrubbed and refreshed. He'd obviously changed his mind about the leisure centre and gone back to Bob's instead, because he was in clean clothes. He stopped by her checkout on his way to report for duty.

'That's better,' Bea said, approvingly, and Ant's pink, freshly soaped face seemed to glow a little brighter.

'I smell nice, too.' He wafted his jacket to and fro.

Dot turned round in her swivel chair. 'That smells like my wild rose shower gel.'

Ant grinned. 'Is that yours? I thought it was Bob's. Sorry, Dot.'

Dot laughed. 'Don't be silly. You can use whatever you like. You smell lovely.'

For a moment, Bea pictured herself lying next to Ant, her face nestled into his neck, breathing in the floral, musky smell.

'You all right, Bea?' His face crinkled with concern. 'Are you having a funny turn?'

'No, I'm fine. I'll see you for lunch. Bacon sarnie in the café, or chips in the park?'

'You choose. My treat.' He set off towards the back of the store with a decided spring in his step.

Dot smiled and turned back to her till. 'You two . . .'

'What?'

'Nothing.'

'Shut up.'

'I didn't say a thing.'

Bea was glad of the banter, which helped to lighten an otherwise dark morning. Assuming the video of Charles wasn't faked — which it clearly wasn't — what on earth was going on? Why would Charles think that his wife was buried in the allotments? She and Queenie had only seen him the day before, sitting in Kingsleigh cemetery. In between customers, she racked her brains trying to remember what he had actually said. *I wanted to sit and think and this seemed like the right place.* Something like that. He hadn't specifically said that he was visiting a grave.

Bea froze as the implications of this sank in. If Charles knew that Catherine wasn't buried at the cemetery, but was, instead, at the allotments, had he put her there?

'Excuse me, is this till open?'

She looked up to find a woman dressed top to toe in what was probably officially described as greige, but which looked like the colour of a muddy puddle.

'Yes. Sorry, I was miles away.'

The woman pressed her lips together as if she was suppressing a sarcastic comment. Bea, who would normally rise above such things, went into battle, in her own way.

'I love your outfit,' she said, her voice so sweet and smooth that Dot turned round to watch the fun. 'Where did you get it?'

'Oh this? Thank you! It's designer, I forget which one. I got it at the Outlet Village, you know, near Shepton.'

'Ah yes,' said Bea, whose only experience of shopping there had been a trip to buy discounted school shoes when she was at primary school. 'You look amazing.'

The woman's face displayed the small, constrained smile of someone who knew that all compliments were well and truly deserved. Indeed, so good was she feeling that the natural order of things had been restored, that she started to chat with Bea.

'Did you hear about that old man?' she said, keeping her voice low. 'They've arrested him for murdering his wife.'

Bea was shocked out of her little game. 'Arrested? Are you sure?'

She looked around for confirmation from the other people in her queue and Dot's. They all shook their heads, with one diving onto her phone to check the latest news.

'Well, he's being questioned anyway,' Mrs Greige corrected.

'That's not the same thing,' Bea snapped. 'It doesn't mean he did it.'

'I bet he did, though.' There were murmurs of agreement from the queue.

Although Bea had had the same thought, somehow it was different hearing it discussed so openly. It seemed so disrespectful — to Charles and to the woman at the allotments, whether it was Catherine or not.

'We don't know, do we?' she said, then bit her lip to stop herself saying any more. She processed the woman's shopping as quickly as possible, restricting further interaction to the absolute minimum. Then she worked her way through her customers as efficiently as she could. For a Monday morning, the store was really busy, which was both a blessing — Bea had hardly any time to sit and think — and a curse — without a lull and with the constant chat about Charles and bodies and murder, she started to feel panicky.

Eventually, she put her 'Checkout Closing' sign onto her conveyor belt and leaned across towards Dot.

'Dot, I need a break,' she said. 'I'm feeling a bit . . .'

She didn't need to say exactly how she was feeling because Dot understood. 'It's fine, darling. Take as long as you need. I'll tell Neville it's women's problems if he asks.'

'Thanks, babe.'

She logged out and made her way through the store, intending to shut herself into a cubicle in the staff restroom, but then realised that some cool, fresh air was what she really needed. She let herself out of the side door and stood leaning against the wall, eyes closed, breathing.

'Um . . . are you okay?'

She opened her eyes to find Tyler looking at her. He was wearing a Costsave high-viz jacket and had the ruddy-cheeked look of someone who had been physically active all morning.

'Just having a breather,' she said.

'That's what Ant says when he's off for a fag break,' he said. 'Do you want me to fetch him?'

'No, it's all right. I'm only here for a minute. I'll go back in soon.'

He turned to go off across the car park.

'Hey, Tyler,' Bea called, 'were you out with the boys last night, up at the allotment?'

'No, I stayed in. I didn't think I could get out without Mum knowing and she wouldn't have liked me going. Besides, I wasn't keen. I don't really like going up there, not since . . . you know.'

Bea did know. Tyler had been caught up in the incident that still haunted her. It hadn't occurred to her that he might feel the same way, but now he'd said that, she felt stupid for not realising.

'Me neither,' she said. 'I know it was all over months ago, but I still have flashbacks to it.'

'I have nightmares. Mum says I yell out in my sleep.'

'I'm so sorry. It's hard, isn't it?'

'Yeah. The thing Scout keeps telling me, though, is that it was horrible, but we all got out of it in one piece. We're still here. We got through it. She's right, you know. We did.'

Bea smiled. 'She's a smart cookie.'

'She is, and she lost more than any of us, but she's doing brilliantly at school. I'm really proud of her.'

Bea pushed away from the wall and stood up straight. 'And I'm proud of us, Tyler. We're still ploughing on, aren't we? And I'd better get back to it before Neville kicks off.'

She held up a hand and he high-fived her with a satisfying smack. 'Tell Ant I said hi and I'd like chips and park. He'll know what I mean.'

'Will do. See you later, Bea.'

Bea went back inside. Without noticing, her breathing had returned to normal, and she was feeling lighter and more human again. For the next hour or two, she put thoughts of Charles to the back of her mind as much as possible and instead deflected any discussions about the allotment murders by doing a bit of opinion canvassing, asking her customers what they liked most about Kingsleigh and what needed to change.

By the end of the morning, her not-very-scientific study had established that, on the whole, people liked living in Kingsleigh, and, more than anything else, they wanted free parking and an end to dog poo on the pavements.

CHAPTER THIRTY-THREE

'I take it you were investigating.' Bea dipped a chip into a pool of ketchup and popped it in her mouth. A hungry sparrow hopped about near her feet, hoping for crumbs.

'Yeah.' Ant had demolished his chips in record time. He extended an arm and tipped the cardboard tray out over the grass, much to the sparrow's delight. 'We took Saggy's metal detector up there because Dylan had found a ring in his potato patch. We all wondered if there was more where that came from. Never even occurred to me there'd be another body.'

'Hell of a shock.'

'You can say that again. I keep seeing it — a white patch in the soil. Thought it was a stone, but then . . .'

He put the empty chip tray on the seat next to him and leaned forward, holding his head in his hands.

Bea gently rubbed his back. The sparrow's activity had attracted a couple of pigeons now. Bea watched them, shielding her unfinished food with her free hand, just in case one of them decided to chance their luck. After a while Ant sat up again and she withdrew her arm. 'And this was on Dylan's plot?'

'Yeah.' He ran his hands through his hair. 'But right at the edge, near the boundary fence where you wouldn't normally dig. It — she — could have been there for years.'

'Do you think it is Catherine?'

He pulled a face. 'Charles seemed pretty certain.'

'How did he know it was her?'

'We found an earring before we found the . . . skull. When I told him about it, it was like an electric shock. You could see it going right through him. Then when I said about Dylan finding the ring, that was it. He just kept saying he had to talk to the police. He wanted to see the body, too, see where she was.'

'Poor Charles. Ant, do you think — it feels awful saying this — but do you think he's the one who buried her there?'

Ant ran both hands over his head.

'Going from his reaction, unless he's a really good actor, I honestly think it was a surprise. I don't think he knew she was there, but maybe that's because I don't want him to have done it.'

'Me neither,' said Bea. 'All these years we've known him, and been calling round, looking after Goldie. You even saved his life, Ant, when he collapsed at Costsave. If it turns out he's a murderer, I just don't know what I'll do with myself.'

'He can't be, though, can he? Not Charles.'

'But . . .'

'What?' He turned to look at her.

'Well, if he didn't kill her and bury her at the allotments . . . how did he know she was dead? It doesn't add up, does it?'

The question hung in the air between them.

'But,' she carried on, thinking aloud, 'if he'd killed her, surely he'd put her in his own plot, so he could guard it, make sure that no one else disturbed it?'

'Good point.' Ant had got up to put his tray in the bin. He plonked himself down again next to her. 'Honestly, Bea, it was fine investigating Dylan's death with the boys, but none of them have got it up here like you have.' He tapped the side of his head.

Bea put down her chip fork, suddenly not hungry anymore. 'I'm not going back to it, Ant. I can't. I felt a bit funny again at work this morning, with what you discovered last night. I wasn't even there, but the thought of it made me feel panicky.'

He turned his body so he was facing her, resting one arm along the back of the bench. 'I'm not trying to pressure you, Bea, honestly. It's just that the investigation and, well, everything, really, is better *with* you. I've missed you.'

She smiled. 'What if that's just how it's got to be? What if we're going on very different paths, Ant? If I get onto the council, I'll have to spend evenings in meetings and weekends sorting out people's problems. I won't have loads of spare time to hang out with you.'

He shrugged. 'It's fine, isn't it? I've been thinking about this. I'd be dead proud of you. I don't want to stop you doing anything. Although I do think you need to have fun sometimes. The council sounds pretty pigging dull to me.'

'Some of it will be dull, but they do some important stuff. I've been looking into it all weekend. I want to find my own campaigns and things to work on, but I also think it would be good to carry on the projects that Dylan started, you know, as a sort of tribute to him.'

Ant's face brightened. 'That's a good idea. What sort of stuff?'

'All his ideas for a greener town, and he was trying to set up a museum. You know how bonkers he was about all that local history stuff.'

'It could be named after him or have a little plaque or something.'

'Yes, but we're a long way off that, Ant. The minutes of the last meeting were all about feasibility studies and things.'

Ant yawned. Bea wondered if he was faking it to express his true feelings about her council aspirations, but soon realised that a nice full stomach and the all-nighter were catching up with him.

'Are you going to be able to get through the afternoon?'

He stretched his arms and legs out. 'Just about. I'll buy a can of Monster or something on the way back. That'll pep me up.'

They both stood up. She offered her cold chips to Ant, but he was too tired to eat anything else and she put them in the bin, much to the excitement of the pigeons and sparrows, who started flapping about at its pillar-box opening as she walked away. They headed towards the alleyway to the high street.

'If Charles didn't do it, are you going to try and find out who did?' said Bea.

'I dunno, we were a bit at sea with Dylan's death. I reckon we should carry on with that one. More chance of finding out about something that happened last week than thirty-nine years ago.'

'Unless they're connected.'

'Not likely, is it? A serial killer who took the best part of forty years off?'

'As far as we know . . .'

'God, I hope there aren't any more bodies up there. I think two's enough, don't you?'

'Two's two too many.'

'Truth.'

They emerged into the high street and prepared to cross the road. Bea stepped out just as the green council van pulled out of a parking place.

Ant put his arm across her to stop her going any further, and the van blasted its horn and went on its way.

'What the hell is wrong with that guy?' said Bea.

'Van drivers, innit?' said Ant. 'I quite fancy driving one, actually. I've pretty much cracked reading. Perhaps I should learn to drive next.'

They crossed over and were soon back at Costsave.

'That was really nice,' said Ant. 'Chips in the park, and a good old chat.'

'Yeah,' said Bea. 'It was.'

'Do you want to . . . I mean would you like to . . . ?'

Bea looked at him enquiringly. They were standing outside the staff entrance now.

'Are you going in or just standing there?' It was Eileen, who had sneaked up behind them.

159

'You go ahead.' Ant opened the door for her and held it.

She narrowed her eyes. 'Thank you, but I want a word with you later. Actually, now will do. You keep away from my Dean. I've just nipped home to see him and he's traumatised. He could only just about manage one cheese toastie and a jam doughnut with his cup of tea. I had to practically hand-feed him.'

Bea could see Ant was struggling to keep a straight face. 'I'm sorry to hear that, Eileen. Will you please tell him that I hope he feels better soon.'

Eileen sniffed. 'I will.' She looked him up and down, tutted under her breath and disappeared through the door.

'Like a mother bird feeding its baby worms,' said Bea. 'That's quite the image, isn't it?'

'You have to remember, though, that Dean is a *very sensitive young man.*'

'Oh, I know,' she said with a grin. 'What was it you were trying to say just now? We've only got a couple of minutes.'

Ant shuffled his feet about, scraping at some gravel with his toes.

'It doesn't matter.'

'Ant! Spit it out!' She gave him a hard stare.

'It was just, I was thinking perhaps we could go out. *Out* out. On a date. If you wanted to. I mean, not if you don't. No pressure. Forget I said it. Silly idea.' He held the door wider, inviting her to go inside and end his embarrassment.

'A date?' Bea said, and he half closed his eyes, bracing for her reaction. 'Why not? That's a lovely idea.'

CHAPTER THIRTY-FOUR

Ant returned to the stores feeling like a new man. Ever since the day Dylan's body had been discovered he had felt destabilised, unanchored. It was partly the shock of losing someone so unexpectedly, realising that life can turn on a sixpence. And then, seeking comfort with Bea had somehow driven them apart, destroyed the easy friendship that, he realised, had come to be the bedrock of his life. Today had brought another shock — finding the second body was about as bad as things could get — but now there was a glimmer of hope. He and Bea had managed a reasonable conversation. It felt like they were back on track and maybe, just maybe, the track was leading somewhere very, very good.

He and Tyler were covering for Dean's absence, as well as doing quick forays into the yard to keep the trolley situation under control. They made a good team and being busy meant that Ant wasn't able to give in to the urge to find a quiet corner and have a nap. When Neville came to check on them, he nodded approvingly at their efficiency in dealing with the waste cardboard and plastic that the shelf-replenishment team had produced.

161

'It's looking spick and span in here,' he said, standing with his back to the shelving that hid Dean's man cave and the operational centre of their investigation. 'Well done.'

He turned and was leaving them to it just as Bob appeared in the doorway. 'Ah, Bob, feeling better?'

'Hello, Neville, I wasn't off sick this morning — I was helping the police. I didn't mean to leave you in the lurch and I rang Syd to check that she could cover for me. I'll take it as a half-day's leave.'

Neville sniffed. 'I'll talk to George about it and check that that's acceptable.'

'Oh, I've just seen her,' said Bob, breezily. 'She said it was fine.'

Neville winced slightly. He never took kindly to members of staff bypassing him. 'Good, very good,' he said, giving the impression that he meant exactly the opposite. 'And is that why you were looking for me?'

'I was actually looking for Ant. I need to tell him something.'

Neville checked his watch.

'I'll literally be ten seconds,' said Bob, walking firmly past Neville, who stood his ground. 'Something confidential.'

Neville bristled with hostility but backed off. Ant noted the interesting dynamic between the two men. Bob was a not insubstantial figure and had previously led a staff rebellion that had almost kyboshed preparations for the royal visit earlier in the year. Although Neville was, in theory, his senior, he did defer to Bob, if push came to shove.

Bob and Ant took themselves off to the far end of the stores, where Bob told him that he had just dropped Charles off at home. He had given a statement to the police and hadn't been charged with anything. Although Charles was adamant that the body was that of Catherine, it was now a question of waiting for the post-mortem and other inquiries. 'I think he said something about dental records.'

Ant shivered. 'Is he on his own?'

'Yes, apart from Goldie, and a bunch of press vultures outside his bungalow. I told them to clear off and leave him alone, but they ignored me.'

'Perhaps me and Bea should call in after work, take him a food parcel.'

'That's a good idea. See you later.'

Bob started to walk away, then stopped. 'Are you okay, Ant? It wasn't nice what you went through last night.'

'Um, yes. Just knackered,' Ant said.

Bob stepped forward, slapped him gently on the back and then bustled off to the shop floor.

'He's all right, isn't he?' said Tyler. 'Looks like an old-school wrestler but he's just a big softie, really.'

'Tell that to Neville,' said Ant with a wry smile. 'But yes, Bob's one of the good guys.'

CHAPTER THIRTY-FIVE

'I don't need to wait for the dental records. I know it's her. It's my Catherine.'

Charles wasn't a big man, but to Bea he looked tiny and defeated sitting in his armchair this evening, with his shoulders slumped and his head hanging forward. She and Ant had run the gauntlet of the press outside the bungalow. Ant had sent a bit of abuse their way, while she had appealed to their better nature. Neither approach had had any obvious impact.

It had taken a while for Charles to open the door. In the end, Bea had called through the letterbox and Goldie had convinced him that it was friend, not foe, outside. Bea had made them all a cup of tea and they were now sitting in his front room with the curtains drawn firmly and the TV on to drown out the sound of the people gathered outside.

'From the jewellery?' said Bea.

He nodded and waved in the direction of the tiled mantelpiece. After a few seconds, Bea twigged that he was indicating his wedding photograph. She put down her tea, stood up and fetched it. As she examined the image, she could just about see the engagement ring on Catherine's right hand.

'Ah,' she said. 'The ring.'

'She wore it on her right hand that day. So that the wedding band would have pride of place on her left. After that, though, she wore them both on the left, every single day that we were together.'

'And the earrings?'

'A birthday present. We'd seen them in the window of a shop in Bristol. I saved up and went back and got them for her.'

Bea set the photograph on the table between them.

'Oh, Charles. Do you . . .' Bea didn't know how to say it, wondered if she should ask at all. 'Have you got any idea what happened, how she ended up where she was found?'

He shook his head. 'Someone put her there, thirty-nine years ago. That's all I know. She disappeared without a trace and I never heard from her again, not one word.'

Ant shot her a look.

'She disappeared?' Bea said, gently.

Charles sighed. He was holding his hands in his lap — his tea was untouched on the table — and he scratched at the side of one thumb with the other so hard that Bea thought his nail might break the skin.

'Charles?'

He looked down, unable to meet her gaze.

'I told everyone she'd died in hospital. I was too ashamed to admit the truth.'

Bea glanced at Ant, who looked as alarmed as she felt. What on earth was Charles about to tell them?

'What is the truth?' she said, gently.

'Thirty-nine years ago, on the eighth of September, Catherine left me. She told me that there was somebody else. She'd already packed a case. It was sitting in the hall when I came home from work. She didn't want to just go or leave a note. She wanted to tell me face to face. I think . . . Well, I think it took a lot of courage.'

'Did she say who it was?'

'No. She wouldn't say. I tried to reason with her. I asked her what I'd done wrong, how I could change to make things better. I would have done anything, you know, anything at all to keep her, except . . .'

'Except?'

'She said she loved me but she was *in love* with them. That finished it. You can't change someone's feelings by reasoning with them, can you?'

He looked at her, and Bea found herself meeting his tears with hers. 'No, you can't.'

She moved off the sofa, crouched next to him and put both her hands round his.

'I'm so sorry, Charles,' she said and then she was quiet, because, although she had a million questions on the tip of her tongue, what else was there to say?

CHAPTER THIRTY-SIX

Ant and Bea left Charles's after an hour or so. Bea had made him some toast but he hadn't eaten it and had declared he was going to let Goldie out into the garden and then go to bed. Unwilling to abandon him to the press, they offered to stay, but he'd dismissed them, saying that he wouldn't open the door to anyone and he'd had enough for one day.

'It seems wrong leaving him on his own,' said Bea, once they were clear of the group of reporters and photographers, and had walked to the corner of the rec.

'I know, but he made his feelings clear. I expect he wants some time to himself.'

'Time to process it all. Time to grieve, I suppose.'

'Yeah. Poor bloke. Imagine living a lie all that time, though. You never know what's really going on with people, do you?'

'No. Do you want to come for tea? Queenie would like to see you. And I would. Well, I can see you now, but you know what I mean.'

'Oh God, Bea, don't start getting all awkward again. I'd love to come for tea but I'm too knackered. I don't really know how I got through the day, to be honest. Say hi to

Queenie for me, but I'm going to go back to Bob's and study the inside of my eyelids for as long as possible.'

'Understood,' said Bea. 'I'll see you tomorrow.'

She peeled away and headed across the rec. Night was falling now and it would soon be dark.

Ant watched until she was just a small figure in the distance. Even the sight of her walking away made him feel tingly. Tired as he was, he waited until she'd disappeared across the road at the top of the rec. Then he turned and loped along slowly through the streets. He was so tired that his legs felt like they belonged to someone else. He had to consciously make an effort to put one in front of the other, like wading through water.

When he got to Bob's, the lights were on and his host was busy rattling pots and pans in the kitchen, while Dot sat at the kitchen table, drinking a large glass of white wine.

'There you are,' Bob said, as Ant loitered in the doorway. 'We're eating healthy tonight, if you want some — turkey stir-fry. There's plenty.'

'Oh, no, I'm really tired. I think I'll just—'

'Come and sit down, love.' Dot patted the chair next to her. 'Get some food inside you and then have a sleep.'

At that moment, Ant's stomach rumbled. Dot obviously heard, caught his eye and raised an eyebrow. Ant smiled and collapsed down into the chair.

'Wine?'

'No, ta. Horrible stuff.' He smiled.

He heard the clink of metal against glass and Bob plonked an open bottle of beer in front of him. 'Get that down you.'

'Service is good here, isn't it?' said Dot, raising her glass.

Ant picked up the bottle. 'Yeah, not bad. Cheers.'

The first mouthful of beer was so delicious, Ant thought he might cry. Then, as the alcohol filtered into his system, the warmth of the kitchen seeped through to his bones and the cooking smells filled his senses, a residual spark of energy was ignited. 'It's been a hell of a day,' he said.

168

'How was Charles?' said Bob.

'Wrung out. He told us that his wife left him for someone else all those years ago. We all thought he was a widower, and he kind of let us think that because he was ashamed.'

Dot leaned forward. 'Is that what he's saying? She left him?'

'Yeah. He seemed sincere.'

'But he's seemed like a sincere widower all this time, hasn't he? If someone lies about one thing, they'll lie about others. You can't trust them.'

'So, you think he killed her?' asked Ant.

'They do say it's the most dangerous time for a woman — leaving a relationship. Perhaps he just couldn't bear to let her go, or he lost it when she said there was someone else. It happens. And she ended up right by his allotment plot. I mean, it doesn't need to be any more complicated than that.'

'But this is Charles we're talking about . . . I mean, *come on*.'

'Killers don't all look like big scary ogres, Ant.'

Bob put two plates on the table and went back to the bench to get a third. The food was glistening and steaming, and the smell made Ant's mouth water.

'It was the plot next to Charles's, though, wasn't it? We need to know who rented that one going way back, don't we?' said Bob, as he sat down. 'That's what we need to do.'

'We?' said Dot. 'You mean the police, don't you? I could understand you wanting to find out who killed your mate, but now there are two bodies it's time to step back and let the powers that be get on with it. Even Bea has had enough and I never thought I'd say that.'

'Besides—' Ant shovelled food into his mouth and then held it open and fanned it rapidly with his hand — 'I don't think we've got much chance of finding out what happened thirty-nine years ago. For a start, the person who did it could be dead by now.'

'Careful, it's hot,' said Bob, unnecessarily.

'Unless they're connected,' said Dot.

They both looked at her and she waved her fork at them. 'Ignore me. Forget I said it. I'm not meant to be encouraging you.'

'How could they be connected?' said Bob.

Dot speared a piece of chicken. 'I don't know, but two bodies in the same place, it's fishy, isn't it? So, one line of inquiry would be to figure out who was around at the allotments then and is still around today. Obviously, Charles is top of that list.'

'But we've pretty much ruled him out for Dylan's murder. I can't see Charles hitting someone on the head. He's not got the strength.'

'But there must be other people — Lionel, for one.'

'Yes, definitely Lionel,' said Bob. 'Hey, we need your notebook, Ant.'

Ant badly wanted to eat up and fall into bed, but the food was still too hot so he left the table and dug in his coat pocket for his notebook and pen. He sat back down and turned to the next blank page, but when he tried to write something he found the white rectangle of the paper swimming in front of his eyes.

'Lionel,' Bob prompted, but Ant put down his pen.

'I can't, Bob. My brain's too tired.' He held the pen out. 'Can you do it?'

Bob took the notebook and wrote *1985/2024* at the top of the page, then started a list of names. *Charles, Lionel.*

'How about Cyril?' said Dot. 'He always gives me the creeps.'

'Really? I mean, he's a little uptight, but he's harmless.'

'Put his name down.'

Bob added Cyril to the list. 'I don't even know how long Cyril has had a plot. Like I said, we need to see the records. I wonder where they are.'

'And like *I* said, I expect the police will be able to find them.'

'No harm giving them a helping hand . . .'

Ant let them talk back and forth. As hungry as he was, he couldn't keep his eyes open any longer. The noise of his fork clanging onto his plate made him jump. It had fallen out of his hand as he'd drifted off. He cleared his throat and blinked rapidly.

'Oh, Ant,' said Dot. 'You remind me of my Sal. She used to be so tired by teatime that she'd nod off. I once found her in her highchair face down in a bowl of mushed-up Weetabix.'

'I'm so sorry, Bob, I don't think I can eat this,' said Ant. 'I've got to go to sleep.'

'Fair enough,' said Bob. 'I can eat yours. Don't want it going to waste.'

Dot firmly moved the plate out of his reach. 'I'll put it in a pot in the fridge and Ant can have it tomorrow.'

Ant dragged himself upstairs. He peeled off his clothes, dumped them on the floor and crawled into bed. The sheets were cool against his skin. His brain had pretty much ground to a halt. Thoughts swam in and out of focus. Somewhere there was someone who knew what had happened to Dylan and, maybe, what had happened to Catherine. Or maybe there were two people, living with the worst sort of secret. Maybe Dot was right — it wasn't his job to find out . . . Maybe Bea was right, too. He wrapped his arms around a pillow, thought of holding Bea close and fell into a deep and dreamless sleep.

CHAPTER THIRTY-SEVEN

'Bob, can I have a word?'

Bob, lurking at the tea area in the staff room while he waited for the kettle to boil, pulled a face. 'You sound like Neville when he's about to administer a bollocking. Do I need to put a *Bugle* down the back of my trousers?'

Bea grinned, but it was a nervous one that flashed across her face and was gone. 'It's nothing like that,' she said, and bit the inside of her mouth.

'Go on. What's on your mind? Do you want a cuppa, too? I seem to be making one for everyone else.'

'Oh, yes please. Just milk in mine, no sugar. The thing is, have you put your name forward to be a town councillor?'

Bob smiled as he added a teabag to another mug and then carefully went along the row he had arranged, pouring in boiling water. 'Malcolm Sillitoe approached me, but it's going to be no.' He glanced across at Dot, who was sitting on the sofa reading a magazine. 'I've got too much on, and, to be honest, I'm not a meetings man.'

Bea was surprised how strong the flush of relief was. This was starting to really matter to her. 'Oh, that's good. I didn't want to stand against you. I mean, I think you'd have done a good job.'

172

'Well, as far as I'm concerned, you've got a free run and, for what it's worth, I think you'll be great.'

'Do you?'

'A hundred per cent,' Bob said as he added milk to most of the cups.

'Malcolm practically laughed in my face when I said I was interested. I want him — all of them — to take me seriously, so I've been preparing my application, putting a sort of manifesto together, if that doesn't make me sound too much of a twat.'

Bob frowned. 'Not at all. I'm impressed. Dot said that you were asking people what their priorities are.'

Bea pulled a face. 'Dog poo and parking charges. Neither of which really lights my fire. I'd like to continue Dylan's museum idea. He was so enthusiastic in History lessons at school and he was right — every kid in Kingsleigh should know about our history and be able to see the artefacts. I'm definitely going to dig into that some more. Have you seen the artefacts?'

Bob stirred all the mugs and then picked up the first four, two in each hand. 'Years ago. There was a special exhibition in the church hall for the millennium. Then they all got hidden away again. They're worth seeing. You should go and have a look at them. I think they're back in a storeroom in the basement of the town hall.'

'Ooh, do you think they'd let me?'

Bob shrugged. 'You don't know if you don't ask. That last one is yours—' he nodded towards the flowery mug on the end of the row — 'and the one next to it is for Eileen.'

Bea picked up the two mugs and took one over to Eileen and asked after Dean, who was still off 'with his nerves', apparently. Bob, having delivered his first batch of drinks, picked up another two and headed towards the door, where Ant and Tyler were standing. Ant looked round the room for Bea and winked when he saw her.

Bea raised her mug in greeting. 'Are you coming in?'

'Boys' meeting,' Bob said and ushered them out. Ant turned both palms up, in a 'what can I do?' gesture and Bea turned to Dot.

'What are they up to?'

'Still playing detectives, I reckon. I'm relying on Bob to squash their investigating antics. It's all got out of hand.'

'Gives me the shivers just thinking about it. I'm glad I've opted out of this one. It feels like new things are opening up for me. It feels good.'

Bea was scrolling through her phone as she talked with Dot.

'So it should, Councillor Jordan,' Dot said, with a twinkle in her eye.

'Not Councillor yet,' said Bea. 'Got a good ring to it, though, hasn't it? Actually, I'm just going to ring someone while I think about it. I'll be back in a min.'

Bea went out into the corridor and rang the town council number. She asked to speak with Wendy Fox and was put through straight away.

'Hello, Bea, I haven't seen your form yet,' Wendy said, as she picked up the line.

'No, I'm still working on it. I've been reading about the museum project and wondered if I could see the artefacts. It says "by appointment" on your website.'

'Can you do tomorrow lunchtime? I'll get someone to show you round.'

'Tomorrow at one o'clock?' said Bea. 'I think I can make that.'

'It's funny,' said Wendy, 'because no one has enquired about them for ages, but you're the second person to have a viewing in the last month.'

'Oh! Who was the other one?'

'Dylan. It was one of the last things he did.'

CHAPTER THIRTY-EIGHT

Ant, Bob and Tyler sat with their chairs facing the 'incident wall' with its notes, drawing pins and bits of string, sipping their mugs of tea.

'Dean told me to take it all down,' said Tyler. 'I rang him this morning. "Bin it," he said. "Bin the whole lot."'

'How was he?' asked Bob.

'He still sounded really upset. Said he couldn't sleep, kept feeling sick.'

'I'm not surprised. It was pretty grim,' said Ant. 'I keep seeing it, the skull in the ground. I don't think I'll ever forget it. Poor old Dean was the one who actually touched it.'

'I don't like to say I told you so, but—'

'Yeah, yeah, Bob. I know. It was a silly idea to go up there without permission. But, in a way, it was a good thing, too.'

'What do you mean?'

'Well, at least Charles knows what happened to his Catherine, after all these years. I mean, it's not what anyone would want, but it's some kind of resolution, isn't it?'

They all thought about that for a moment or two.

'I suppose we'd better do what Dean said, take it all down,' said Tyler. 'He'll find it really triggering if it's still there when he comes back.'

'Did he say when that was going to be?' said Ant.

'It sounded like he was going to have the week off, at least.'

'No harm leaving it up there for a few more days, then. I've got some stuff to add. For a start, we didn't tell the police but the night we were up there, we saw the vegetable thief.'

'What?' said Bob.

Ant told them about spotting the torchlight, hiding behind the bushes, and then defending Marvin. 'It was just a young kid in a hoodie,' he said. 'I reckon they're nicking stuff because they need the food. It's not sabotage, and it certainly pisses on Cyril's theory that Dylan was the culprit.'

'Why didn't you tell the police?' said Bob. 'How do you know they didn't kill Dylan? Maybe he caught them in the act and they lashed out.'

Ant shook his head. 'He wasn't stabbed, though, was he? Besides, I don't believe this kid could have done it. He was scared. We basically stood up and said "Boo!" and he ran off.'

'Let's put it on the board, anyway.' Tyler jumped to his feet and darted over to a shelving unit. He retrieved a large plastic box and brought it back to his seat, where Ant could see that it contained an assortment of Post-it notes, pens, pins and string. He took out a pad of sticky notes and dutifully wrote on it and put it up under the existing 'allotment thefts' note.

'We should start a new section, too,' said Ant. 'Add Catherine to the wall. I know we want to find out who killed Dylan, but we can't ignore a second body.' Ant caught Tyler's eye, and they both looked at Bob.

'Agreed,' said Bob. 'We've both spoken with Charles and I'm sure we've got some useful information.'

'Plus, with getting us all banned from the allotment, I feel like I owe him,' said Ant.

'Same again, then?' said Tyler. 'Are we sure the second body is Catherine Hale?'

'It hasn't been officially confirmed yet,' said Bob. 'Just put "Body Number Two", to be going on with.'

Tyler wrote it down and placed it on the wall with plenty of blank space around it. Ant took out his notebook, which Bob had written in the day before. Over the next twenty minutes, in a frenzy of calling out, writing down and pinning up, they created a second spiderweb of clues, notes, dates and ideas.

Aware that the clock was ticking towards the start of their afternoon shifts, they all stood back and looked at the product of their efforts.

'Give me the string,' Bob said.

Tyler handed it over.

Bob pinned one end on the word 'allotment' on Dylan's section of wall and attached the other to the matching word on the second body's section.

'It could be two completely separate cases,' he said, 'or it could be one case that began with one murder thirty-nine years ago and ended with another a week ago.'

'Except we don't know that it's ended, do we?' said Ant. 'In fact, it won't end until the killer is caught. While they're still out there, it's not over. They could kill again.'

CHAPTER THIRTY-NINE

'Ed will take you round the stores,' said Jackie at the reception desk. 'He's one of our grounds staff. He won't be long. Ah, here he is now!'

Bea heard the door open and turned round to see a tall man of about forty entering the office. It wasn't his stature that she recognised, though, but the dark beard and the set of his eyes.

'Oh—'

'You!' he said, speaking at the same time.

'You already know each other. That's good.' Jackie's smile faltered when she saw both their expressions.

'Um, well, we don't actually—'

'She has a bit of trouble with the Green Cross Code and other rules,' said Ed.

Jackie looked puzzled. 'Well, Ed, this is Bea Jordan. And Bea, this is Ed Sillitoe.'

For a moment, Bea considered feigning illness or suddenly remembering another appointment. She had no urge to spend any time at all with this man, who she had already written off as rude and unpleasant. Then she remembered why she was there and decided to give him a chance to redeem himself.

'Hello.' She held out her hand to shake his.

He laughed, rather unpleasantly, but did take her hand and give it a brief shake. His skin was rough, almost like sandpaper in contrast to hers, which was sanitised and moisturised at regular intervals throughout the day.

'Come on,' he said. 'It's through here.' He walked towards a door at the back of the office.

Bea gave a quick glance to Jackie and followed him. The door opened into a gloomy hallway and stairs going both up and down.

'This way,' Ed said, and set off along the corridor and down the stairs. Lights came on automatically as they approached the basement. There were four doors visible on this corridor. Ed went to the furthest one and unlocked it. There were two locks at the top and bottom of the door and a hefty one in the middle.

'Is it just old artefacts down here?' asked Bea.

'No, there's all sorts. All the town council archives, papers going back years and years to when it was Kingsleigh and District Council, and then Kingsleigh Vale Council before that. The old rocks and bones are in here, though.'

'Bones?' said Bea, picturing the Paris catacombs.

'Only kidding.'

He stepped into the room and held the door open for her. Again, Bea had a moment of hesitation. Her instincts told her that being alone in a basement room with Ed was not a good idea. She'd look like a fool if she backed out now, though, wouldn't she? Besides, the town council staff knew where they were, and she *did* want to see the relics.

'Are you coming in?' said Ed, with a hint of a smile. 'I won't bite.'

CHAPTER FORTY

'The bigger stone carvings from the abbey are just kept over there, and those big crates contain the sections of Roman mosaics dug up when the factory was built,' said Ed. 'And we've got the coin collection, and some smaller pieces over here.'

He and Bea walked the length of the windowless room, with Ed pointing out different sections within the store. In the confined space, he seemed taller and broader, almost filling the gap between the shelves along both walls. He filled the air with a particular smell, too — like freshly chopped wood mixed with the sweaty taint of overexertion. Bea was careful to keep herself between him and the door, feeling twitchy at the thought of him blocking her path to the only way out.

Apart from some larger objects wrapped in cloth and sitting on the floor, everything was neatly stacked in boxes and crates, each one labelled with a number and brief description.

'Is there a list of all the objects?' said Bea. 'An inventory?'

'Yes, of course. There's a paper copy up in the office, but it's all online, too. Everything was recorded when it was put here.'

'What about the chalice and the chessmen, and the other thing, the seal?' said Bea.

'They're in the safe.'

'Can I see them?'

He looked at her long and hard.

She forced herself not to look away. 'There's not a problem is there?' she pressed, even though her nerve was on the verge of departing.

His face broke into a cold smile. 'There's not a problem, Bea. Why would there be?'

He turned to the safe, which was set into the wall at the far end and started turning the dial. Bea turned away ostentatiously, like she sometimes did when customers were tapping their pin codes into her card reader. When she looked back, he was pulling the door open to reveal a space with two shelves containing various bags and boxes.

He reached in and pulled out a large box. 'Hold this.'

She took it, surprised at how heavy it was. She held the base while he eased the top off to reveal a large drinking vessel, shaped like a huge wine glass, but obviously made of metal. It was inlaid with intricate designs on the stem and bowl, the sort of pattern you might see on a Celtic cross.

'Oh,' said Bea. 'It's beautiful. What a shame it's stuck away in here.'

'I think one of the museums in Bath had their eye on it, but people here wanted it to stay, quite rightly, I think. Once something like that goes on display somewhere else, you can kiss goodbye to it. You wouldn't get it back.'

'Really?'

He looked at her witheringly. 'Elgin Marbles?'

'That's different. If you're just talking the same county—'

'No, these treasures belong here. They're Kingsleigh's heirlooms. Everyone else can keep their mitts off them.'

He replaced the lid and put the box back in the safe.

'There are the chessmen, too, and the seal. Do you want to see them?'

'If you don't mind.'

There were six chessmen, two white ones and four black ones, made from bone and ebony respectively. Bea had seen

181

some pictures online but it was much better seeing them in real life. They looked like medieval statues, but in miniature, and had a rather unsophisticated charm. If Kingsleigh did ever get its museum, replica sets could be a nice little seller in the museum shop.

'I think they're better than the Isle of Lewis ones. Those are almost jokey, aren't they? These are simple, but dignified,' said Ed.

Bea was surprised to hear such an evaluation. Perhaps she had misjudged him. 'You care about these things, don't you?'

'Of course. It's a privilege to be responsible for keeping them safe and sound. We might work outside most of the time, but the boys and I are very aware that the town's history is just under the surface. You never know what you might dig up at the cemetery or in the park. If the lads find anything they bring it to me. We've added a few bits and bobs to the official collection. This is the last of the big three.'

He took out another box. The seal was a dark, round disc about the size of the base of a coffee mug. This, too, bore intricate carvings although they were worn and damaged so it wasn't easy to see what they were meant to be.

'That was dug up just beyond the boundary of the abbey,' said Ed. 'Probably belonged to the last bishop. It certainly looks like his insignia.'

Bea screwed up her eyes, but still couldn't see a discernible shape or pattern. 'Odd to think of a time when things like this were in use.'

'Well, it was only the top brass. We still use seals in this country, at least the king does. That's what's great about Britain — we still respect tradition.'

'I suppose.' Bea found the idea of using a wax seal in this day and age frankly baffling.

'Don't tell me,' he sneered, 'you're one of those people who likes pushing statues into harbours, are you?'

Bea wasn't sure where she stood on the treatment of the local area's colonial landmarks, but she didn't like being mocked. She also didn't like feeling intimidated by anyone, but here she was, shut in a room she suspected was pretty much soundproof, in an otherwise empty basement, with a large, powerful man.

So, hating that she had to do this, she smiled and said mildly, 'No, I've never pushed a statue over. That's not my style.'

'Glad to hear it,' Ed said. 'Right. That's it. I think you've seen everything.' He put the box back and closed the safe door.

'Well, thank you. I'd better get back,' Bea said.

'Sure. No problem.'

'Was it you who showed the collection to Councillor Bradley?'

'Bradley? He was familiar with them anyway. Did you know he'd written a book about the town's history? He had some of the artefacts photographed for that. I don't know why he needed to see them again. After you—'

Again, he held the door open for Bea and she walked out into the corridor, already feeling a little lighter for being somewhere less confined. They went back up the stairs and emerged into the office.

'Thank you,' Bea said, again. Ed just nodded and walked swiftly towards the front door, obviously keen to get on with his day. Bea trailed in his wake, stopping to glance into Wendy Fox's office.

'Everything all right?' Jackie asked.

'Yes. Fine. It was interesting. I just wondered if Wendy was around.'

'She's on her lunch break. She popped out about ten minutes ago. Do you want me to tell her you were looking for her?'

'No, it's not urgent. I'll catch up with her sometime.'

Bea left the office and walked back along the high street. As she passed the newsagents' she almost bumped into the town clerk, who was coming out of the door and not looking where she was going.

'Oh, sorry, Bea,' said Wendy, reaching her arms out to steady them both. 'How did you get on?'

'It was good, thanks. There's a lot of stuff there.'

'There is.' She let go of Bea's arms and smiled.

'I can see why Dylan Bradley thought a museum was a good idea.'

'Yes, he was very . . . driven. It was very important to him.' She paused for a moment. 'Right, no rest for the wicked. I'd better get on.' She started to walk away.

'Wendy,' Bea called, and she stopped and turned round. 'You said that Dylan had looked at the collection shortly before he died. He knew all about it, surely, so when you showed him round, what was he looking for?'

'Oh, I didn't go with him. With him being a councillor, and a local expert, I just gave him the key. He went down there on his own. He was there for a good hour.'

'Did he say anything when he brought the key back?'

'Not much. He seemed preoccupied. He took the inventory into the meeting room and spent half an hour or so looking at it.'

'Did you ask him what he was doing?'

Wendy shook her head. 'I was in a meeting with the Chair, Malcolm, in my office when he left. Dylan did phone me, the day he died, actually. I missed it and he left a message on my voicemail, said he needed to talk to me. I've been wondering what he wanted to say. I guess I'll never know.'

'What time did he ring?'

'Just after seven. There was one message on my work phone and one on my mobile.'

'Did you ring him back?'

It was as if a cloud passed across Wendy's face. 'When I found the message, I'd had enough for one day. I wish I hadn't left it, for all sorts of reasons.'

Bea gave her a sympathetic look. 'You just don't know, though, do you? You don't expect people not to be there . . .'

A muscle in Wendy's cheek twitched and Bea wondered for a moment if emotion was getting the better of her, but she seemed to make a concerted effort to resist, pressing her lips together and taking a sharp breath in through her nose. She glanced at her watch. 'Malcolm's due in again in five minutes, actually. I must run.' She walked away at a fast pace.

Bea checked her phone and realised that she was already late for her afternoon shift.

CHAPTER FORTY-ONE

'I was going to pop in on Charles after work,' said Ant, loitering by Bea's checkout. 'Wanna come?'

'Yes. Shall we take him a ready meal or something? And a couple of tins of dog food for Goldie. He hasn't been in since . . . you know . . . and he normally buys things from day to day. I'm a bit worried about him.'

'Hmph.'

Ant and Bea both looked at Dot, who was oozing disapproval.

'What's up with you?' said Ant.

'Nothing.'

He raised his eyebrows. 'Come on, something is.'

'It's nice of you to worry about him. I would save my concern for that wife of his, the poor soul.'

'You still think he did it?'

Dot sniffed. 'It's the most obvious explanation, isn't it?'

'I honestly don't believe he knew, Dot.'

Dot sniffed again and swivelled back round in her chair. It seemed the discussion was over. Ant and Bea exchanged looks.

'Let's meet upstairs after work,' said Ant, 'and then grab the stuff for Charles on the way out.'

'Sounds like a plan,' said Bea.

Ant shambled away and Bea greeted her next customer. It was the early-morning panic shopper from the previous week. Bea was pleased to see she'd managed to get dressed today and her demeanour was a lot more chilled. She had a small basket of shopping, mostly tins from the Costsave Value range, but also some of the fruit and veg that were featured in the 'Fresh for 50p' display.

Bea beeped her shopping through. 'How was the Mediterranean pasta?'

The woman looked blank for a moment.

'You were here the other morning.'

The penny dropped. 'Oh, yes. It was fine. Good, actually. Jaden did a good job.' She started putting the tins into the bottom of a reusable bag.

'What's on the menu this week?'

The woman smiled ruefully. 'He hasn't told me yet. You might see me at half eight another morning.'

'I should be able to remember,' said Bea. 'It was the same thing every year. I don't suppose they've changed it. Oh, you can have another one of these—' she held up a bag of half a dozen easy peel satsumas — 'They're in a BOGOF this week.'

'Are they? Is it all right if I nip back?'

'Sure.'

The woman scuttled back to the fresh fruit section and was soon back.

'Thank you,' she said, as Bea rang it through.

She paid with cash and Bea was pleased to see she had enough this time. As she watched the woman leave, carrying her bag of shopping, Bea wondered if Charles would like some easy peelers. He hardly ever bought fresh stuff, although that was probably because he had his allotment. Then she remembered that Ant had said it was going to be taken off him. She'd get him the easy peelers and swing by the cake and biscuit aisle as well.

By five o'clock, she was ready to go. She and Dot walked up to the staff room. Ant waited for them in the corridor while they took off their tabards and collected their coats and bags.

'Sure you don't want to come with us, Dot?' He winked at Bea.

'I'll leave you to it.' Dot set off down the stairs towards the door.

Bea jabbed Ant with her elbow. 'Stop stirring, you monster.'

'Just a bit of fun,' said Ant. 'Right, let's get him some bits.'

They ambled round the aisles together, then used one of the self-service tills. Outside, it was a pleasant, warm afternoon, and they strolled along the high street in good spirits. Bea told Ant about her visit to the town council stores. She didn't mention the creepy vibes she'd got from Ed Sillitoe, or the fact that he really seemed to know his local history.

Ant said that he'd got Dylan's copy of his own book.

'Oh, Ed mentioned that. I'd be interested in reading it.'

'I started, but it's a bit heavy for me. It's kind of nice that it's his though. He's marked some of the pages, so it feels really personal. I can lend it to you. It's at Bob's. I'll bring it in to work tomorrow.'

The conversation flowed so easily between them that they were at Charles's before they knew it. Bea was pleased to see that the reporters and photographers had left their posts. How quickly the news cycle moved on, but it was a good thing, in this case. She knocked at the door.

There was no answer, so she knocked again and she and Ant both heard Charles's voice.

'Go away! Leave me alone!'

She leaned down and pushed the letterbox open.

'Charles, it's me and Ant. Can you let us in?'

After a long minute, the door opened and Bea's sunny mood evaporated in an instant. The house was in darkness and Charles looked like a broken man — his face grey, his hair unkempt, his clothes crumpled and stained. Beside him, Goldie seemed to match his mood, peering out but barely wagging her tail.

'Hello, Charles,' Bea said. 'Can we come in?'

'I don't know.'

'We've brought you some food.'

'I'm not a charity case.'

Bea looked at Ant. This was not the Charles they were used to. Ant stepped forward. 'All right, mate. Let me just put this bag in your kitchen, anyway. Can I put the kettle on, too? I'm desperate for a brew.'

His breeziness seemed to do the trick.

'Suit yourself.' Charles stepped aside to let them in.

'Does Goldie need to go out?' asked Bea. As she and Ant walked through to the kitchen, the whiff of stale air, unwashed armpits and dog farts (she hoped it was dog) filled her nostrils. 'Okay, I think she does.'

She opened the back door and Goldie trotted gratefully outside into the back garden. A gentle breeze brought some welcome fresh air into the room.

Charles had gone into the lounge and was sitting in an armchair.

Bea followed him. 'You could open your curtains now,' she said. 'The reporters have gone.'

He didn't respond, so Bea took the initiative, drawing back the mustard-coloured curtains and letting the sunlight in. She reached up and opened a little top light. 'It's lovely and warm outside.'

Again, Charles just sat, staring at the carpet in front of him.

'I missed you in the shop today.' She looked at him for a response, but he gave no sign that he'd even heard her. She wasn't sure what to do or say, faced with such a brick wall of despair, and was very glad to hear Ant approaching from the kitchen.

He came bearing a tray with mugs of tea and Jaffa Cakes. 'I can't remember if you take sugar or not, Charles,' he said, putting the tray down on the coffee table. 'Charles? Do you want some sugar in yours?' He looked at Bea, who shook her head. 'Here you are, mate. This one's yours. It's only half a cup. I can get you some more.'

Ant picked up a mug and held it towards Charles, who ignored it. Ant took one of Charles's hands and gently placed it around the warm mug. 'There you go,' he said. 'Try this.'

To Bea's surprise, Charles's hand gripped the mug and he raised it to his mouth. Ant sat down next to Bea on the sofa and they both watched as Charles took a sip and then another one.

'Are you hungry, mate?' Ant said.

'No. Don't know,' said Charles.

'Try this.'

Ant broke a Jaffa Cake in two and handed one of the halves over. Charles took a very small bite. Gradually, sip by sip, bite by bite, Charles came back to them. When he finished his tea, he said, 'Thank you. That was lovely,' and Ant darted back into the kitchen to fetch him some more, while he ate the other half of the Jaffa Cake.

Goldie wandered in from the garden and reached her long snout across the coffee table towards the packet.

'I can't remember the last time I fed her,' said Charles. 'Would you mind?'

Bea jumped up and rattled around the kitchen, opening a new tin of food for Goldie and putting fresh water in her bowl.

'We got a couple of ready meals for you,' she said, when she went back into the lounge. 'Would you like me to heat one up for you?'

'In a minute, maybe.'

'It'll be better now the reporters have gone,' said Bea. 'I expect you felt a bit trapped here.'

'They all think I did it,' said Charles. 'They think I'm a murderer. Can't blame them.'

'We don't,' said Ant. 'Do we, Bea?'

'No, of course not.'

'I keep thinking that I should feel better, finally knowing what happened to her, but I don't. It feels like history repeating itself. I lost her once, thirty-nine years ago, and now I've lost her all over again. I never stopped wondering where she was. Sometimes, I even thought she might come back to me. Foolish, I know.'

'I'm so sorry,' said Bea, exchanging a sad look with Ant.

'And all this time, she was close by. Literally yards away from me when I was up at the allotment. And I never knew. I can't believe I didn't sense it.'

'You know, there might be an obvious way of finding out who did it,' said Ant.

Bea felt a tingling in her spine. She may have sworn off investigating, but she hadn't lost her instinct for it.

'What's that?' said Charles.

'We just need to know who had the plot next to yours thirty-nine years ago. Do you remember?'

Bea listened with bated breath.

'I wish it was that simple,' said Charles. 'I didn't have an allotment then. I only got one some years after Catherine left. I started it to give me something to do, a new interest. I was so sick of staring at my own four walls. I was living up in Fouracre Road, then. The allotments were literally at the end of the road, so it seemed like an obvious thing to do.'

'And you were given a plot so close to her,' said Bea. 'What are the odds?'

'It's sickening, isn't it? She was right by me the whole time.'

'Or maybe there's some comfort in it?'

'I don't know, Bea. I can't see it like that at the moment.'

'No, of course not. Life can be so cruel.'

'And now it's all over. I suppose it's like a chapter ending, or a whole book. I got a letter from Lionel this morning, Ant, confirming that I've forfeited my plot by not being able to look after it. Did you get one, too?'

Ant winced as if he was in pain, which in a way, he was, thought Bea. The emotional pain inflicted by a guilty conscience.

'I don't know. I haven't been back to Bob's yet. I expect it's waiting for me. I'm so, so sorry for this, Charles. It's totally my fault and I'm completely gutted.'

Charles shook his head. 'No, lad. It's not your fault. It's Lionel who's taken this decision, and in a way, he's right. The rules say that you have to tend your own plot and I'm just not up to it anymore. I haven't been for a few years now. It's unfortunate the way it's all happened, but . . . maybe it's time. The only bit I really resent is him saying it's with immediate effect. With the show days away, that's more than bloody-minded. That's vindictive. I mean, what's going to happen to Marvin?'

'Immediate?' said Ant. 'That's ridiculous.'

'That's what it says,' said Charles. 'The letter's in the kitchen, if you want to see it.'

Bea got up and fetched it. She scanned it quickly and read part of it out loud for Ant's benefit. '*Your status as allotment holder is revoked with immediate effect. Any personal items remaining on the site 48 hours after this notice is issued will be removed.* Bloody hell, you can tell he's a twat, just from this letter. It does say you can appeal, though, at the bottom here, in very small print.'

'I've already started writing my letter,' said Charles. 'I ran out of steam, though. I mean, what's the point? Lionel's right. I'm too old to look after the plot.'

'You should still write it,' said Bea. 'Have your say. Let us know when you've done it and one of us can hand deliver it. Now, Irish hotpot or fish pie? I didn't know which you'd prefer, so I got both.'

Charles let her heat up the fish pie, and they left him tucking into it. Bea was pleased they were leaving him in a better state than they'd found him in, but was still worried.

'I suppose you've got your evenings to yourself now that you're banned from the allotments,' she said as she and Ant headed across the rec.

'Yeah, well, I thought I'd nip up there now, actually. I mean, I've only had the verbals from our friend Lionel. I haven't *seen* any letter he's sent to me . . . yet. So, I reckon I can still go up there and check on Marv. It might be a question of killing two birds with one stone as well.'

'What do you mean?'

'Hopefully, the man himself will be there and I can ask him ever so nicely to let us look after the plot until the show. Charles has been through enough. Anyone with an ounce of kindness would allow him to take part one last time.'

CHAPTER FORTY-TWO

Ant had to be content with only killing one of his 'birds', though, because up at Fouracre Road, Lionel was nowhere to be seen. As he walked through the gates and towards Charles's plot, he was aware that he was causing a bit of a stir. His ban was obviously common knowledge. A few people deliberately blanked him, which hurt, but others made a point of saying hello. He was pleasantly surprised at those who were still friendly. Cyril was not one of them. Being so close, it was too rude not to acknowledge Ant at all, but he clearly disapproved of Ant's presence.

'All right, Cyril?' Ant called, not breaking his stride as he made a beeline towards Marvin.

'Ant,' Cyril said, 'I'm surprised to see you here.'

'Can't keep a good man down.' He was by the marrow patch now. The dark green leaves seemed bigger than ever and he had a nasty moment when he wasn't sure that Marvin was still there, but then he got a glimpse of the marrow's stripy body through a gap. When he crouched down and parted the jungle, there he was in all his glory. A quick check over reassured Ant that he was as big, bold and beautiful as ever. After all their hard work this year, it would be a travesty if they couldn't enter

Marv into the show. He took a snap on his phone and sent it to Charles and Bob with the message, *Looking good.*

He fetched the watering can from Charles's shed and gave Marvin a good soaking. He fancied he could almost hear the plant sucking up water through its roots. He watered the beans and tomatoes, then had a quick look over Dylan's plot, which was cordoned off at the far end.

As he was tying up a wayward runner bean plant, a thought occurred to him. Lionel had been there when Dylan's sons had given permission to Bob and him to keep looking after their dad's plot and enter some of his produce into the show. Was this the loophole that they needed to keep coming up here? His spirits started to lift at this possible solution.

He looked around again, hoping to spot Lionel and plead his case there and then, but he couldn't see him. He did see someone in patched dungarees making their way over, though, and his spirits lifted further.

'Hi, Lisa.' He grinned as she got near, then rearranged his features as he saw her expression. 'What's up, mate? Are you okay?'

'Have you had a nasty letter from Lionel? Cos I have.' Lisa fished a folded-up piece of paper out of one of her pockets. 'I've been given notice to quit, for breaching the allotment rules.'

'That's crazy,' said Ant. 'I mean, I know what we've done wrong, but what rule have you broken?'

'Profiting from my allotment, using it to run a business. I mean, it's true, but it wasn't something I planned or did deliberately. It's just that during lockdown, things really took off, and it wasn't always easy to get supplies, so it made sense to grow my own. I'd been growing veg till then and just changed things over to flowers. At the back of my mind, I knew it probably wasn't allowed.'

Ant frowned. 'But it was bloody obvious you were growing flowers here for the last couple of years. No one said anything, did they?'

'Yeah, I mean, I couldn't exactly hide them. Why ban me now?'

'I think it's because you're seen as Team Dylan,' said Ant. 'You tried to put those flowers down and we were there together. I think Lionel's got it in for all of us.'

Lisa sighed. 'If that's what it is, he's taking petty to the next level.'

'Sounds about right. Have you seen him today? I want to have a word.'

'He was here earlier, apparently, but he's gone now. I honestly don't know what I'm going to do. Know anyone with a patch of land for rent?'

'No, sorry, but I'll let you know if I hear about anything. Listen, I've just about finished here and then I'm going to go and find Lionel and have it out with him. It's not fair to chuck us out just before the show, not with everything going on with Charles. Shall I put in a word for you?'

Lisa sighed. 'I don't think there's any point. I know I've got to find somewhere else. Thanks, though.'

'Do you know where he lives?'

'Yeah, it's on the letter.' She unfolded the paper and gave it to Ant.

'Fifteen Edinburgh Avenue,' he read. 'Fifteen. Okay, I've got it. I reckon I'll head up there.'

Lisa narrowed her eyes. 'Is that really a good idea, Ant? It might be seen as a bit . . . aggressive?'

Ant handed the letter back to her. 'I'm not going to scream and shout on his doorstep. I'm just going to ask to have a word. You should have seen Charles today. He's broken. It's awful. I got us into this mess, so I'm going to get us out of it.'

CHAPTER FORTY-THREE

Bea looked at the form Wendy Fox had printed out and handed to her. It was surprisingly sparse. The first section was all straightforward facts — name, address, contact details. Then you had to confirm you were eligible, and finally set out why you wanted to be a councillor '*stating your connection to Kingsleigh and any relevant knowledge, experience and skills.*'

The last section felt like a cross between a job application and the personal statement on a university form. Bea remembered filling one out when she was in the sixth form — was it only three years ago? Her teachers, including Mr Bradley, had encouraged her, and her mum had read through her submission with her and cheered her on as she pressed 'send'. In the end, it hadn't worked out. Whether Queenie's excitement was genuine or fake, at that stage Bea was her carer, her only connection to the outside world. If she'd left home to go to Birmingham or Hull, Queenie would have been completely isolated, trapped in her own home by her agoraphobia. There was no way Bea could live with that on her conscience. Besides, she told herself, it had all worked out for the best. Queenie was a lot better now, and Bea loved working at Costsave. Most days, it just felt like it was all meant to be. She had to admit, though, now and again, she wondered 'what if?' and she found herself thinking, 'Is this it?'

Which is why, she told herself now, she was filling in this form. There was more to life than Costsave. She had more to give.

She looked at the blank form again. It might be better to fill it in online. So much easier to correct mistakes, but she could use the paper form to draft her answers and make notes.

Right, time to concentrate. She took her favourite pen (the one with a wibbly, fluffy flamingo on the end) and filled in the easy bits, then she paused and, using her pen as a pretend microphone, asked herself, 'So, Bea Jordan, why do you want to be a councillor?'

The blank space on the form was intimidating her. She reached for the nearest notebook and found a new page. On the top she wrote, *I want to be a councillor because . . .* and then started making bullet points, but with each one she couldn't help hearing a little self-sabotaging voice.

I love this town and want to help . . . Lame?

I am Kingsleigh born and bred . . . Some sort of pun here? Bred/Costsave/Bread? No, no jokes!

I want to speak for ordinary people — people like you and me . . . God, so patronising. Why was this so hard?

I'm young . . . Too young? What did she know about anything?

I work hard . . . Costsave wasn't going down the mines, though, was it? It was a right laugh a lot of the time.

Kingsleigh is a great place to live . . . And die. Bea couldn't help thinking of the series of crimes she'd investigated and now the two bodies in two weeks at the allotments.

She sat back and read through the list. It was very thin. She wasn't sure she could use any of it. The last point was playing on her mind. She was only doing this now because Dylan Bradley had died. Two bodies in two weeks.

She started flipping through the notebook, which was the one she'd used for her last investigation. There were pages and pages of notes — dates, times, places, lists of suspects, possible motives. Damn, she was good at this!

One of the 'desirable' skills for a councillor was the ability to conduct research. Well, she'd definitely shown an aptitude for that, but could she put it on a form?

She wondered if Ant and the others were being as organised as they could be in investigating Dylan's death. She hadn't wanted to have anything to do with it — for good reason — but she and Ant had been a good team. Should she swallow her pride and ask to get involved?

Suddenly she had a flashback to the cold, dark shed. She saw the flash of a gun going off and had the metallic smell of blood in her nose. Her heart started to race and her hairline prickled with sweat.

No, she thought. *Leave them to it*. She was going down a new path, a positive one. If she wanted to do justice by Dylan Bradley, then she should mention on this form that she wanted to see the projects he'd started come to fruition. She'd pin her colours to the Kingsleigh Museum idea.

She flipped back to her list. Yes, she thought, the museum, and while she was at it, it wouldn't hurt to mention car parking and dog poo.

CHAPTER FORTY-FOUR

Edinburgh Avenue was one of Kingsleigh's most desirable addresses. It was among a small network of roads containing detached houses set back from the road. The less exclusive ones were link detached, joined by the umbilical cord of their garages, while some were separated by a gnat's whisker of clear space, just enough not to breach the Trade Descriptions Act. The further away from the town centre you got, the posher they became, until at the far end they were the stuff of *Homes and Gardens*, with huge gardens at the back and circular drives, laurel hedges and electric gates at the front.

It wasn't a neighbourhood Ant regularly hung out in. He did have memories of visiting once or twice with his dad, but that had been after dark and decidedly unofficial. Now, as he looked at the two-storey house, with its mock-Georgian portico around the front door, he had a suspicion he'd been there before. He tried to dismiss it. Even if he had, that was all in the past, and it was one of the jobs that hadn't resulted in an arrest or a conviction.

He needed to focus. He wasn't there to grovel but was prepared to say sorry and appeal to Lionel's better nature. Despite his recent actions, Ant suspected that Lionel might be the type of person who enjoyed being publicly and visibly magnanimous. Ant was here to give him the chance to look good.

His mouth was dry as he opened the heavy wooden gate and approached the front door. *Come on, Ant*, he told himself. *You can do this.*

He grasped the dark metal door knocker and rapped loudly a couple of times, then stepped back a little onto the gravel drive. After a moment or two, the door opened and a middle-aged woman wearing what seemed to be a uniform of some sort looked out enquiringly. She had badge on her tunic top, which bore the company logo of Kingsleigh Home Care as well as her name, Fatima. 'Hello,' she said. 'Can I help you?'

'Um, I was hoping to see Lionel Gittins. I'm sorry, have I got the wrong house?'

Fatima smiled. 'No, you've come to the right place. Mr Gittins is in the back garden. Do you want to go round? I'll tell him you're here.'

'Oh, right. Yeah, thank you.'

'No problem.'

Fatima closed the door and Ant followed the path round the side of the house. There was another gate to negotiate, a wrought iron one set into a door-sized gap in six-foot-high brick wall. When Ant tried it, he found that it was padlocked, but he soon saw the familiar figure of Lionel approaching on the other side.

'Oh, it's you. What do you want?'

'Can I have a word?'

Lionel hesitated for a moment. 'Yes. Yes, all right.' He took a key out of his pocket and undid the lock, then opened the gate. 'Come in, then.'

Ant stepped through into one of the most beautiful gardens he'd ever seen. It was like something out of a magazine or *Gardeners' World* on the telly (which, to be fair, he always switched away from if he was on his own, although Bob was a fan). A sweeping lawn ran from a paved terrace outside the back of the house and down towards a wilder area, which seemed to be dotted with fruit trees, and was separated from the main garden by a rose-covered trellis and arch. Halfway down was a pond on two levels with a little cascade from one to the other. Weed-free borders fringed the lawn, with a mixture of foliage and flowers that drew the eye.

'Blimey, Lionel,' said Ant. 'Nice place.'

'Thank you.'

'Have you been here long?'

'Thirty years. We brought the kids up here and we've got it just how we like it. Do you want a tour?'

Ant looked at Lionel to check that he was serious, but it seemed like he was. 'Yes, please.'

They walked slowly around the garden, with Lionel pointing out plants and features he was particularly proud of. The bottom section was an orchard with paths cut in longer grass. Apples and pears were ripening up nicely.

'It's a bit of a nuisance really,' said Lionel. 'There's too much fruit to deal with and any rotting apples attract wasps, but Mary loves it.'

He looked through the rose arch towards the house, where a woman was sitting just inside by an open French window. Fatima was tucking a blanket over the woman's knees.

'She's got Alzheimer's,' said Lionel. 'We managed on our own for five or six years. Well, with help of friends and neighbours. The Sillitoes next door were very kind. But it got too much. We've got carers coming in now. It means I can still get out to the allotments and know that she'll be safe.'

Ant was blindsided at his honesty. 'I'm so sorry,' he said. 'I had no idea. I don't think anyone does.'

A brief, tight smile appeared for a second or two on Lionel's face. 'It's not a secret, but we don't broadcast it and it doesn't really come up in conversation. We're not ashamed, but it's . . . private. It feels better that way.'

'Of course. I won't tell anyone.'

'You can tell people. I just don't want a fuss. Now,' he said, with a change of tone that indicated the previous topic of conversation was closed, 'what did you want to see me for?'

'Well, you can probably guess,' said Ant. 'I came to apologise again, and to ask that you let Charles keep the plot until the end of the month, so that he can enter the flower and produce show one last time.'

Lionel was listening but didn't say anything. Light filtered through the leaves of the apple tree above him and created dappled shadow on his face.

'I went to see him today,' Ant continued. 'He's so sad. I think the whole Catherine thing has broken him.'

'I see,' said Lionel.

'He said he'd write and appeal, but honestly, it's all my fault. Me going up there without asking permission — that's what riled you. I want to put it right. I just thought maybe I could do that by asking you directly.'

Ant couldn't read the look in his eyes. 'Plus,' he went on, 'we promised Dylan's sons that we'd look after his plot until the show, and I don't want to let them down. I don't really want to let anyone down, although I seem to be good at it.'

Faced by continued silence, he started to feel deflated. He'd given it his best shot, but coming here had, perhaps, been yet another error of judgement. It had taken quite a bit of courage but the nervous energy he'd summoned up was seeping away now. He looked at the ground and scuffed his feet on the path, making contact with an early fallen apple, sending it scudding into the longer grass.

'It's okay,' he said. 'I understand that I've stuffed up. I shouldn't have bothered you at home.'

'Actually, I'm rather glad that you did,' said Lionel. Ant looked up again. 'I'm not a monster, Ant. Perhaps you can see that now. Charles must be going through agony. It's a terrible thing, isn't it? I was very angry when I made that decision. The committee backed me up, because they always do, but perhaps I was too hasty. Please, tell Charles and Bob that the ban won't start until next month. And they can, of course, appeal it, in the usual way.'

'Really? Are you sure?'

'I'm sure. I was intemperate.'

Ant wasn't sure of the exact meaning — he'd try and remember to look it up later — but he thought it meant Lionel realised he'd been a bit of a dick.

'Thank you,' he said. 'I really mean it. And Lisa too? She told me she'd had a letter as well.'

'Lisa's got the rest of the month. She can appeal, if she wants to. I'll let you out.'

They started walking back up the garden towards the side gate.

'One thing,' said Ant, pleased that he'd remembered it. 'Do you have the allotment records going back years?'

'I've got the records from 2015 onwards. Why do you ask?'

'Charles wanted to know who had the plot where Catherine was found.'

As they got nearer to the house, Ant could see Lionel's wife more clearly. She had obviously nodded off in her chair, her head slumped forward a little, with her pale scalp visible through her wispy white hair. Fatima fussed round her, tucking her hands — whose long, elegant fingers were little more than skin and bone, bearing rings that now looked too large — under the blanket.

'Ah,' said Lionel, 'the police have already asked about that. It's not that straightforward. That section of land wasn't used as allotments then. The existing site was extended in the late eighties, I think. I'm not sure of the exact date.'

'What was it before that, then?'

'Just farmland, I think.' Then he frowned. 'No, that's not right. It was council property. They had a garage and kept vehicles and mowers and whatnot there.'

'Oh, okay.'

'If you're still interested in the records, they're in the library's local history section.'

'Yeah, maybe not. Thank you, anyway.'

Lionel undid the padlock again and let Ant out. As he turned to say goodbye, he was locking up again. It was obviously part of a strict routine, a way to keep Mary as safe as possible, although she was too sleepy today to wander anywhere.

As he set off up Edinburgh Avenue, back towards town, Ant realised that he was seeing Lionel in a different light. You never knew what people's lives were like behind their public face. He was as guilty of making assumptions as the next person. He'd try not to, from now on, although whatever pressures people were facing at home, there was no need to be, as Charles called it, 'a little Hitler'.

Ant checked his phone. It was nearly seven o'clock. The library's hours had been cut again recently, and there was no way it would still be open now. In light of what Lionel had said, he wasn't sure there would be any point digging about in the records, but, even if there was, it would have to wait for another day.

CHAPTER FORTY-FIVE

'You three have got a spring in your step,' said Ant, catching up with Bea, Dot and Bob as they walked along the high street.

Dot squeezed Bea's arm. 'Bea's nearly written her application to be a councillor. Isn't it brilliant?'

'Er, yes. It's amazing. You're really going for it, then?'

'I am,' said Bea. 'I think. I couldn't quite press send last night. I don't know what was stopping me.'

Bob tipped his face to emphasise his double chin and put on a Churchillian voice. 'You have nothing to fear except fear itself.'

'What?' said Bea.

'Churchill, wasn't it? Or was it someone else? Maybe Roosevelt. I can't do an American accent.'

'You can't do a very good Winston, to be fair,' said Dot. 'No offence intended.'

'None taken, my dear.' Bob leaned over and pecked Dot on the cheek.

'What's happened to your car, Bob?' said Ant.

'New fitness regime starts here,' said Bob, patting his ample stomach. 'No more fry-ups, walking to work. Five fruit and veg every day.'

'Seven,' said Dot. 'You need to eat seven these days and do ten thousand steps.'

'Blimey,' said Ant. 'Shame about the fry-ups. You've got a talent for them.'

'He's got a talent for all sorts of things,' said Dot, with a wink, 'which is why I want him in tip-top shape.'

'Ugh, spare us!' said Bea, laughing. 'You're in a good mood, too, Ant. What's going on?'

'I pulled it out of the bag yesterday. Went to see Lionel and pleaded for us to keep the allotment until after the show, and he agreed.'

'That's a big result,' said Bob. 'He can be an awkward old sod, and once his mind's made up, that's usually it. How did you do it?'

'Just said sorry again and told him how sad Charles was. Appealed to his better nature.'

'I'm rather surprised he has one.'

'Turns out he's human, like the rest of us,' said Ant. 'I saw a different side to him, actually.'

All three of his companions looked across to him.

'You never know what someone's dealing with, do you? People might have all sorts going on at home. It's made me realise I should make allowances. Not judge too harshly.'

'What's going on with Lionel, then? Or shouldn't we ask?' said Bob.

'His wife's ill,' said Ant, not quite knowing how much to say.

'Ah, I'm sorry to hear that. I had no idea.' They were nearly at Costsave now, their mood slightly lowered by Ant's news about Lionel. 'Anyway, that should cheer Charles up a bit.'

As they crossed the car park, Bob and Dot went ahead and Ant fell into step with Bea.

'I brought Dylan's book for you.' Ant dug in his pocket and handed it over to her.

'Thanks. Crikey, it's a bit dog-eared, isn't it?'

'Yeah, like I said, he's marked some of the pages. I can't work out why, though. Shall we have a look at break time?'

'Okay. Do you want to read my application before I send it in?'

Ant beamed, pleased to be asked. 'I'd love to. I think it's really brave to put yourself out there.'

Bea beamed back. 'Or stupid.'

'No, not stupid. Never stupid. You're the smartest person I know.'

They were outside the staff door now. Bob and Dot had disappeared inside.

'Give over,' said Bea. She suddenly darted forward and kissed his cheek, then pulled open the door and started running up the stairs. Ant stood there for a moment, shell-shocked, then dived inside after her.

'Hey!'

She paused, halfway up the stairs and looked back at him. He kissed his hand and blew it towards her. She reached out and pretended to catch it, then turned, carried on up and headed into the women's locker room.

He got ready for work and took his place for the staff briefing, next to Bea. George and Neville's words of wisdom went largely in one ear and out of the other, as he just enjoyed standing close to her, imagining a future with her . . .

He suddenly became aware that someone had said his name. He focused towards the front of the room and found Neville glaring at him. 'I'm looking at you, Anthony.'

Now, everyone else was looking, too.

'Why? What? What have I done now?'

Bea leaned closer. 'No smoking on-site,' she whispered.

Ant held his hands up in surrender. 'It's a fair cop.' A ripple of amusement passed through the room. 'I need to give up, anyway. Filthy habit.'

Neville was clearly not amused, but George had moved on to the next item. The briefing was soon over and they all filed out to start another day.

'Do you want me to give up smoking?' Ant asked Bea as they waited at the top of the stairs.

'It's not up to me, Ant. It's what you want to do. If you want to give up, I'll try and help.'

'Food for thought,' he said.

There was a pleasant chill in the air as he patrolled the car park, rounding up stray trolleys and picking up litter. In the middle of winter, this job was pretty miserable. Today, though, there was just a hint of autumn and it didn't feel sad, the end of something — rather, it was a welcome sign of things moving on, moving forwards.

Just before break time, he heard a familiar voice and saw Saggy approaching, holding a bulging plastic-wrapped parcel. He, too, seemed to have a spring in his step.

'All right, mate?' Saggy said.

Ant pretended to look at his watch. 'You're up early. It's not midday yet. What's going on?'

'Just making a drop-off in your lockers. Sweet little deal.' Saggy nodded towards the block of Pay and Pick Up lockers to one side of the front entrance. 'Are you ready for a fag break?'

Ant puffed out his cheeks. 'No can do. There's a bit of a clampdown on smoking at work. Better leave it for a day or two.'

'Shame. Shall we have a drink this evening?' Saggy continued. 'My treat.'

This was a very unusual offer, and one not to be sniffed at. 'Sure. Must have been a good deal.'

'You know the sports socks I was selling?'

'Know them, I'm wearing them!' Ant looked down to the expanse of white sock visible between his trainers and the bottom of his trousers.

'Yeah, well, I've still got a couple of boxes. I'm selling them on eBay. Just got rid of a job lot of them.'

'Do people buy socks on eBay?'

'Course they do. People buy everything. And sell everything. Proper cheered me up, after . . . you know . . .'

'Nice. I've got my reading class after work, but we could meet after that. Half seven?'

They high-fived and Saggy went towards the store. *There must be something in the air today*, thought Ant. *Finally, things are on the up.*

At half past ten, he went inside and found Bea in the staff room. She had her nose in Dylan's book. He made a cup of tea and sat down beside her.

'What do you reckon?' he said. 'Do you know why he marked those pages?'

'I'm not sure. He's circled references to about twenty items or artefacts, mostly little things like coins and pottery. He's put numbers by some of them. They look like dates, but they're from this year, not historical. He must have had a reason.'

Tyler joined them. 'Oh, I've finished reading that book now. I learned quite a lot. There's more to Kingsleigh than meets the eye.'

'Yeah, but in this copy, Dylan marked loads of pages. Look—' She handed the book to Tyler.

'That's weird,' he said. 'What are the dates?'

Bea shrugged. 'We don't know, but I might take a stroll down the high street and ask Wendy Fox about it at lunchtime.'

CHAPTER FORTY-SIX

Just before noon, a rumour started sweeping around Costsave. It reached Bea via a customer scrolling on their phone while they waited in her queue. Out of the corner of her eye, Bea caught the customer's expression change and she uttered a quiet, 'Ooh.'

Bea cocked an enquiring eyebrow at her.

'They've taken someone in for questioning in connection with the murder of Dylan Bradley,' the woman said.

The other two people at Bea's checkout looked round.

'Does it say who?'

'No. Hang on, I'll check the community sites.'

Bea continued beeping her current customer's shopping through while everyone else waited.

'Okay, people are saying it's an elderly man. No names yet.'

Bea fumbled a jar of jam. It fell onto her checkout, tee-tered on the edge and then dived onto the floor, where it shattered, sending glass and jam out in all directions. Her customer squealed and stepped sharply backwards, starting a ripple effect. For a moment Bea thought that her queue was going to perform like human dominoes, and they'd all end up on their backs, but with a bit of staggering and clutching on to one another, they all managed to stay on their feet.

'Whoa, that's the most excitement I've had since my honeymoon in Rhyl!' said one of them.

'You need to get out more,' said another.

'Or stay in more.'

'What's Rhyl like, by the way? I've never been.'

'I'm so, so sorry, everyone. I don't know what happened there,' said Bea. She pressed the button to start the light on the top of her till flashing, but it wasn't needed. From his customer services desk, Neville had observed the kerfuffle and was leaning forward towards his microphone. Now his voice boomed around the store, 'Cleaner to checkout six. Cleaner to checkout six.'

Before long, Eileen appeared with the cleaning trolley. Quickly assessing the situation, she swept past Dot's checkout, went round the front and parked up by the mess in front of Bea. She dealt with it with admirable efficiency. It had been a long time since she'd been on cleaning duties as her regular job, but she clearly hadn't lost her talent for it.

'No point crying over spilled jam,' she said, briefly surveying the now-clean patch of hard floor, checking for any stray pieces of glass.

'Thanks, Eileen. You're a star. You covering today?'

'Only for half an hour while Coral's on her break.' She moved a little closer. 'Did you hear someone's been arrested?'

Bea's heart was thumping hard in her chest. It was surely Charles, but was he really in the frame for Dylan's death as well as Catherine's?

'That's what they're saying. A man in his seventies.'

Seventies? Charles was older than that, wasn't he? Now she came to think of it, she wasn't sure.

'Is it okay to pay now?' Her customer wasn't being snarky, just prompting Bea.

'Oh, sorry, yes, of course. Card, is it?' Bea rang up the total and selected the payment type. She mouthed, 'Thank you,' to Eileen, who set off with the cleaning trolley along the front of the store, stopping to pick up bits of cardboard and cabbage leaves on her way.

After that, lunchtime couldn't come fast enough, but, of course, time seemed to enter a new dimension and each minute felt like an hour. Bea tried her best to be her usual cheery self with her customers, but it was an effort. She didn't have to fake things with one customer, though. She was genuinely delighted when the young mum she'd offered advice to made a beeline for her checkout.

'I tried the parent and toddler group,' the woman said. 'It was great. We've been twice now. Everyone's really friendly and I've even found someone for Callum to have a playdate with. They're coming round to ours this afternoon. That's what these are for.' She showed Bea a box of Costsave luxury dark chocolate and ginger cookies. 'Me and Fraser's mum, not the kids. They can have grapes and apple slices.'

'I'm so pleased,' said Bea.

The clock had finally ticked round to five to one when she spotted someone very surprising approaching her checkout. He was walking slowly and seemed unsteady on his feet, even using his walking stick.

'Charles!' Bea said, when he made it within earshot. 'This is nice! I wasn't expecting you.'

Beside her, she thought she heard Dot sniff and mutter under her breath.

Charles managed a watery smile, and put a pint of milk, a sausage roll and a packet of gravy bones on the conveyor belt.

'I thought I should make the effort and show my face,' he said. 'I can't stay indoors for ever.'

'It's lovely to see you here,' Bea said.

Dot swivelled round in her chair. Bea could feel her eyes drilling into the two of them.

'Have the police been to see you today?' she said.

'Me? No, but that's partly why I've come here. We had two police cars to the bungalows this morning. I heard the noise and was just in time to see them march him out — I'm not sure if he was in handcuffs or not.'

'Blimey, Charles. Who was it?'

'It was Cyril. They're questioning Cyril.'

CHAPTER FORTY-SEVEN

'Did you hear about Cyril? He's the guy we saw up at the allotments that day, isn't he?' said Bea.

'Yeah.' Ant spooned another heap of sugar into his tea.

'Do you think this wraps it all up? If Cyril killed Dylan. Is he one of the ones who's been there for years? Could he have killed Catherine, too?'

'He could well have. He's a miserable old sod and he's on our list.' He moved his fingers across his mouth to indicate zipping them up.

Bea dug him in the ribs. 'You can tell me about your investigation, if you like,' she said. 'I don't want it to be off limits between us. I don't want anything to be off limits.'

Ant raised his eyebrows, digesting that.

'While you think about that,' she continued, 'I'm going to ring Wendy and ask her about the notes in Dylan's book. Perhaps it's something else that can go on your investigation board, if Cyril doesn't end up being charged.'

Bea took out her phone and selected the town council number. As it started ringing, she got up and walked into the corridor. When she came back, she didn't sit down again, but grabbed her tea and gulped down the remains, then put the empty mug by the sink.

'She says she can see me now. I reckon I've just about got time. See you later, Ant.'

Ant gave her a thumbs up. Without her to talk to in the staff room, he thought he might as well check out the Four Amigos' nerve centre and see if anyone had any thoughts on the latest development. In the stores, Bob and Tyler were ahead of him, and today they were joined by Dean, back at work for the first time since their gruesome midnight discovery.

They were all sitting facing the incident board. Ant pulled up a chair next to Bob.

Someone had added an asterisk to Cyril's name and a note beside it — '*Questioned by police*' and today's date.

'Do you know why they've pulled him in?' said Ant.

'Rumour has it that he was heard to threaten Dylan,' said Bob. 'In fact, it was Lisa. She said she'd overheard them arguing a couple of weeks ago and Cyril had said, "If I find out it was you, I'll kill you."'

'The tomato thief?' said Ant. 'It wasn't Dylan, though.'

'Did you tell the police? It feels like it's pretty relevant now. In fact, not telling them might be withholding evidence.'

Ant sighed. 'I'd better ring someone, hadn't I? But I don't see what difference it will make. The point isn't who is or was the tomato thief, it's the fact that Cyril *thought* it was Dylan. He was getting in a knot about it in his head.'

'They still need to know, son. You know it's the right thing to do.'

'Yeah.'

'I can back you up,' said Dean, unexpectedly. 'Saggy and me saw the thief, too. It wasn't just you.'

'I'll do it after work. Perhaps you guys could hang around, just in case,' said Ant.

There were mutterings of agreement.

'The thing is,' Ant went on, 'if Cyril did it, hit Dylan round the head, because he thought he'd nicked his tomatoes, where does that leave Catherine?'

'Two separate cases,' said Bob, 'and one big coincidence? I reckon we might never find out who killed her. It's so long ago now.'

Dean burst into laughter, and they all turned to look at him. Ant reckoned he wasn't the only one thinking that Dean had returned to work too soon. 'That can't be it!' Dean said. 'I just don't believe that some old codger would kill his neighbour because he thought he'd nicked his tomatoes. I mean, come on! A row, yes, maybe a little shove, but not something like that.'

'Perhaps the police have proof. Maybe there's forensic evidence that points to Cyril. We'll have to wait and see,' said Bob.

'How are you feeling, Deano?' said Ant. 'Back to full strength?'

'I'm at about fifty per cent, mate, but I didn't want you lot messing up my stores . . . Thought I'd better come back and make sure everything was okay.'

'What a trooper.'

Dean blushed a little, unused to praise from his friend.

'Your devotion to Costsave should get some sort of recognition. Shall I have a word with Neville?'

Dean's expression soured, as he realised Ant was gently ribbing him. 'Yes, all right. I was upset, but it was also pretty sweet having a bit of time off, not going to lie. I've got Mum where I want her, as well. She won't let me lift a finger to help at home — washing up, bins, she's doing it all.'

Ant felt a passing wave of sympathy for Eileen, not a feeling he was used to.

'So, the board's still up and we're still digging, are we?' Dean said. 'Although, not literally.'

'Yes, I reckon,' said Tyler. 'I was thinking about the things highlighted in Dylan's book. They weren't the big stuff, were they? They were little bits and bobs. What was that all about?'

'Bea's on the case,' said Ant. 'She said she didn't want to get involved, but she can't help herself. She's gone to see Wendy Fox about it. I'll let you know what she says when she comes back. And I'm off to the library this evening for my reading session. I might ask to look at the allotment records while I'm there — I mean, it's all practice, isn't it? I'm seeing Saggy in the Ship afterwards, if anyone wants to come.'

'Dot's signed us up for badminton in the leisure centre,' said Bob. 'Then I'm going to nip up to the allotment and do the watering and checks.'

'And I said I'd help Scout at the diner tonight. Her brothers are going out for the evening so they could do with an extra pair of hands.'

'Report back tomorrow, then?' Ant got to his feet. 'Good to have the old team back together.' He reached for Dean's empty mug to take it back to the staff room, but instead Dean went to fist bump him. Then Tyler and Bob leaned in, too, and all four hands met in the middle.

'The dream team,' said Dean.

Ant gathered up the mugs and as he headed out of the stores he felt a little warm glow. Dean's journey from stores oddbod to part of the gang was a surprising one, but it clearly meant a lot to him. Life was strange, thought Ant, but it wasn't all bad.

CHAPTER FORTY-EIGHT

Wendy frowned as she leafed through Dylan's book. 'What are the dates?'

'I don't know,' said Bea, 'but I wondered if we could check one or two of the items that were ringed.'

'Yes, let's do that,' said Wendy. 'I'll look a couple of them up on our system and then grab the keys for the stores.'

Bea sat in the chair opposite her and watched as Wendy concentrated on her PC screen for a few minutes, consulting the book, checking the information online and writing things down on yellow sticky notes. She attached the notes into the book, marking the relevant pages, then got up.

'Could you pass me my jacket?' Wendy asked her. 'It can be chilly in the basement.'

Bea reached behind her and eased a rather nice navy jacket off its peg on the coat rack in the corner, noting that the label said Armani. Impressed, she passed it to Wendy, who put it on and picked up a bunch of keys from a key safe on the office wall. Then she ushered Bea through the door at the back and down the stairs to the basement.

This visit felt very different from Bea's previous one. On her own with Ed, she had been on edge the whole time. Now, she and Wendy talked easily and freely, making Bea feel that perhaps she would fit in as a councillor, after all.

Wendy let them into the furthest storeroom. 'Let's start with this one.' She opened Dylan's book at a page marked with one of her sticky notes. *'Three Roman coins, found in 1973, in Kingsleigh cemetery.* Dylan's ringed them and written *10/02/24* in the margin. Now, they should be over here . . .' She walked over to a set of boxes on shelves and ran her fingers over the labels, examining the reference numbers.

She pulled out a small, shallow box. 'Can you take this and I'll open it up?'

Bea held the box while Wendy levered off the lid. Inside, the soft lining showed round indentations that would be perfect for displaying coins. However, that's all there were — spaces where coins should be.

'Oh,' said Wendy. 'This isn't good. We'll keep this one out and have a look at the next one.' She replaced the lid and Bea continued to hold the box, while Wendy turned to the next marked page. *'Fragments of mosaic,'* she read out, *'depicting a fish and water.* Okay, it should be this side.'

She bent down to the lower shelf on the other side of the room, pulling out a box labelled *'Mosaic'* and with a reference number that matched the one she'd noted down. The box was larger and she slid it across the floor towards Bea, then took the lid off. This, too, was empty.

'Ah,' she said. 'We've definitely got a problem.' She stared at the empty box, deep in thought. 'I'll check some more.'

It was the same with the next item, a belt buckle, believed to be medieval and found in the ruins of the abbey, and the next — more coins, half a dozen this time. By now, there was no mistaking the pattern.

'So, Dylan had found out that some of the town's treasures were missing,' said Bea, rather stating the obvious. 'Do you think that's what he wanted to talk to you about?'

'Could be. I wonder what the dates are, though? Do you think they are when he discovered each item was missing?'

'I don't know. They must be significant. This is theft, isn't it?'

They looked at each other, surrounded by empty boxes.

'It certainly looks like that,' said Wendy. 'And, if so, it's extremely serious.' The skin of her face seemed to sag as she said, 'Oh God, we should check the safe.'

'I think it's okay,' said Bea. 'Ed showed me the chalice, the chessmen and the seal when I was here before. They seemed fine.'

'I need to see them with my own eyes, just for my peace of mind.' Wendy went over to the safe and unlocked it. After a minute or two rummaging around, she sealed it up again. A little colour was returning to her face. 'They're okay, thank goodness. Let's put everything back for the time being. If this is ongoing, I don't want the thief to know we're on to them quite yet.'

Wendy set about putting the boxes back where she found them.

'Who has access to the storerooms?' asked Bea.

'It's only members of staff,' said Wendy. 'Anyone else has to be accompanied by one of us.'

'You said you let Dylan come down here on his own?'

'True. He is — was — the exception, because of his status as a councillor and local historian. I don't think anyone else has been here. To be honest, there was only low-level interest in our artefacts for years until Dylan started his museum campaign. Most people had forgotten they were here.'

She looked around the room, satisfied that it appeared undisturbed. 'Before we leave,' she said, 'I need you to promise that you will keep this between us for now. This is big, Bea. This seems to be theft on a large scale. If it gets out, it will rock the council and the town.'

'Of course,' said Bea. 'What are you going to do next?'

'Well, first I'll check each item Dylan identified, establish the scale of the loss. May I keep this book?'

Bea nodded.

'Then, I'll have to tell the Chair, and I expect we'll take it to the police. I can't imagine the impact a scandal like this will have. Unless we can avoid it somehow.'

'I don't understand how you could avoid it, though.'

'If I could identify the person responsible — and, like we said, there are only very few people who have access to stores — and recover the items, then there would be no harm done in the end.'

Bea was worried. 'Catch the thief yourself? Wendy, I've been involved in investigations before and it's a dangerous game.'

'At the moment, I'm one step ahead, though. Whoever it is doesn't know that I know. As long as that stays the case, it may be possible to set a trap. I must swear you to secrecy, Bea. Discretion is one of the essential qualities for a councillor, after all. In this case, if you tell anyone, it could jeopardise my investigation.'

Wendy looked at her with utter seriousness, and, Bea thought, a glitter of excitement in her eyes. She remembered the thrill of her earlier adventures, before it all got too much, and realised that she had met a kindred spirit.

'I swear I won't tell,' she said. 'But I'm not sure you should do this yourself. If we're right, and Dylan had found out about the thefts and was about to tell you, it could be the thing that got him killed.'

'You're right,' said Wendy thoughtfully. 'I'll need to tread carefully.'

'Very carefully. If I were you, I wouldn't come down here on my own, or even with just one other person. It feels very cut off. And if you do set a trap, I'd be happy to be there too. Safety in numbers and all that.'

Wendy put a hand on Bea's shoulder. 'Thank you. To be honest, I think the staff and most of the councillors are a little bit scared of me. But I may take you up on that.'

'Please do. I've put myself in too many silly situations. You feel like you're not afraid of anyone, that you can look after yourself, but when people are cornered or desperate, it can quickly turn nasty.'

Wendy locked up and they went upstairs, back into the office, which seemed light, buzzy and refreshingly normal after the intensity and claustrophobia of the storeroom. As Bea turned to thank Wendy again, the front door opened and Ed Sillitoe appeared. He frowned when he saw Bea and Wendy closing the door to the stairs.

'Back again?' he said. 'Is there a problem?'

'No, no problem,' said Wendy, breezily. 'I was showing Bea around the archives. She was asking about the history of the council, so I dug out some of the old records.'

Bea was impressed at the seamlessness of Wendy's lying.

'Takes all sorts,' he said, mildly, then put some time sheets in a labelled in-tray.

Bea started towards the door. 'Thanks, Wendy.'

'No problem. Let's stay in touch.'

They shared a split second of unspoken understanding before Bea turned and left.

222

CHAPTER FORTY-NINE

'So, did Wendy have any ideas about the notes in Dylan's book?' said Ant. He and Bea were walking down the high street together after work. 'You were gone a while. Thought I was going to have to cover for you.'

'Made it back by the skin of my teeth,' said Bea. 'She couldn't think of anything straight away. She asked me to leave the book with her, I hope that's okay.'

Ant chewed the side of his mouth. 'Well, yeah, I suppose. But I want it back. It's kind of special.'

'I'm sorry, Ant. I should have rung you to ask. She's only borrowing it.'

'It's okay. I reckon we can trust the town clerk, can't we?'

'Actually, yes,' said Bea. 'She was quite excited when I explained what we'd found. Apparently, Dylan phoned her the evening he died. She had a couple of missed calls. She's wondering if this is all connected somehow. Between you and me, I think she rated him. She's a bit scathing about some of the councillors, but she seemed to admire him as someone who wanted to get things done.'

'Well, if you look at most of the old fossils on the council, you can see why she'd like him. It's the same up the allotments.

There are so many people up there that I swear were born old — you can't imagine them ever being kids or teenagers.'

'Talking of which, any news on Cyril?'

'Not that I've heard. I think we'd know if he'd been charged.' Ant had ground to a halt outside the bakery shop window. 'Look at that, one curry pasty left. Won't be a minute.'

He darted inside and soon emerged carrying a paper bag. 'Just a little brain food. Honestly, reading's getting easier and easier, but it's still hard work, especially at the end of the day like this.'

'You've stuck at it, though. That's actually really rather brilliant,' said Bea, smiling.

'I'm on the last book of the reading scheme now. When I finish, that's it! I'll be released out into the world of books.' He spread his arms out, paper bag dangling from one hand and ran down the pavement in a zigzag line, much to the irritation of a couple of pedestrians coming the other way.

'Watch it,' said one, who narrowly missed receiving a slap in the face with the pie bag.

'Sorry, mate. Sorry.' Ant stopped running and turned to face Bea, who was enjoying the near miss. He waited for her to catch up with him, but she deliberately swerved and walked as far away as possible.

'Nothing to do with me,' she said. 'I've never even seen you before.'

She was joking, but it cut him to the quick. The thought of rejection — even faked — was too much.

'Don't say that, Bea.' He darted across and grabbed her hand. 'I couldn't bear it if you didn't want to know me.'

'Don't be daft. I was teasing.'

She didn't try to take her hand away. Instead, he felt her squeeze it, and suddenly everything was all right again.

'Am I too immature? For you, I mean. Or just generally.'

'Bloody hell, Ant, this is a bit deep for an after-work chat.'

'Yeah, sorry. Forget it.'

She was still holding his hand.

'You're not immature, you're just very, very silly and I wouldn't want you any other way. You're also kind, resourceful and brave. One of the bravest people I know. I don't want to change you, Ant. I reckon you're all right just as you are.'

Objectively the pavement was still there under his feet, but he had to see it to believe it, because it felt as if Kingsleigh High Street had melted away and he was walking on air. He didn't think he'd ever felt like this before. He wanted to take it all in, so he could remember it for ever — hand in hand with the girl of his dreams.

Bea was looking at him intently. He wondered if there was something wrong with his face. Had he got something on it? Perhaps he had started crying without realising.

'What?' he said.

'You can say something nice back, you know. I mean, if you can think of anything.' He felt her grip loosen, but she hadn't yet broken away.

'Oh shit! I was just letting it sink in. No one ever says anything nice about me. I don't know how to take it. I'm sorry, Bea.' He panicked, words swimming around inside his head like a shoal of fish, twisting, turning, out of reach. 'I reckon you're all right, too.'

She smiled. 'That'll do.'

'God, I'm awful,' said Ant, mortified.

'But I like you,' said Bea. 'That's something my dad used to say in a funny voice. God knows where he got it from. "You are awful, but I like you." Then he and Mum would laugh like drains. I should ask her about it.' Her expression softened. 'I wish you'd met him, Ant. I think you two would have got on.'

Now Ant really did think he might cry. 'I wish I had, too. The way you and your mum talk about him, he sounds like a top bloke.'

'He was. We were very lucky.'

They had walked the length of the street now and were outside the civic centre. Bea's phone started ringing. She let go of Ant's hand and fished her mobile out of her bag.

She frowned. 'I don't know the number. It's local, though.'

'You answer it. I've got to go.'

Ant wondered about swooping in for a crafty peck on the cheek but decided not to push his luck.

Bea smiled at him and then stabbed at the phone. She must have pressed too many times as it went to speaker and as he started to walk away, Ant could hear the caller.

'Bea? It's Malcolm. Malcolm Sillitoe. Are you busy this evening? I was wondering if you'd like to call round for a drink.'

Ant stopped in his tracks and turned round. Bea raised both eyebrows and turned her mouth down at the corners. Ant smothered a laugh.

'Oh, um, I'm not sure,' she said.

'I've been hearing good things about you. I always like to meet a potential new councillor, find out a bit more about them, see how we can work together.'

She raised her shoulders to her ears and held up her free hand in a 'What should I do?' gesture to Ant, who mirrored her body language. He himself would run a mile from a chat with Sillitoe, but people like him would be part of Bea's new circle, if she became a councillor.

'Oh, right. That would be great. I haven't put my form in yet, though.'

'No, no, I understand. This is just a "getting to know you" chat. Nothing formal. Why don't you pop round in half an hour.' He gave her his address.

'Okay,' said Bea. 'I'll see you then.' She killed the call. 'Bloody hell, do you think it's all right to go like this?' She looked down at her work clothes, which today were a black belted mac over plain black trousers and a black jumper. Ant thought she looked rather chic.

'All right?' he said. 'Perfect, I'd say.'

She flashed him a smile. 'I'd better get going, then. It's a bit of a stump to the posh side of town and I don't want to rush and get all hot and sweaty.'

Ant could feel anxiety radiating out from her. He went back to her, stuffed the pie into a pocket, and put his hands on the top of her arms.

'Bea, you're as good as anyone on that council. Don't let him intimidate you. The chances are he'll bore you to death. Do you want me to ring you in an hour, so you've got a get-out excuse if you need one?'

'Oh God, yes. That's a good idea. Thanks, Ant. I'll speak to you later.'

This time he did lean in and planted a kiss just next to, not on, her mouth. 'You've got this.'

CHAPTER FIFTY

When Bea knocked at number seventeen Edinburgh Avenue, Malcolm opened the door instantly. It was almost as if he'd been waiting in the hall for her.

'Bea!' he said, like he was greeting a long-lost pal. 'Do come in.'

'Thank you,' Bea said. One of her old schoolfriends lived in the same road, and when she was younger Bea had enjoyed her visits to their big, sprawling house with a garden you could get lost in. It was a noisy household, with dogs and cats and kids milling around and a kitchen that always smelled of home cooking. In contrast, the Sillitoe house was quiet and orderly and had an air of austere calm, which made Bea feel untidy and somehow not worthy. She took a deep breath and tried to remember what Ant had said to her. *You're as good as anyone on that council.*

A woman with short hair dried into soft waves and wearing a tastefully patterned shirt dress was hovering behind Malcolm inside the hallway. 'Can I take your coat?' the woman asked. 'I'm Christine, by the way.'

'Thank you.' Bea put her bag down on the shiny parquet floor and shrugged off her mac.

Christine took it and hung it on a rack tucked away in a recess under the stairs. 'I'll leave you two to it,' she said and sort of melted away into the depths of the house.

'Come in,' Malcolm said, indicating the second door off the hall. Bea got a glimpse of a book-lined study and then went into an elegant lounge. The overstuffed sofas and chairs were upholstered in blood-red velvet. Their dark wood bowed legs ended in little clawed feet, which each sat on discs to protect the carpet. Occasional tables in the same dark wood were scattered about the room, bearing metal coasters, twiddly table lamps and, in one case, a copy of the *Radio Times*. On the mantelpiece over the fireplace a selection of china figures were arranged artfully either side of a handsome carriage clock. Malcolm and Christine clearly enjoyed the finer things in life.

'Do sit down,' he said, pointing to one of the chairs.

Bea lowered herself down onto an unforgiving cushion.

'Sherry?' Malcolm went over to a sideboard and poured some into two glasses before she'd had a chance to answer. It seemed rude to say no at this point, so Bea took the glass she was offered.

'Cheers,' she said.

'Your good health,' said Malcolm.

From where she was sitting, Bea could see through the French windows into the garden, which reflected the same style as the house. The planting was colourful but restrained, with various stone features dotted around, drawing the eye towards a rather impressive rockery and pond. One of the sculptures looked vaguely familiar, reminding Bea of a Mediterranean ruin, consisting of artfully placed chunks of stone and a pillar with carving around its base.

'The sculptures are mostly Ed's work,' said Malcolm. 'He's modelled them on the abbey ruins. We think he's very talented.'

'Er, yes. Yes, he certainly is.' She had a fleeting thought. What if they weren't replicas in the garden? What if Ed was less of a sculptor and more of a thief? She took a sip of her sherry, which was surprisingly smooth and almost pleasant.

'I hear you've been taking an interest in the town's heritage?' It was said casually, and yet Bea's senses were suddenly alert.

'Well, if I'm lucky enough to become a councillor, I'm interested in finishing some of the things that Dylan Bradley started, as a sort of tribute to him. It seems to me that the project dearest to him was the town museum.'

'Yes indeed. It was definitely his baby. He was very . . . tenacious in trying to move things forward. And you've had a couple of tours of the stores? Seen our treasures for yourself?'

A couple of tours. So, Ed must have reported back to his dad that he'd seen her there today. Bea felt that she was engaged in some sort of dance to which she didn't know the moves. Why would Ed tell Malcolm about her visit if it wasn't important to them both? Was he monitoring her interest in the artefacts because he knew some of them were missing?

'Yes, Ed was kind enough to show me round. It was very interesting.' She could feel warmth surging up her neck and could picture the blotchiness of her skin.

Malcolm looked at her, but said nothing for a long time, during which Bea became acutely aware of the clock ticking on the mantelpiece. The noise seemed to grow louder and louder until it was ringing in her ears. Finally, Malcolm's mouth twitched into something approaching a smile. 'I misjudged you to start with, Bea. Bob was singing your praises when he rang me to say he didn't want his name to go forward. He said how clever you were, how quickly you picked things up.'

'Bob said that, did he? Very nice of him.' Bea drank some more sherry. Smooth as it was, it wouldn't have been her first choice, but she realised she'd have to finish it or risk causing offence.

'And I think that we could work together very well, don't you?'

'Um, yes. I'm sure we could.'

'I can help you, Bea. Be a sort of mentor. I realise you'll want to have an impact, but sometimes it's better to take the long view, lose the battle in order to win the war. Do you get what I mean?'

Bea hadn't got a clue what he was talking about. Maybe it was the sherry, which had almost gone now. Maybe she was just tired after a long day at work. 'Sure,' she said.

Malcolm laughed. She'd heard it before, when she'd raised the idea of being a councillor with him for the first time — a staccato, mirthless sound. 'There's a lot to take in at first. I hope I haven't put you off. I think you'd be a tremendous asset to the council. I'd be happy to endorse your application.'

'Oh, that's great.'

Above the ticking of the clock, Bea could hear another sound now. The harsh engine noise of a large vehicle pulling up on the Sillitoe's drive.

'Ah, here's Ed,' said Malcolm.

Bea drained her glass and put it on the coaster next to her. 'Actually, I've got to be going.' She stood up to find that she was slightly unsteady on her feet. 'Thank you for this. It's been . . . nice.'

'Why don't you stay for another drink?' Bea started walking towards the door.

'My mum's expecting me back. I told her I was coming here but she'll worry if I'm late.'

'Of course.'

As Bea reached the hall, the front door opened as Ed let himself in. He stopped, silhouetted in the doorway. 'Oh, it's you,' he said. Then, to Malcolm who was now behind her. 'What's she doing here?'

'Just a "get to know you" chat, Ed. I'll tell you about it later. Your mother's in the kitchen, if you want to say hello. I'll see Bea out. Unless you'd like a lift home, Bea? You're looking rather flushed. I'm sure Ed wouldn't mind.'

The thought of being alone in the cab of the council van with Ed Sillitoe acted like a shot of adrenaline to Bea. The sleepiness she had felt before was gone in an instant. 'No, I'm fine, thank you. If I could just have my coat . . .'

Malcolm retrieved Bea's mac from under the stairs and held it for her. She felt her flesh creep a little as he came close enough for her to thread her arms through the sleeves.

'Thank you.' She darted along the hallway, squeezed past Ed and crunched her way across the gravel drive. As she reached the pavement and headed back towards the middle of town, her phone rang. She rummaged in her bag and saw that it was Ant.

'This is your friendly get-out call. I'm your mum having a funny turn, if you need me to be.'

'Oh, Ant!' she gasped, keeping her pace as fast as she could manage without actually running.

'Bea? Are you okay?'

'Yes, I've just left, but it was as weird as hell.'

'What happened?' Ant sounded alarmed. 'Is he an old perve or something? Did he try something?'

'No, it wasn't that and there wasn't anything I could really put my finger on, but I won't be going for drinks at his house again.'

'Do you wanna come to the Ship? I'm just waiting for Saggy to turn up.'

'No, I'm going to go home.' The thought of a shower and then an evening in her PJs in front of the telly almost made her cry. 'I'll see you tomorrow.'

'All right, Bea. You take care, though.'

'I will.'

'Love you, Bea.'

'Love you too. Bye.'

CHAPTER FIFTY-ONE

'Is there anything better than a pint of cider?' Saggy looked at his glass lovingly, having taken his first mouthful.

'Two pints?' said Ant.

'I'll drink to that.' They clinked their glasses together and both took another swig.

'How've you been, mate? Since, you know . . .'

Saggy wiped his mouth with the back of his hand. 'Bit rough. I'm selling the metal detector. I just can't see myself ever using it again.'

'That's a shame. I mean, if it helps, it's not likely that you'd ever make another find like that.'

Saggy helped himself to a salt and vinegar crisp from the packet that Ant had torn open and placed on the table between them.

'Are you kidding me? In Kingsleigh? There are bodies all over the place. You keep finding them.'

'Fair point.'

'Are you and the lads and Bob still looking into it?'

'Yeah, we've got quite a few lines of inquiry. I've just been doing a bit of research in the library, actually.' Ant brought out his notebook.

'You're a proper little bookworm now, aren't you? Who'd have thought you had it in you?'

'Education, mate,' said Ant. 'That's what it's all about. School wasn't for me, but now I'm educating myself. No one's telling me to do it. It's all coming from in here—' he held his hand against his chest — 'and it feels good.'

'Fair play to you. I know what you mean. All those years of lugging books to and from school and sitting in endless boring lessons, and it turns out it's all on the internet. Everything's there. You can lose yourself for hours.'

'Yeah, but I'm talking about learning stuff not squeezing one out to whatever pervy site you've found now.' Ant grinned.

'Shut up! That's not all I use the internet for. You're not the only one with an enquiring mind.'

'Just a bit of bants, mate. You've gotta give that hand a rest sometime.'

There were only little bits of crisp left now. Ant picked up the packet, folded it to make a channel, held it up to his mouth and tipped his head back, getting a satisfying mouthful of vinegary, salty crumbs.

'What's in your notebook, then?' asked Saggy. 'What did you find out?'

'I was looking at the old records. Carole helped me find them.'

'That's good of her, considering you did a bunk and didn't tell her.'

'She's been really nice about it. I apologised and everything. It's only Neville who's a bit shirty with me, which isn't a big surprise. Anyway, we found the site plan from 1985 and it looks like where Catherine was found was outside the old site, like Lionel said. So, anyone could have put her there. It didn't need to be someone who was using the allotments. Which is a shame as I did find a list of allotment holders for that year. I took some snaps of it on my phone, but just having a quick look, there were quite a few familiar names — Cyril, Lionel, and even Malcolm Sillitoe. He's Chair of the town council now.'

'It *could* be Cyril, then. Far as I know the police are still holding him. Between you and me, though, I reckon it was your friend Charles.'

'No, mate.' Ant shook his head firmly.

'Come on, Ant. You've got a bit of a blind spot there. You told me that he said she was leaving him. There's your motive. There's your opportunity. And you just said, anyone could access the spot where she was left.'

Ant shook his head. 'He seemed genuinely gobsmacked when she was found, though.'

'He's had nearly forty years to rehearse that, Ant. Sometimes the most obvious solution is the right one. Are you getting another round in?'

'I thought you were flush?'

'Yeah, but you're the one with the regular income. Don't be tight.'

Ant went to the bar, pondering Saggy's take on the case. He still couldn't find it in him to believe that Charles would be capable of hurting anyone. When he carried the pints back, along with another packet of crisps, he was deep in thought.

Saggy took his second pint. 'Cheers, mate. Before you were so rude about my internet habit, I was going to say I found something for you to put in your notebook.'

'What's that?'

'While I've been spending time on eBay, expanding my empire, I found someone local selling old coins.'

Ant didn't feel as impressed as Saggy obviously expected him to be. 'Oh yeah? Why would I write that down?'

'Because, Professor Einstein, they are the sort of coins you find with a metal detector and dig up. The sort of coins that someone like your friend Dylan Bradley would have got excited about.'

'I still don't see what that's got to do with his death, or Catherine's.'

'Well, I did a bit more digging — *geddit?* — and there are quite a few listings for Kingsleigh going back several years.

There's a healthy trade in old bits and bobs here. Not just that, though. On one of the detectorist forums, Dylan had put up a "Wanted" post. Hang on, I took a screenshot. Here it is. *"Wanted: Good money paid for artefacts relating to Kingsleigh, Somerset. Any condition, any era considered."'*

Ant leaned forward. 'Okay, well, that *is* interesting. Can you send me the screenshot?'

'Sure.'

'I'll write it down, too.' Ant found a pencil stub in his pocket and carefully wrote, *Dylan. Buying and selling.* He'd have to remember to tell the boys about it tomorrow, add it to their incident board. In the meantime, though, there was a pint to finish, and maybe he'd have room for another one, if Saggy was paying.

Later, as he walked back to Bob's, he mulled over the case, or two cases. It was turning chilly now. His hands were cold. He dug them into his pockets, then remembered how warm Bea's hand had felt in his. She really hadn't sounded good when he rang her earlier. He checked his phone. It was nearly eleven. A bit late to ring on a work night, but it would go to voicemail if she was already asleep. He dialled her number and felt butterflies mixing with the cider in his stomach when he heard her voice.

'Ant?'

'Hey, Bea. Is this too late? Were you asleep?'

'No, I was up. Where are you?'

'Just walking back to Bob's. I wanted to check that you were okay. You sounded rattled earlier.'

'Yeah. I was. It was weird vibes at Malcolm's. I think he only asked me up there because his son, Ed, saw me at the town council offices earlier. I think he reported back to his dad, and it was like he was sussing me out or something.' Her voice trailed off.

Ant wondered for a moment if they'd lost the connection. 'Bea? Are you still there?'

'I'm still here. Ed turned up at Malcolm's as well. He gives me the creeps. I got out as quickly as I could.'

'Do you really want to get involved in this council stuff, Bea? They sound a bit dodgy to me.'

'Well, I sort of am involved already. You know I went to see Wendy Fox . . .'

'Yeah.'

'The thing is—' she paused — 'No, I'm not supposed to tell you.'

'You've got to tell me now. You can't leave it like that.'

'I promised I wouldn't.'

'Just whisper it. That doesn't count.'

At the other end of the line, Bea chuckled. 'All right,' she said. 'Just *swear* to me that you won't tell anyone else.'

'I won't.'

'We looked up some of the items that Dylan had ringed in his book. They should have been in the town council's storeroom, but they weren't. They're missing.'

'Oh really,' said Ant, and it felt for the first time in this investigation that things were starting to fall into place. 'Saggy just told me that someone in K-town is selling old stuff like that online, and that Dylan was getting involved. Are you thinking what I'm thinking?'

'Yeah,' said Bea. 'I think I am. Can you send me some links? I can report back to Wendy. If we can find out who is dealing in this stuff, I reckon we'll have identified our thief, and maybe the person who killed Dylan.'

'We?' said Ant. 'You and me? Or you and Wendy?'

'Wendy wants to set a trap and catch the thief red-handed. I think we might have found the way to do it now.'

'Bea, do you think it's time to call the cops? We're on to something here, but it could be dangerous.'

'It's not really up to me, Ant. I shouldn't even have told you what I did.'

'But you did, and I know what you know now, and you know what I know, and it looks like it joins together.'

'I'll talk to Wendy in the morning and see what she says. Don't tell anyone else yet. Remember, you promised.'

'Okay, cool. But I'm starting to feel very uneasy about all this, Bea.'

'It's fine, Ant. Wendy's the most sensible, competent person I've met for a long time. She'll know what to do. Anyway, it's getting late now. I'll see you tomorrow, yeah?'

'Yeah, okay. Night, Bea.'

'Night.'

He'd reached the front of Bob's house now, but before he went inside, Ant made another call. He didn't give away any secrets, but he wasn't happy just to leave things in other people's hands. If he was right about what was going on, the stakes were very high indeed.

CHAPTER FIFTY-TWO

The first thing that Bea saw when she checked her phone the next morning was a message notification from Ant.

Item for sale. A link was attached. She clicked on it and it opened a page featuring a small spoon with a plaited design to the handle. It was described as '*small wooden spoon, possibly seventeenth century*'. The seller was KT23 and the location was Kingsleigh, Somerset.

She reached for her laptop and checked in the town council online archive list. Bingo! The spoon listed was either the same or very similar to one that should have been safely tucked away in the storeroom.

Even though it was only just gone seven, she tried Ant's number. Surprisingly, he was awake.

'Saggy found it,' he said. 'He sent me the link. Looks like it's from the same seller, and it's only been up for three days. So, they're still active. If we want to catch them, this is our chance.'

'It can't be "we", Ant. Remember, you don't know anything about this. I'll tell Wendy about this listing, though, and see what she says. The obvious thing is for one of us to pose as a buyer and arrange to meet them.'

'You'd have to use a fake profile, I reckon. People will know who Wendy Fox is, and to be honest, a lot of people in Kingsleigh would recognise you, Bea. Taylor's a bit of a computer whizz. He could tell you how to do it.'

'Ant, we can't tell anyone else!'

'We don't have to say what it's for.'

'I don't know. I'll talk to Wendy. I'll see you later.'

She was about to ring off when Ant said, 'Bea, will you let me know what you decide? Whatever you choose to do, I'd like to be your backup, or at least be on standby, in case you need me. I won't tell the others.'

'Okay. We'd better get a move on, though. I haven't even got out of bed yet.'

'Plenty of time!'

Bea smiled to herself. They were always going to have different attitudes to timekeeping. Some things would never change.

There was a 'Closed' sign up in the town council office door when Bea walked past on her way to work, but some movement inside caught her eye. She stopped and peered in, cupping her hand across her forehead to cut out the reflection. At the back of the office, Wendy Fox was emerging from the door to the basement. She squinted as she spotted Bea, then smiled in recognition and came over to unlock the door.

'Bea! That was good timing. Come in. I got here early to check the other items in the book. They're all gone. All of them, but I've got a new theory. Do you want to sit down for a minute?'

'I can't really stay,' said Bea. 'I've got to be in work in ten minutes. What's your theory, though?'

'I was thinking about this book,' Wendy said, brandishing Dylan's copy. 'We thought that Dylan was on the trail of the thief, but what if it was actually him? He was the one taking things from the stores, under the cover of doing local research. It could have been going on for years. And I trusted him. He was in and out so frequently — the only councillor who went there without one of the staff.'

'So that book is a record of his crimes?' said Bea, trying out the idea for size. It didn't square at all with her knowledge of the man. As a teacher, he had been known for his straight-forward approach and fairness. From everything Ant had said about him, he carried these qualities with him in everything else he did. If he *did* turn out to have been pilfering valuable artefacts, Ant would be gutted.

'Exactly!' said Wendy. 'I mean, I didn't want to consider it. Dylan was an excellent councillor and, I thought, a really good guy, but it's kind of obvious, isn't it? Sometimes you have to think the unthinkable and put personal feelings aside. It's here in black and white, or, rather, pencil.'

Wendy looked Bea directly in the eye, with an air of tri-umph. 'I mean, we'll have to come clean about it at some point, think about a carefully worded and timed statement, but maybe there's a way to do it without trashing the repu-tation of the council. Something along the lines of "historic losses now resolved" or something like that. It's possible that we might not even have to name Dylan. I know it's sentimen-tal, but it would be a shame to have people think badly of him. He did a lot of good.'

Bea was aware of time marching on. She was pretty sure she'd be late now, even if she ran the length of the high street, which wasn't going to happen anyway. But she couldn't leave just yet. There was a flaw in Wendy's theory, which couldn't go unchallenged.

'I don't think that adds up, though, Wendy,' said Bea. 'The thing is, I was hoping to see you because I think I've found some of the items for sale online. It's been going on for ages.'

Wendy pursed her lips. 'So, that's where Dylan was sell-ing them. It all fits together, doesn't it?'

'It would do, if there hadn't been a new listing three days ago. Whoever has been trying to sell these things is still active. For obvious reasons, it can't be Dylan.'

'Oh Bea.' Wendy looked crestfallen. 'This is awful. Just for a moment then I thought that it was all tied up. I mean, it was still shocking but we could deal with it, learn some lessons and move on. The thought that it's one of my staff, my trusted team, is just devastating.'

'I'm sorry,' said Bea. 'But that's how it looks. The thief is still out there, and it has to be someone who has access to the stores. It's also possible that they killed Dylan to silence him. I think we should tell the police what we know.'

Wendy's face was ashen. 'I'll need to tell Malcolm.'

At the mention of his name, a shiver went up Bea's spine. Yesterday's visit to the Sillitoe house had been so uncomfortable. All her instincts told her that Malcolm or Ed, or perhaps both of them, had something to do with this.

'Do you have to tell him?' she said. 'Surely Ed is one of the suspects. He's got free access to the stores. And Malcolm himself knows where the keys are . . .'

Wendy frowned. 'You're right. God, this is a difficult situation, Bea. As a clerk, Malcolm is my line manager. But then I need to weigh up my responsibilities to the other councillors, my staff and the people of the town as a whole.'

'Surely, if we're talking about criminal offences, that overrides everything?'

She sighed. 'Yes. You're right, but I've got a duty to do things in the least damaging way possible. I wonder if we should go ahead with the sting idea? If we knew who we were dealing with, it would help me negotiate all the angles. If there's an item for sale now, why don't we buy it, arrange the handover and see who turns up?'

'Yes, I agree that we could set that up, but we can't do this on our own. It's too dangerous. We need backup. We could ask people we trust — I've got some mates that would help — or we could go to the police. It's time to call in reinforcements.'

242

CHAPTER FIFTY-THREE

'Testing, testing, can you hear me, Wendy?' Bea tipped her chin down a little and spoke quietly, hoping that the tiny microphone would pick up her words. It was attached to a wire that trailed round her neck and inside her coat to a battery pack clipped at her waist. She listened for a response through her wireless earbuds.

'Loud and clear, Bea.' Wendy was sitting in her Audi in a quiet spot on one side of the car park.

'Ant?' said Bea. 'Can you hear?'

'Yup. Roger that.' Despite her nerves, Bea smiled. He was really embracing his undercover persona. In fact, she could see him lurking by one of the trolley parks. Although his shift had finished a couple of hours ago, he'd held on to his Costsave high-vis jacket which he was wearing over the top of a hoodie, looking exactly like he did when he was at work. It was, Bea thought, excellent cover for surveillance.

Similarly, Dean was taking Tyson for a very slow, sniffy walk along the edges of the Costsave site. No one would give him a second glance or suspect that he was dawdling with a purpose. He'd just passed a man in overalls who was rodding a drain in the road outside, and Bea could see he was having trouble getting Tyson to move away from the tempting smells. Further round, Tyler was sitting astride his bicycle, apparently absorbed in his phone. He looked a little bit like he was engaged on county lines business, just waiting for his next call, which, Bea thought, looked authentic for Kingsleigh, but made her feel a bit sad. It was so easy for kids Tyler's age and younger to get drawn into things that set them on the wrong path. She was glad that he, at least, was on the straight and narrow. Last but not least, Saggy was sitting with Bob in Bob's Vauxhall estate, or 'nerve centre' as Saggy liked to call it, on the opposite side of the car park to Wendy. Bob had been extremely reluctant to take part but had been persuaded by Dot, who had appealed to his protective side. 'I couldn't live with myself if anything else happened to Bea,' she had said, 'and neither could you.'

It had been surprisingly easy to set up. Tyler had created a fake email and a new eBay account for Bea. She had then made an offer for the spoon, which she and Wendy judged was high enough to be tempting but not too high to raise suspicion in the seller. Bea had taken great delight in sending Wendy a text immediately after checking her own phone one lunchtime. *Offer accepted. Game on.*

The seller had agreed to leave the parcel in one of the Pay and Pick Up lockers at seven that evening and message when it was done. It had been Ant's idea to arrange the deal in the Costsave car park after their suggestion of a face-to-face hand-over had been rejected. The block of Pay and Pick Up lockers had been in place for six months or so, over which time he had often casually watched people leaving and collecting parcels there. Most of it was innocuous, of course, but occasionally his street sense alerted him to someone whose dealings might not be strictly legitimate. Some packages, he thought, might well feature on the national register of stolen goods or spark excitement in a police sniffer dog. Not that it was any of his business.

It was five to seven. The store wasn't busy, but there was a steady stream of early-evening shoppers. Bea pretended to examine the racks of plants near the store entrance. They were a mixture of extremely tired summer flowers at knockdown prices and new 'Colour Your Winter' plants that were just in this week. Bea checked the time on her phone again and looked at a tray of plants with a few daisy-like blooms drooping on the end of wilting stalks. They were so sickly and sad that she felt sorry for them. She was no gardener, but perhaps these poor specimens would revive if she gave them a bit of water and love at home. Already marked down, they would cost next to nothing with her staff discount.

'Bea! What are you doing here?'

She spun around to see Neville looming at her. 'I just, er, spotted these earlier, and Mum said she fancied the sound of them,' she said, improvising wildly.

'Well, you know what they say,' he said with a smirk. 'You touch it, you buy it.'

'What? Really?'

'No, it's not official Costsave policy, but if you squeeze that leaf any harder it will come off in your hand.'

'Oh, yes. Sorry.' Bea let go of the leaf and it came away and fell to the ground by her feet. 'Oops.'

'I'll pretend I didn't see that. Those plants aren't at their best, are they? I think I'll tell Tyler to remove them from sale tomorrow. Goodnight, Bea.'

'Night, Neville.'

Bea watched Neville stalk away across the car park. She hoped that he wouldn't spot Ant and quiz him on why he was still apparently on duty long after he'd clocked off. 'Sorry about that. Did I miss anything?' she said into her coat.

'No. All quiet,' said Wendy.

'What's the time?'

'Seven o'clock. Eyes peeled, everyone.'

Bea looked across the storefront to the lockers, but there was nobody near them. A woman got into a car nearby and Bea heard the gentle whine of an electric engine starting up. The noise was suddenly drowned out by the throaty noise of a larger vehicle. A dark green council van pulled into a nearby space and Bea's stomach lurched. 'Jesus,' she said, 'it's Ed Sillitoe. Bloody hell, I think we've got him.'

'Keep calm, Bea.' Wendy's voice was steady and reassuring in her ear. 'Just stay where you are. Keep your distance. Has everyone got eyes on him?'

'Camera ready here,' said Saggy, who had been proudly showing off his long lens to the boys earlier. He was starting to relish his role as the team's tech guy. The little spy kits of microphones and earbuds had been surprisingly affordable. He'd intended to sell them on after tonight, but perhaps he'd keep them for future ops.

The van door slammed and Ed strode towards the store. He didn't deviate from his path towards the lockers, but kept right on towards the entrance.

'He's heading straight for me,' said Bea. 'What do I do?'

'Just look at the plants,' said Wendy. 'It's all good.'

Bea tried to turn her back towards Ed as he approached and focused her attention on a withered leaf.

'I wouldn't bother if I were you. They're all a bit past it,' she heard Ed saying, and realised he was talking to her. 'Oh, it's you—' He laughed. 'No offence, Bea, but I don't think plant care is your thing. If I was your boss, I'd keep you on the checkouts.'

'Haha, yeah, right.' She tried to think of something more intelligent to say, but he wasn't stopping to chat and had already crossed the threshold and grabbed a basket. He walked through the fresh produce and disappeared round the end of the aisle.

'Did you get that? Is my cover blown?' said Bea into her lapel.

'Maybe he's playing it cool. Getting some shopping before he goes to the lockers,' said Wendy.

'I don't think he was carrying anything.'

'It's going to be a small package, though. Could be in a pocket. Stay put. Let's see what he does next.'

Bea couldn't stand the thought of Ed seeing her hanging round the plants when he left, so she walked away from the lockers and pretended to study the community noticeboard. After a couple of minutes, Tyler squawked, 'Subject emerging from front door. This is it, guys.'

She glanced sideways and there he was, now carrying a plastic bag. Without looking left or right, he headed back to his van, climbed in, put his shopping on the seat next to him and drove off.

'Shit,' said Bea. 'Is that it?'

'Just shopping then,' said Ant. 'Not our man.'

'I think he suspected something and changed his plans,' said Bea. 'I'm sorry. I blew it.'

'Let's just wait a minute.' Wendy's voice was cool and reassuring.

Bea sighed loudly. 'How long shall we give it?'

'Another ten minutes.'

'I've got chops going cold at home,' said Bob. 'Dot said she'd do dinner for half past. Five minutes, then I'm off.'

Bea read all the cards on the board, which reflected Kingsleigh society in all its glory. Babysitting and dog-walking services advertised, items for sale, piano lessons offered. She made a mental note of someone selling an electronic keyboard. She'd always fancied learning to play. Perhaps this was a literal sign that it was time to get started.

'Okay,' said Wendy, eventually. 'I think I'm calling it. Time to go home, everyone. Sorry it was a waste of time.'

Bea heard sounds of agreement and frustration through her earpiece, but she wasn't quite ready to give up. 'Why don't I send them a message through the app? Just to ask if there's a hold-up. Hang on.'

Ant had already abandoned his post by the trolleys and was walking towards her. When he got close to Wendy's car, he stopped and she wound down her window. Bea quickly opened the app on her phone, found her notification of the agreed sale and clicked on the 'Message' button.

Can't find delivery notification. Is there a problem? She pressed send. Above the general grumbling from the others over the wires, she thought she heard the ping of someone's phone.

Then through her earpiece she heard a very loud, 'What the fuck?' from Ant. 'I'll take that, thank you.'

'Ant?' she said. 'Are you okay?' She looked across towards him. He was still standing by Wendy's shiny black car, but now he had his hand up in the air and was holding something aloft.

'How dare you?' Wendy's normally calm voice was filled with fury. 'Give that back. That's private property.'

What on earth was Ant playing at? Bea didn't know what was going on, but it looked like Ant was making a complete fool of himself. She started running towards them, as did Tyler and Dean. She heard a couple of car doors slam as Saggy and Bob abandoned their car, too, and legged it across the site.

As Bea got near to the car, the driver's door opened and Wendy stepped out. Ant backed away. He was holding a phone.

'Give that back. Now.' Wendy was trying to speak with icy authority, but Bea detected an undernote of something else. Was it panic?

'Ant,' Bea called out. 'What the hell are you doing? Give Wendy's phone back.'

Ant danced further away. 'She's your seller, Bea. She's the one you've been messaging.'

His words didn't make sense.

'Don't be silly. She helped me set it all up. It was her idea to catch the thief.'

'That's right,' said Wendy. 'I knew it was a mistake involving other people, Bea. We should have kept it between ourselves. Come on, now. Give it back to me.' She held her hand out towards Ant.

'Bea,' said Ant, 'send your seller another message. It doesn't matter what it says. Do it now.'

Bea looked from Ant to Wendy and back again.

'Do it. Please.'

248

She still had the app open. Just to prove him wrong, she typed another message — *Where are you?* — and pressed send.

The phone in Ant's hand pinged loud and clear, and, finally, the truth started to dawn on Bea. Wendy had access to the town council treasures. She could easily remove them, little by little over time. And when anyone got close to finding out what was going on, she manipulated them, duped them, or, in Dylan's case, got rid of them.

'Oh my God,' Bea murmured. 'Guys, we need the police. Somebody ring them.'

'No need,' said Bob. 'Hey! Over here!'

The man in overalls, who had been clearing the drain, was already observing them. He put down his tools, hopped over the low boundary wall and came jogging towards them. He was joined by another, who had been leaning against a lamppost having a vape. Then Tom appeared from around the corner of the building, where the staff entrance was.

Bea was confused, then both disappointed and relieved. One of her friends, sworn to secrecy, had squealed and told the police about their secret operation. The watchers had been watched all along.

Wendy wasn't done yet, though. When the first officer to reach them identified himself, she straightened her jacket and said, 'Ah, good. Officer, I'm Wendy Fox, clerk to the town council. I want you to arrest this man. He's stolen my phone.'

Ant looked at her evenly. 'You've all just heard her admit it's hers. And this is the phone used by the person who is selling stolen goods. You are the thief, Wendy Fox, and I think—' here his voice wavered — 'I think that you killed my friend.'

CHAPTER FIFTY-FOUR

Bea, Ant and the others spent a long evening giving statements at Kingsleigh police station. They were allowed to go home in dribs and drabs and it was almost midnight when Bea shambled out of the interview room, feeling like a limp rag and not relishing the thought of the walk home. She was relieved to see Ant and Bob waiting for her in the lobby.

'Your carriage awaits,' said Bob. 'Couldn't let you walk on a day like this.'

'Thanks, Bob.'

'You all right, Bea? Need a hug?' said Ant.

'I just want to go home,' she said, but quietly slipped her hand into his as they left the building and walked over to Bob's car. She sat in the front passenger seat, while Ant climbed into the back.

'Wendy Fox. I still can't believe it,' said Bea. 'I was completely taken in by her.'

'Don't beat yourself up,' said Bob. 'She had everyone just where she wanted them. The councillors, the staff, the rest of the town.'

'Was it you who told the police about our sting, Bob?'

'It was me,' said Ant, much to her surprise. 'I rang Tom.'

'Blimey, Ant. You've changed.'

'I know, but having seen what happened to Dylan, I couldn't bear the thought of the same thing happening to you. Obviously, I still think he's a tosser but talking to him seemed like the lesser of two evils.'

'Aw . . .' Bea twisted in her seat a little and reached her hand behind. Ant held on to it and gently stroked her thumb. 'Did you know it was her?'

'I thought she was a bit sus, but then I wondered if I was just jealous — you hadn't wanted anything to do with the boys and me and our investigation, but suddenly you and her were a chummy little team.'

Bea could see that it could have looked that way. 'I was flattered that someone like her rated me. She was so encouraging, like having a mentor or something. I was impressed with her nice suits and all those letters after her name. Then, when I went to her with the book, it became our little secret — she trusted me. I can't believe I was so naïve.'

'Like I said, you weren't the only one.' Bob put his indicator on and turned into Bea's road. 'Everyone thought she was beyond reproach. That's why she got away with it for so long. It only went wrong for her when Dylan noticed that things had gone missing.'

Bea shuddered. 'She even tried to pin it on him,' she said. 'She tried to convince me that he was the thief and that it would all just quietly go away because he'd died.'

'She had some nerve, I'll give her that.'

'Why do you think she killed him at the allotments?'

'Unless she confesses, we might never know,' said Bob, 'but I imagine she knew he was on to her. She either arranged to meet him or went up there on the off chance. Perhaps he tried to reason with her. Maybe she offered him in on the deal. Whatever went on, she must have realised that he wasn't going to keep quiet. She had to silence him.'

'Bloody hell. It all adds up, doesn't it?' said Ant.

'Yeah. It's just a shame that poor old Dylan got the worst of her. A crying shame,' said Bob. 'Here we are. Home safe and sound.' He pulled the car up to the kerb outside Bea's house. The downstairs lights were still on and they all saw the curtains move and Queenie's anxious face peer out. Bob raised his hand in greeting and Bea undid her seatbelt and clambered out.

'Thanks, Bob,' she said.

'No problem. See you tomorrow. Well, later today.'

Ant had got out of the back seat and moved round to take Bea's place next to Bob.

'You were very brave today,' he said to Bea as they stood on the pavement.

'And you were very sensible. Thanks, Ant. What would I do without you?' She leaned forward and kissed his cheek. 'Night, night.'

'Night, Bea.'

He watched as she walked up the path to the front door, which was now open. Queenie stood on the threshold, silhouetted against the warm glow of light.

'Come on, lad,' Bob said. 'Stop mooning out there and get in. It's past my bedtime.'

Ant sighed and got into the car. 'What a day,' he said. 'You don't fancy grabbing a quick kebab on the way home, do you?'

CHAPTER FIFTY-FIVE

The staff briefing was over, but, like naughty children at school, Bea, Ant, Bob, Dean and Tyler had been asked to stay behind. The previous evening's incident had been glossed over by George when she'd addressed the whole staff team. She'd merely thanked all those involved in assisting the police, reassuring customers and keeping Costsave open and running during the operation. Now, however, Bea could see the displeasure glittering in her eyes and she wasn't the only one to notice.

'Here we go,' Ant whispered in her ear. 'Bollocking incoming.'

The room fell silent. George took her time, looking at each one in turn, before she started. 'You know why you're here. Part of me admires the way you work together. You support one another and obviously have each other's backs.' Bea relaxed a little. Perhaps this wasn't going to be so bad after all. 'The other part of me is utterly dismayed at you using the store's private land, without permission, to run an amateur detective "sting"—' she used her index fingers to form speech marks — 'in some cases dressing up as store employees, arranging to meet someone that you suspected was violent and therefore wilfully endangering both staff and customers.'

Yikes, thought Bea. Perhaps they had pushed it too far this time.

'I'm dismayed. I'm angry. I'm very, very disappointed. You may not have noticed, but as a manager I'm constantly trying to give staff the opportunity and space to excel. I admire initiative and teamwork. However, I expect to see this expressed in your work here, in supporting the vision and values of Costsave. I do not expect to see staff acting like they're in an episode of *Starsky and Hutch*.'

Beside her, Bea sensed Ant twitch. She glanced up and the little muscles beside his mouth were working. She dug her elbow into his arm to try and bring him back into line, but George had noticed something was up.

'Something funny, Ant?'

Ant pressed his lips together firmly in an effort to regain his composure, before answering. 'No, George.'

'No. It's not funny. Where was I?'

'*Starsky and Hutch*,' said Neville, helpfully.

Ant made a snorting sound. On the other side of him, Dean emitted a high-pitched wheezing noise, as he, too, wrestled with growing hysteria.

'Thank you, Neville. Oh, it's no good. I've lost my thread. I hope you've all understood how I feel, though.'

Neville turned his head and whispered something.

'Oh yes,' George added. 'We have discovered unauthorised notes and pictures fixed onto the wall in the stores, in what appears to be an unofficial rest and recreation area. I need to remind you that there is one staff room at Costsave and one only. I want this area shipshape by the end of the day. Is that clear?'

Dean and Tyler mumbled their agreement.

'The bottom line is that you can do whatever you want in your spare time, if it's legal, but you cannot and must not drag Costsave into anything that might damage our reputation, or cause harm to staff or customers. I will be adding a note on all your records.'

'Is that an official warning?' said Bob.

Neville looked at him warily, tightening his grip on his clipboard.

'No,' said George, 'it's a note.'

Bob nodded. 'Fair enough.'

'Now, please get to your stations as quickly as possible, and let's say no more about it. Except, Bea, can you stay here, please?'

Ant tightened his jaw and stood a little straighter. 'You can't pick on Bea,' he said. 'If she's in extra trouble, then I reckon we all should be.'

George sighed. 'I wish to speak with her on an unconnected matter.'

Ant held his hands up and joined the others in filing out of the staff room. He sent Bea a backwards glance as he left. She raised her eyebrows and shrugged.

'Do you want to join me in my office for a minute?' said George.

It wasn't really a question. Once in there, George closed the door. 'Do sit down.'

Bea found her mouth getting dry. What on earth was coming next?

'A little bird told me that you are applying to be a town councillor,' said George.

'Oh, um, I was looking into it, but I don't think it's really for me,' said Bea, feeling a rush of relief as she said the words. 'I like working here, I really do, but I was just feeling like I wanted — needed — something more. Sorry, that sounds awful, doesn't it? I do want to make a difference somehow. Whatever I do, it won't affect my job here, though. I mean, if it's volunteering or something.'

George smiled. 'I'm sorry to hear you've changed your mind. I was just going to wish you luck.'

'Oh!'

'And it's perfectly okay to want more. You absolutely shouldn't apologise for that. You've got great potential, Bea.

I'm not sure about your detective work, but I can see you rising up the ranks at Costsave, if that's where you picture yourself. But whatever path you choose, think big. That's my advice.'

Bea couldn't hide her surprise. 'Right. Well, thank you.'

'And I'd like you to think you can come and talk to me about career options. We can chat informally, or Costsave runs a mentoring scheme — you might want to look it up, see if you think a more formal arrangement would be helpful.'

'Oh, wow.' Bea grinned. 'Thank you.'

The phone on George's desk rang and she nodded to Bea before she reached to pick it up. Bea understood that she was dismissed and tottered out of the office, then headed downstairs to the safe haven of checkout number six. She pondered what George had said on her way. She realised she had been thinking of Wendy Fox as a sort of mentor — had been wildly impressed that someone like that would take her under her wing — but it seemed like there was a better role model closer to home.

Dot looked at her searchingly as she reached the checkouts. 'You okay, love?'

'Yeah, I'm fine.' Bea started going through her morning opening-up routine. 'Just had a bit of a pep talk from George. A nice one. I think she might be trying to encourage me to go for promotion. She kind of liked it when I said I wanted more out of life.'

Dot's elegantly drawn eyebrows shot up. 'You actually said that to her?'

Bea smiled. 'Yeah. Cheeky cow, aren't I?'

'No — well, yes — but why shouldn't you want more? You're young. You're smart.'

'Pack it in, Dot. I'm blushing.'

'I'm only sorry I pushed you in the direction of the council. I had no idea there was all that going on.'

Bea waved her hand. 'Don't be silly. Nobody knew. It's not a completely bad idea, either. It's just, with everything, I think I'll give it a few years. Both the Sillitoes might not be murderers, but they still creep me out a bit and I don't think I could hack endless meetings, especially not after a day at work. I'd much rather be tucked up on the sofa watching the telly.'

'Or tucked up with Ant?'

Bea quickly looked round, checking no one else had heard. 'Shush. Maybe. He's actually asked me on a date. We're going to see how that goes.'

Dot smiled to herself, remembering Ant's lighter on Bea's bedroom floor.

'What?'

'Nothing, darling. I just think it might go very well. You two are good together.'

'We'll see.' Bea was smiling too.

'Ooh, talk of the devil.' Dot nodded towards the door. 'Blimey, he looks grim.'

Expecting Ant, Bea turned round to see Malcolm Sillitoe picking up a wire basket. Dot's assessment was true. Malcolm looked like he'd aged ten years overnight as he walked straight-backed but very slowly through the fresh vegetable display. He disappeared from view and Bea got on with serving the trickle of early customers, but, after ten minutes or so, he appeared at her checkout.

'Good morning, Bea,' he said, as he placed his shopping on the conveyor belt — a large jar of coffee and a dozen iced doughnuts. Suddenly, Bea had a flashback to Wendy buying the same. At the time, it had helped Bea form a picture of her as a caring boss. How deceptive first impressions could be.

'Morning, Malcolm,' she said. 'Treats for the troops?'

'Yes. We're partially open today. Wendy's office is out of bounds — the police are in there now, gathering evidence — but we're trying to maintain our service to the public. The staff are obviously very shocked. Wendy's deputy is covering her post for the time being.' He paused. 'I hear you were involved in unmasking her.'

'Sort of. It was my friend, really — Ant — who realised first. I was absolutely gobsmacked. I never suspected her.'

He put both hands on the side of the checkout as if he needed some support to stay standing. 'Me neither, Bea,' he said, 'although Ed told me last night that he had realised some of the artefacts were missing. He thought it might be her and had been trying to keep an eye on things but hadn't got any firm evidence.'

Bea felt her face colouring up. Ed had been her number-one suspect. Perhaps, he, in turn, had suspected her of teaming up with Wendy. What a tangled web.

'Has she been charged yet?'

Malcolm nodded. 'The police told me this morning. She's been charged with theft and murder. It seems Dylan Bradley was on to her, too.'

'What an evil woman,' said Bea. 'You just can't tell looking at people, can you?'

'No.' He took a deep breath and stood up straight again. 'Now, what do I owe you?'

Bea told him the total and he paid with his card, then gathered up his goods.

'Malcolm,' she said, 'before you go, I should tell you that I've decided not to apply to be a councillor. I don't think it's the right time for me.'

'That's a shame,' he said. 'That's definitely the council's loss. Thank you for letting me know.'

He turned and walked towards the door, with the weary gait of someone carrying a lot more than a jar of coffee and a box of doughnuts. In fact, he looked like he had the weight of the world on his shoulders.

CHAPTER FIFTY-SIX

At break time, Ant went straight to the stores to help disassemble the incident room. Dean and Tyler had already started, taking out drawing pins and bits of red string. The sticky notes were still up.

They all paused and looked at the wall.

'Wendy Fox wasn't even on our main suspect list,' said Tyler, sadly. 'I didn't even think it could be a woman . . . I guess it was the violence of the murder. When I told Scout, she just said that I should know better, shouldn't I? And it's true.'

'Deadlier than the male, aren't they?' said Dean.

'Not all women,' said Ant.

Dean pulled a face. 'Maybe not deadly, but scary.' He started counting on his fingers. 'Wendy Fox, George, my mum . . .'

He got the laugh he was going for, but it was muted and brief. Taking apart the man cave felt like the end of an era that they'd all enjoyed.

'I wonder who dobbed us in?' said Dean. 'One of the nightshift lot, I suppose.'

'Probably no one, mate,' said Ant. 'You know how Neville prowls round this place, poking his nose in. He probably found it himself.'

'He did indeed.'

They all jumped and swivelled round at the sound of Neville's voice. He was standing a couple of metres behind them, clipboard clutched to his chest. 'I've known about your little hidey-hole for quite some time, but I was prepared to turn a blind eye. You went too far, though. You always go too far.'

Ant felt that the last remarks were directed at him. 'Neville, is this about me leaving? About everything going wrong between us?'

Neville sniffed loudly. 'Of course not. This is about your behaviour as an employee of Costsave. I would never let any personal upset impinge on my role here.'

Personal upset. The words struck Ant hard. He and Neville had forged a rather touching friendship earlier in the year, but he'd managed to trash it through his own behaviour.

'Neville,' he said, 'I never meant to hurt your feelings. I was rude and I was thoughtless. It was a terrible way to repay your and Carole's kindness to me. I'd like to make it up to you both, if I can. I'd like to make you understand that I'm truly sorry.'

To his surprise, Neville started blinking rapidly. 'That's all I needed, Ant. A sincere apology.'

'I did say sorry before.'

'You said the word, Anthony. You didn't mean it.'

There was a hint of petulance in his tone, but Ant lifted his hands up. 'You got me. It's true. I do mean it now, though. I've had a chat with Carole, too, and I think she accepted it.'

'Yes, she told me. She also said I was being too hard on you.'

Ant smiled. 'She's a bit of a diamond, isn't she?'

'She certainly is.' He got a large white cotton hanky out of his trouser pocket and blew his nose vigorously. 'Right, keep up the good work. I'll come back at the end of the day and make sure it's all gone.'

'Do we *have* to take it down?' said Tyler and they all looked at him.

'Of course,' said Neville. 'You heard George this morning.'

'Only, it's not all over, is it? I get that we can take the Dylan stuff down, but the other side, the Catherine side — we still don't know who killed her, do we?'

Now they all, including Neville, faced the wall. Catherine's name was in the middle of a sea of Post-it notes.

'It's a very cold case, though, isn't it?' Neville said. 'Difficult to find new clues after all this time. I wonder if Charles knows more than he thinks he does. You seem close to him, Ant. It might be worth having another chat with him . . .' He paused. 'What am I saying? This isn't work appropriate. It has to go.'

'We could bung all this up in our garage, if you like,' said Dean.

Ant shook his head. 'No, I think Neville's right. It was a long time ago. We did what we set out to do — we found out who killed Dylan. We probably need to leave it now.'

Bob appeared carrying four mugs of tea on a tray. He did a double take when he saw Neville. 'Oh, sorry,' he said, looking down at the tray. 'I just brought this to encourage the troops. I know we shouldn't have hot drinks in here.'

Neville waved a dismissive hand. 'It's fine, Bob. Just for today.' He walked past him and out of the stores.

Ant watched him go. 'You know, I almost think he'd like to be part of the gang.'

The others laughed nervously. 'Absolutely not,' said Dean. 'You've got to draw the line somewhere. If he's allowed to join, I'm out.'

Ant tipped his head from side to side as if weighing up the options.

'Shut up, Ant,' said Dean, even though he hadn't said a word.

'What shall we do with all these notes?' said Tyler.

'I'll take them,' said Ant. 'I'll stick them in the back of my notebook. And close the cover. I wanted justice for Dylan and that's what we got. Job done. And on Sunday, we'll celebrate him at the show. If his French beans don't win, I'll eat my hat.'

CHAPTER FIFTY-SEVEN

'Big day tomorrow. Nothing more we can do now until the morning,' said Bob.

He and Ant stood and admired their lush green plot. People were dotted across the whole site — examining, assessing, chatting with their neighbours or just standing or sitting quietly. Two plots along from theirs, Cyril and Lionel were deep in conversation. Cyril, of course, had been released without charge and had been spending hours at the allotments making up for lost time. When they'd got there this evening, Charles had made a point of walking across and shaking his hand. Cyril had asked Charles's opinion on his remaining tomatoes and they'd studied them for a few minutes, discussing the aesthetic merits of various options.

'Look at them. Two old friends comparing trusses,' said Bob, fondly, and Ant tried to suppress a snort of laughter. 'Charles is going to miss all this, although there's nothing stopping him coming up here as a visitor. I'm going to miss it, too.'

When Charles wandered back to their plot, he walked slowly up and down, stopping here and there to examine a particular plant or brush a stray fly off a leaf. Finally, the three of them gathered next to Marvin. Ant wondered if he detected tears gathering in Charles's eyes.

'You've both done a wonderful job,' Charles said. 'I wish I could have pulled my weight this year, but it was all down to you.'

'Not at all, Charles,' said Bob. 'You've directed the whole operation from start to finish. We were just the manual labour.'

Charles smiled. 'Lionel was right, though. I'm not up to the job anymore. I haven't been for a few years. This is it, fellas. This is the end.'

'Not quite yet. I'm going to pick you up at seven o'clock sharp, remember, and we'll head straight up here.'

Ant screwed up his eyes and wrinkled his nose. 'Seven in the morning?'

'That's when it all happens,' said Bob. 'Selecting, cutting, trimming, cleaning — when everything is fresh and cool and at its best.'

Ant groaned. 'Can't we do it this evening? Bung everything in the fridge or something?'

'Absolutely not! And we've got to do Dylan's as well. We haven't got this far to fail at the final hurdle just because you want a lie-in. Come on, Ant. One last push.'

Ant sighed. 'Okay. I guess Marvin wouldn't fit in the fridge, anyway.'

They all looked down at their pride and joy, which they had fed and watered all summer, cosseted in a bed of straw, kept clean and slug-free. He was looking magnificent.

'Look at our boy,' said Ant. 'What a unit.'

'Best marrow I've ever had on this plot,' said Charles, proudly.

'It's going to be quite something harvesting him,' said Bob. 'A real moment. Come on, everyone, let's go home, get a good night's sleep. Early start tomorrow.'

'Do you mind if I just pay my respects one last time?' Charles was facing the bottom of the plots now, where a patch of freshly dug soil was the only remaining sign that a body had been found there.

'Of course. Take your time.'

Ant and Bob watched as he made his way unsteadily down the path. He was using two sticks now, leaning heavily on them. Beyond the perimeter hedge, the sun was setting, turning the sky blush-pink.

'Poor sod,' said Bob. 'I said I could help him arrange the funeral, but they haven't released the body yet. It's a hell of thing to deal with when you're eighty-three.'

'I kind of wish we hadn't found her. I mean he knows where she ended up, I suppose, but not who did it. It's not really a resolution, is it? It's all so sad.'

'It's very sad.'

They stood for a while. Ant couldn't help glancing back at Dylan's shed. Knowing who had killed him helped a little, but not that much. It didn't take away the great weight of loss, the shock of someone being there one minute and gone the next, the continuous feeling of missing him. He shivered and realised that the air temperature was dropping fast now as the sun finally disappeared.

'We should go. It's getting cold.'

'I'll fetch him,' said Bob. He walked down and talked to Charles before they both made their way back to him.

'It feels wrong leaving Marvin overnight. What if something happens to him?' said Ant.

Bob took him firmly by the arm. 'No more overnight shenanigans,' he said, in a tone that wouldn't brook any argument. 'Home and sleep now. Tomorrow is going to be a good day. Let's face it, we're all due one.'

CHAPTER FIFTY-EIGHT

'For God's sake, Mum, it's not the Chelsea Flower Show!'

Bea had been horrified by the outfit Queenie had chosen for the flower and produce show — a rose-patterned dress, pale pink jacket and a large straw hat decorated with a mound of plastic flowers. She herself had opted for smart casual, with a nice spotty blouse over her favourite jeans. But now, surveying the surprisingly large number of people waiting to be allowed into the marquee, she was rather proud of her mum, who wasn't the only one who had dressed up a bit. The smattering of hats and fascinators added an extra touch of colour to an already good-natured and cheerful crowd.

Ant had explained earlier that the competitors were going to be let in first and given ten minutes to walk around and see how their exhibits had done in the judging. Places in each class would be indicated by cards left next to the entries — red for first, and yellow for runner-up.

They met up with Ant near the ice cream hut. He charmed Queenie with a compliment and a kiss on the hand and then rather sheepishly planted a peck on the cheek for Bea, but was too nervous to speak much after that. They stood together watching people file into the park. Luckily it was dry underfoot, but Ant spotted Fatima having difficulty getting Mary's wheelchair across a rather bumpy patch of grass. He darted forward, retrieved a blanket that had fallen off Mary's knees and took over pushing duties until they reached a tarmacked path. When he came back to Bea and Queenie, he was visibly sweating. 'That's Lionel's wife, Mary, with her carer.'

'Mary? Oh, I used to see her in the Legion,' said Queenie. 'I wonder what's happened to her.'

'Alzheimer's,' said Ant. 'Lionel told me when I visited.'

'Oh, that poor woman,' Queenie said sadly. 'Nice to see her out and about, though.'

Ant was frowning.

'What's up, love?'

He wiped his face on his sleeve. 'Nothing. I'm just fed up with waiting. Want to get in there now and see the results.'

'Not long now,' said Bea. 'It's nearly ten to two.' She gave him an encouraging squeeze on the arm, but his face remained set in a grim expression.

Queenie gave a little shriek and Ant jumped like someone had applied a cattle prod to somewhere tender.

'What?' he said.

'It's Dot and Bob! Look! Dot's another member of the hat club! Cooee!'

'Is that all?' Ant rolled his eyes while Queenie trotted along the path to meet Dot and Bob as they walked along with Charles. Dot's headgear was a fancy fascinator involving flowers and a couple of jaunty feathers. It went very nicely with her shiny purple dress, which had a peplum at the waist.

'You're very jumpy, Ant,' said Bea. 'Want an ice cream to take your mind off it?'

'I couldn't, Bea,' he said shakily. 'I haven't eaten all day.'

Dot and Queenie stopped to take hat selfies, while Bob and Charles pressed on. As they reached Ant and Bea, the men all shook hands, which Bea thought was both oddly formal and a nice touch.

'This is it, gentlemen,' said Charles.

'I don't know if I can look.' Ant suddenly appeared in discomfort, braced his shoulders and tipped his head down. Then an alarming noise emerged from his mouth. 'I'm sorry, guys, I burp when I'm nervous.'

Bob patted him on the back, like he was winding a baby. 'Better out than in, Ant,' he said. 'Take it easy. Perhaps we should make our way through to the front. They'll be letting competitors in soon. Come on, boys.'

He and Charles started walking towards the crowd. Ant held back. He was squinting and seemed to be staring at something.

'What is it, Ant?' Bea said.

'I've just seen the tomato thief,' he said. 'At least, I think so. That lad over there, in the grey hoodie.'

Bea looked over to see a family group sitting on the grass near the play area. She recognised the woman as the one whose son had needed last-minute cookery ingredients. She was sitting with three children, one of whom was a wan-looking lad of about thirteen.

'Oh!' she said. 'That's Jaden. He's the thief, is he? I had a chat with his mum a week or two ago. She was—' she hesitated — 'well, like a lot of people at the moment, she was a bit strapped for cash.'

'I thought it was something like that,' said Ant. 'Nicking stuff cos his family needed it. I mean, it's still wrong but it's part of a bigger wrong, isn't it? Kids going hungry.'

'What did you see him take that night?'

'A cauliflower. One of Dylan's.'

Bea slapped her forehead. 'Cauliflower cheese!' she declared.

Ant looked at her quizzically.

'The Food Tech syllabus. It's the same every year. Tomatoes for Mediterranean pasta, cauliflower to go with a nice cheese sauce. He was taking things for his school cooking lesson.'

Understanding dawned in Ant's expression. 'What's next week, then? Do you remember?'

Bea racked her brains and then suddenly she could picture herself in the Food Tech classroom with her ingredients laid out, ready to use. 'Oh my God, Ant, I do! Mediterranean pasta, cauliflower cheese and then . . . stuffed marrow. Looks like Marvin had a lucky escape!'

'Bloody hell. I thought someone had been eyeing him up. Turns out they were. If Jaden had actually swiped him, though, I don't know what I would have done. It doesn't bear thinking about.'

'Well, luckily, he didn't. Are you going to say anything to him or tell anyone?'

Ant puffed his cheeks out. 'I reckon that lad's got enough going on without any extra hassle.'

An announcement came over the loudspeakers mounted on poles outside the tent.

'*Would all competitors make their way to the marquee. Competitors only, please.*'

Ant burped again, louder this time.

'Go on,' said Bea. 'It's the moment of truth. I'll catch you later. Good luck!'

CHAPTER FIFTY-NINE

'And now we're coming towards the end of a marvellous after-noon. It's nearly time to reveal who has won Best in Show. But before then, I need to thank everyone who has made this possible, including our sponsors . . .'

Lionel was in full flow on the stage, enjoying every minute. Despite her supposed disinterest in all things gardening, Bea was buzzing about the results of the competition. Cyril's remaining tomatoes had come through to secure a popular win. Dylan had posthumously won one category with a fine selection of runner beans, lovingly chosen, cleaned and displayed by Ant and Bob, another decision which had been well-received and met with a heartfelt round of applause. Charles (and by proxy Ant and Bob) had been an honourable runner-up in a couple of classes, but, of course, had won the vegetable marrow class with Marvin. It was all good fun, but the real thrill was yet to come. Ant had explained to Bea that the grand finale was like Crufts — Marvin would now be judged against the winners of all the other categories. Only one would be declared Best in Show and win a magnificent silver cup.

Bea's stomach felt all fluttery in anticipation. She could only imagine what Ant was feeling. He was standing next to her, jiggling one leg. When she glanced across, he was biting his lower lip so hard that a little bead of blood had appeared.

'Are you okay?' she said. 'Nerves getting to you?'

He licked the blood away, but it started oozing back. 'Bea, can I show you something?'

'Don't you want to watch the big reveal?'

'This is more important.'

Puzzled, she let him take her hand as they threaded their way through the crowd towards the back of the tent. He positioned himself next to Fatima and Mary Gittins, and drew Bea to his side.

'Look at her right hand,' he said in a low voice, tipping his head towards Mary.

Bea looked down. Mary's hands were resting in her lap. Her skin was pale, almost translucent and marked with age spots, but her nails, though short, were beautifully manicured. On the ring finger of her left hand she was wearing a simple gold band and a ring with a single diamond, while the same finger on her right hand bore a gold ring with a red stone, which looked a little battered and scratched.

Why did Ant want her to look at a ring on someone else's hand? Bea scrunched up her face in a 'I don't get it' expression and looked at Ant.

He raised his eyebrows and tipped his head towards Mary again.

Bea took another look.

Her right hand. A battered ring with a red stone.

Suddenly she felt a rushing sensation in her head, like she was on a big dipper at a funfair or diving deep underwater. She turned away from Mary and whispered into Ant's ear. 'Oh my God, Ant, is that the ring Dylan showed you? Does this mean what I think it means?'

'Yes,' he whispered back. 'She must have got it from Lionel. And he—'

'Took it from Dylan. *Oh no.* What do we do?'

'Nothing yet. We can get Tom over here when it's all finished. I'm not mad, am I?'

'You know what you saw, Ant. You're not mad.'

She gave his arm a little squeeze. They both faced forward, although Bea's mind was racing too fast to concentrate on what was happening on stage.

'. . . think we can all agree that it's been a fantastic show. And now it's time to announce the big one . . .'

Charles was sitting at the back of the tent, too, on an uncomfortable-looking plastic chair. Out of the corner of her eye, Bea saw him get to his feet and shuffle along to her and Ant.

'Bea, can you hear what he's saying?' he asked. 'I can't hear him properly. Do you know who's got Best in Show?'

Bea looked back at the stage.

'He hasn't said yet. I think he's just about to.'

'. . . And so, Best in Show — and this was a unanimous decision — goes to . . . Charles Hale for his magnificent giant marrow.'

Everyone in the tent started applauding, with whoops and whistles thrown in. Even Mary, in her chair, started clapping. Despite Ant's bombshell — the implications of which were still whirling and swirling around her mind — Bea was caught up in the moment.

'Oh! Charles! It's you! You did it! Ant! Marvin won!'

'I did? I did!' said Charles. 'We did!'

'. . . Please make your way to the stage . . .'

'Ant! Come with me! Where's Bob?'

Leaning heavily on his sticks, Charles started walking towards the stage. He had to pass Mary and, as he did so, she held her hand out to congratulate him. Charles paused, leaned one stick against the other, and gently took her hand, leaning forward to kiss it, like the old-fashioned gentleman he was.

Bea found herself holding her breath. *Don't look*, she thought. *Keep walking*.

'Come on, Charles,' said Ant. 'You're needed down the front.'

'Wait a minute,' said Charles. He still had Mary's hand and he was looking at the ring on her fourth finger. 'Mary, where did you get that ring?'

Mary looked up at him, questioningly, her eyes pale and watery.

'I don't think she understands,' said Bea. 'Why don't you go and get your prize? We can deal with this later.'

Charles let go of Mary's hand and grabbed Ant's arm, clutching on with surprising strength. 'Ant, call the police. Are the police here?'

'Come along, Charles,' Lionel's voice boomed from the stage. 'We haven't got all day . . . Is there a problem? Can someone help him?'

'There's a problem all right,' muttered Charles. 'Help!' he shouted. 'Police!'

The crowd turned their back on Lionel and were looked towards the source of the shouting, standing on tiptoe, and craning over one another to see what was going on. Bea could see Tom in the far corner of the tent. Their eyes met and she nodded, urgently. He started making his way towards her. Meanwhile, Lionel abandoned his microphone and left the stage, pushing his way through the throng as best he could.

All Bea could see was a crowd of faces turned her way. Charles, Mary, Fatima, Ant and herself were centre stage now as a gap appeared in the mass, and Lionel emerged. 'What's going on?'

Charles waved one of his sticks in the air between them, like he was wielding a sword. 'Your wife is wearing my wife's ring. How do you explain that, you bastard?'

A gasp rose up from the people within earshot.

Lionel stood stock still, then seemed to sway a little from side to side. Bea wondered if he was about to faint.

He visibly pulled himself together. 'Where on earth did you get that?' Lionel was ignoring Charles and addressing Mary. 'Take it off! Take it off at once!'

He lunged forward, dashing the stick out of Charles's hand, sending him tottering towards the side of the tent. Then he reached down towards Mary, but she clamped her left hand over her right and formed a tight fist.

'I said take it off!' Lionel repeated, trying to prise her hands open.

'Stop it, Lionel!' said Bea. 'You're hurting her.'

Lionel froze again, stung by Bea's words.

'I'm sorry,' he said, and his voice seemed to carry genuine remorse. 'I'm sorry. I never meant to hurt you.'

'Is that what you do?' Charles was holding on to a tent pole for stability. 'Is that what you did to my Catherine? You lost your temper? You hurt her?'

The crowd uttered a collective 'Oooh' and then fell silent as everybody strained to hear.

'I don't know what you're talking about,' said Lionel.

'Don't you?' said Charles. 'Let's ask Mary.'

'Don't you dare upset her,' said Lionel. 'She's not well. She doesn't understand.'

Charles persisted. 'Mary,' he said, quietly but clearly, 'where did you get that ring?'

You could have heard a pin drop. But instead of a pin, after a long pause, it was Mary's voice that broke the silence.

'Catherine gave it to me,' she said, looking down at her clasped hands. 'She left it on the floor for me to find.'

'The floor?' said Lionel. 'It must have dropped out of—' He was almost talking to himself now. 'Never mind. Give it to me.'

Mary looked up and Bea could suddenly see a glimpse of the woman that she used to be — clear-eyed, sure of herself, and defiant.

'She loves me, Lionel, and I love her.'

Lionel looked at Ant and Bea. 'She doesn't know what she's saying.'

'We had a whole summer together,' Mary continued. 'The windows wide open while we lay in each other's arms. No one's ever loved me like her.'

'She's rambling now. Fatima, take her home, please.' Lionel's voice was getting louder, trying to drown out that of his wife. Bea was fascinated by Mary, though. It was as if a veil had lifted and Bea had no doubt whatsoever that she was speaking from the heart.

She wasn't the only one transfixed. Everyone was listening.

Fatima crouched so that her face was level with Mary's. 'Not yet, Mr Gittins. Let her speak. Mary,' she said, very gently, 'what happened to Catherine?'

'We were going to go away together. Start a new life. I'd packed my bag, all ready. Lionel was meant to be at work, but he came home and found us. He begged, pleaded, said he'd kill himself if I went. I couldn't leave him, not then. Catherine agreed to go on ahead and wait for me. Lionel took her to the station, put her on the train but . . . she never sent word. I never saw her again. I wonder where she is . . .'

Tom had got to the front of the crowd now. He stepped forward and put his hand on Lionel's arm.

'Lionel Gittins, I'm arresting you on suspicion of murder. You are not obliged to say anything, but anything you do say may be taken as evidence. Do you understand?'

Lionel didn't respond. His eyes were fixed on Mary. 'I've always loved you, Mary. I couldn't bear to lose you.'

Mary stared down at her hands, and the scratched, but still beautiful ring. 'I wonder where she is . . .'

Lionel turned his attention to Fatima. 'Will you make sure she gets home safely? And don't forget to lock the gates.'

Fatima looked at him evenly. 'Of course, Mr Gittins.'

Tom gently but firmly guided Lionel's hands behind his back and handcuffed him.

Charles had recovered his balance and moved away from the side of the tent, his second stick returned to him by a member of the crowd. He stood in front of Lionel. 'How did you do it? Did she suffer? Tell me, you bastard. You owe me this, at least.'

Lionel's face seemed to sag, but he showed no other trace of emotion. 'It didn't take long. I drove past the station, parked up and . . . put my hands around her neck.'

Charles let out a long, anguished sigh. 'All this time,' he said. 'All this time, I never knew.'

'I'm sorry,' said Lionel. 'You deserved better. We both did.'

Now a spark of fire glittered in Charles's eyes. 'Don't put us in the same bracket, you miserable excuse for a man. We're not the same. We never have been.'

'True. You're a weak man.'

'Why, you—' Charles raised one stick as if he was about to strike Lionel. Then he changed his mind, lowered the stick and rested heavily on it. 'A weak man cannot resist their basest instincts. A weak man wants to control people. A weak man lashes out. I'm not the weak one here.'

'Come on,' said Tom, steering Lionel out of the tent. 'Let's get you out of here.'

He frogmarched him through the opening in the canvas and out into the bright sunshine, leaving chaos and confusion behind them.

People were milling around, buzzing with the excitement of what had just happened. Bea was about to turn to Fatima and ask if she needed help getting Mary home when Ant barged past her and out of the tent.

'Ant! Wait!'

She hurried after him. He'd drawn level with Tom and Lionel and was walking along beside them. She ran to catch up.

'It was Dylan, too, wasn't it? Were you just going to sit back and let Wendy Fox take the rap for you?'

Lionel carried on walking, tight-lipped.

'I want to know!' Ant shouted.

'Ant, please, get out of the way now,' said Tom.

'She was going to prison anyway,' said Lionel, and Bea felt a shiver run down her spine.

'Why kill him in the first place? He was a good guy,' said Ant.

'He showed me the ring, told me he was going to hand it into the police in the morning. He wouldn't listen. I just wanted everything to stay buried until the truth couldn't hurt Mary anymore. It was always about Mary.'

'But it all came out anyway.'

Lionel was looking at the ground in front of him, but there was an expression of disdain on his face now. 'I never thought that a group of no-hopers like you would find her.'

They were nearly at the roped-off parking area now. Tom held his hand up in front of Ant. 'Ant, if you don't leave us alone now, I'm going to have to arrest you too. *Let it go*. I've got a job to do.'

Ant stopped. Bea stood next to him and slipped her hand into his as they watched Tom lead Lionel up to his car, where he loaded him into the back and drove off.

Ant shook his head. 'I can't believe it, Bea. I just can't believe it.'

'I know. It's hard. But it's over now. You did it. You caught him.'

He ran his free hand through his hair, still struggling with his emotions. 'I don't know what to do now.'

'Let's take a walk,' said Bea. 'You and me.'

CHAPTER SIXTY

'You think people are complicated, but it's very simple in the end. Love, money, jealousy, revenge. It all comes down to one of those,' said Ant.

They had walked away from the tent and down the sloping grass to the river. Now, hand in hand, they followed its course upstream, under the road and through a quieter section of the park that ran along the back of the civic centre.

'So, Dylan died because of something that happened thirty-nine years ago,' said Ant. 'Bit ironic for a historian.'

'Not the sort of history that featured in his book, though,' said Bea. 'Two wives falling in love. One husband who could let go, the other who couldn't. It's so sad. It could have been so different.'

'Yeah. I never thought Charles did it. I'm glad I was right.'

'I had a few doubts, to be honest. I mean, you never really know people, do you?'

'Well, I was pretty sure he was a kind person. Turns out he was, and is.'

'And both he and Lionel lived with their secrets for all that time. It must have been stressful, mustn't it? Unless they managed to just blank it out, bury it somehow.'

'Nothing stays buried for ever though, does it? Things come to the surface eventually.'

They'd reached the point where the footpath led over an old bridge, in a part of Kingsleigh where Victorian cottages clustered around the riverbank. When they got to the bridge's apex, they stopped and leaned on it, elbows resting on the rough stone surface. The rushing water made a pleasant chattering sound as it flowed over the pebbly riverbed and between the supports of the bridge.

Bea peered into it. She caught sight of a dark shape flitting out from one patch of reeds to another. 'There!' she cried. 'A fish. Did you see it, Ant?'

'No.' He leaned over a bit further, then he laughed. 'Here, are you the sort of person that shouts out, "Sheep!" or "Horses!" when you're on a train or in the car? You are, aren't you?'

Bea smiled. 'Might be.'

He shifted back from the edge a little and turned to face her. 'There's so much I don't know about you.'

'It's not all good,' said Bea. 'Maybe you won't like me if you find out more.'

He was looking deep into her eyes now, and she felt a fluttering in her stomach almost as if the little fish was dancing and darting in there.

'I seriously doubt that,' he said. 'Me, on the other hand . . . you heard Lionel. I'm a no-hoper.'

Bea reached up and put her index finger against his mouth. 'Shh, Ant. He's a bitter, twisted old man. He wouldn't know hope if it bit him on the bum.'

He gently kissed her finger. 'You don't share his view, then?'

She smiled and kissed him lightly on the lips. 'I don't share his view. Now, are we going to finally fix a plan for our date night? I reckon you've got potential.'

CHAPTER SIXTY-ONE

Extract from the *Kingsleigh Bugle*, 26 September 2024, page 10.

[Photo shows pupils gathered around an elderly man standing in front of an enormous vegetable marrow displayed on a table.]

PRIZE MARROW INSPIRES
YOUNG CHEFS

Pupils and staff at Kingsleigh Comprehensive were delighted to receive the gift of a prize-winning marrow this week. It was grown by Charles Hale, 83, on his allotment and weighed 35 kg. Known affectionately as Marvellous Marvin, the marrow beat stiff competition at the flower and produce show to win Best in Show. Charles decided to donate the marrow to the school to be used in Food Technology lessons.

At the handover this week, Charles said, 'This is the finest marrow I've ever grown and I'm thrilled that it will help a new generation of children learn to cook. My late wife, Catherine, was a splendid cook, who delighted in using simple ingredients to produce delicious meals. I hope that these young people will understand where their food comes from and that home-grown, fresh produce is the best. The secret ingredient in any recipe is love. If they learn to cook with that, they won't go far wrong.'

THE END

ACKNOWLEDGEMENTS

I would like to thank everyone at Joffe Books for the love and care they have poured into *The Supermarket Mysteries*, especially my two editors, Steph Carey and Jasmine Callaghan. Thank you also to my wonderful agent, Sarah Hornsley at PFD, who is the best person a writer can have by their side.

I'd also like to thank the fellow writers who have continued to support and encourage me, especially Emma Pass, Sheena Wilkinson, Sophia Bennett, Colin Scott, and the hosts and writers at London Writers' Salon's Writers' Hour.

As ever, a big thank you to my family, and perhaps most of all to the readers who have embraced the Costsave crew and followed their ups and downs. The best part of being a writer is hearing that people connect with your stories, and I know that many of you have taken Ant, Bea and their friends to your hearts.

Rachel Ward
September 2024

THE JOFFE BOOKS STORY

We began in 2014 when Jasper agreed to publish his mum's much-rejected romance novel and it became a bestseller.

Since then we've grown into the largest independent publisher in the UK. We're extremely proud to publish some of the very best writers in the world, including Joy Ellis, Faith Martin, Caro Ramsay, Helen Forrester, Simon Brett and Robert Goddard. Everyone at Joffe Books loves reading and we never forget that it all begins with the magic of an author telling a story.

We are proud to publish talented first-time authors, as well as established writers whose books we love introducing to a new generation of readers.

We won Trade Publisher of the Year at the Independent Publishing Awards in 2023. We have been shortlisted for Independent Publisher of the Year at the British Book Awards for the last four years, and were shortlisted for the Diversity and Inclusivity Award at the 2022 Independent Publishing Awards. In 2023 we were shortlisted for Publisher of the Year at the RNA Industry Awards.

We built this company with your help, and we love to hear from you, so please email us about absolutely anything bookish at feedback@joffebooks.com

If you want to receive free books every Friday and hear about all our new releases, join our mailing list: www.joffebooks.com/contact

And when you tell your friends about us, just remember: it's pronounced Joffe as in coffee or toffee!